BORN OF MAN

Stephen Gray was born in Cape Town in 1941. He completed a Masters degree in English at Cambridge, and was a member of the Writers Workshop at the University of Iowa. Since 1969 he has lived and worked in Johannesburg where he lectures in English. He has written plays for the Market Theatre, and edited both *The Penguin Book of Southern African Stories* and *The Penguin Book of Southern African Verse*. His new volume of poetry is *Apollo Café*. His previous novels include *Time Of Our Darkness* (Frederick Muller/Century-Hutchinson 1988)

Born of Man is his first work to be published by GMP.

First published July 1989 by
GMP Publishers Ltd,
PO Box 247, London N17 9QR

World Copyright © 1989 Stephen Gray

British Library Cataloguing in Publication Data

Gray, Stephen, 1941–
  Born of man
  I. Title
  823 [F]

ISBN 0–85449–107–4

Printed and bound in the European Community by
Nørhaven A/S, Viborg, Denmark

BORN OF MAN

STEPHEN GRAY

GMP

I

Christmas will have us by the balls soon enough. Can bloody New Year be far behind?

I swore to Jannie I wouldn't let this annual ravishment go by without a letter to all of you – our such good, long-lost friends. None of you'll be at our festive board, *alas*. The way South Africa is now maybe it is better you stay away! – we respect your decision.

Mind you, the way I am now there won't be quite the bash we were wont to have, either. It's been *one hell of a year* for those who stayed put.

The historic old gravel pass down into the Valley is just the same as when we bought here in 1984. But those of you who vibrated your rotten arses down would hardly recognise our little sanctuary. The Bairnsford Nursery sign is pretty eyecatching these days. You are lured in to your financial ruin by guess what? – acres of erect cannas with red tips.

Casual retail trade still ticks over, but to our old friends we'll sell wholesale on the side, don't worry.

Actually, gang . . . it's easier for me just to focus on *one* of you. Who was always the best listener, the best? – Klaus my baby! Hell, it would be nice to see *you* stroll down the dusty path again.

Jannie says if I just explore this thing, I can adjust for everyone else. The printer does sixty characters *a second* . . . so they can get *theirs* (suitably revised) later. But don't be alarmed if you get billed for 1 000 Duke's Folly without discount in the rush!

This is all part of my festive season therapy, me *typing* like this. I'm terrified. I don't know how my old secretary did it. Thank God I can go back and process the words . . . My fingers are like limp sausages . . . If I relax for an instant: aaaah, *you see??* – a string of drunken blather. You'd find that familiar.

Hey, what's the difference between a blowjob and lunch? You mean you really don't know? My darling, come to lunch *immediately*.

Danny and Martie, those traitors, will get you up to date on every single sensational event – they're going to visit you, spending their ill-gotten gains. I have a good mind to pip them to it with this! They don't have a clue how things really affected us.

Mind you, I was so terminally blotto that when Jannie screamed at me that I'd *gone blue* . . . all I could think was, well, that completes the story, doesn't it? Honestly, I was past feeling. They hacked my heart out (this was at the Trescott) and it pumped about like a Portuguese man-o'-war with the last of its willpower . . . I was four hours on that table! The surgeon (he's a new friend of ours, but thereby hangs a tale – yes, the same one who did Kev) . . . took Polaroids of what he was doing to me, can you imagine? This was only a fortnight ago. I assure you, if I hug myself, I *do* feel the cross-stitch down the front.

You wouldn't recognise old me. I can already walk without getting breathy. I've lost FIFTY-TWO KILOS! Now I can tag onto Jannie and Kevin, and even to toothy Timothy. You see, I have time to do nothing better than type.

Anyway, my dear Klaus, because we do know that you will not return, for profoundly political reasons that I can't even follow . . . this (whether you like it or not) is for *you* . . . And for Paul, of course, should he moon over your delectable shoulder. I have absolutely nothing against Paul, as you know – thanks to the courtesies, he gets what you get. But Klaus . . . when I think of the way, after New Year only two years ago, you and Paul came to do your farewells . . . oh God . . . they say the first two years are the most difficult, don't they? – well, good luck to you. But even my *new* heart flaps around a bit. These partings are worse than surgery. I'd better not express the accumulating sense of loss I feel *word for word* (assuming I could). Dear Jannie can read this out as easily as me. He just thinks you're terrible traitors – he'll put in a recurring AND DON'T COME BACK, KLAUS! (This machine is really for him, so I better be discreet.)

The point of this letter, Klaus my darling with the most moulded buns in the whole of the Alps, and a St Gotthard Tunnel you can cuddle in the whole night through . . . keep clean now, and have Paul tested for the big A *monthly*, you hear . . . is DO NOT BELIEVE A WORD MARTIE AND DANNY TELL YOU IN TANDEM IN BOURGEOIS LITTLE CUCKOO-TICKING CHOCOLATE-COATED ZURICH. Klaus, my love, THEY'LL GET IT ALL ABSOLUTELY WRONG. (Like your paper did – *that's* another score I intend to settle.)

We couldn't *really* let them know what was boiling up,

could we? When you've got something that will ROCK THE WORLD, wouldn't *they* be the first to spoil it, as indeed they *nearly* did? We weren't going to have two of the dilliest gossip-queens, even if they do have *contacts*, spill the beans in their cups at the Pink Flamingo any old Saturday night, just to fuck us all with the impact! By then we trusted *nobody* – we *couldn't*.

After last New Year, when it all really got underway, I suppose, Dannie and Martie were simply not invited. Of course, that was far too suspicious for them. They evaded Timothy at the gate, Timothy who so efficiently escorted anyone off who trespassed one foot beyond the selling area. These two – they slap the vicious dogs aside, my dear, with their handbags, and before you know it there's a *big surprise* on the patio. Two droopy old *ghouls* come to suck *blood*! The three of us got such a fright. *Kevin's gone* – you never saw anyone in his condition *go* so fast. And shocks were very bad for him by that stage.

'What's *she* got that *we* could catch,' says Martie, tripping in the ferns.

'It's so rural here, probably rabies,' says Danny.

'Rinderpest, the stupid cow. Can't she greet her *old friends*?'

'Kevin's gone even shyer these days,' I say.

'Shyer, why?' says Danny.

'We tried to phone,' says Martie.

'That's the advantage of a party line,' Danny says. 'Someone's going to get *fed up* and tell us why you don't answer.'

'We're incommunicado,' says Jannie, coming with two more cups and pouring.

'Your neighbours in the Valley think you're dead,' says Danny.

'We're just not serving J and B any more,' I say, lying in my teeth. 'Kevin can't face old pisscats coming through the Bougainvillaea at him.'

'But he was always so abstemious,' says Danny, taking a teacup, his hand rattling the saucer.

'Bad as that, is it?' says Martie. 'Mind you, after what he's been through . . . poor Kevin. That Henno, he was the ultimate lout. I told him, Kev my boy, BAD NEWS. He'll love you and leave you without the family silver. Don't do it, Kev . . . I told him straight.'

'He was such a nice boy,' says Martie. 'Good at his job, too.'

'I told him straight,' says Danny.

7

'I suppose it was last New Year's Eve . . . finally *broke* him,' says Martie.

We – you notice – are giving nothing away.

Then Danny says, 'You can say what you like . . . but relationships are either *right* from the start, or they are *wrong*. We know that now, don't we, my dear?' He slides his toe across the floor to Martie.

Martie shakes his head so vigorously in agreement his teeth clatter.

'We're so happy for you,' says Jannie.

'Klaus and Paul, that's another example. Made in heaven,' says Martie.

(From me to you, my Klaus . . . I can delete this bit later. No girl ever forgets her first bliss. When you made your entry, fresh from CH aus, do you know how the lights twinkled in my little disco? From my shoulders fell my stole, to be trampled on by the hordes. My heel cracked, so I had to balance on one . . . and you just picked me up and carried me away . . . That was heaven, though no marriage was made there. So soon the passion descends . . . into friendship and drink! Didn't I start a bracket? I'll have to close it. There.)

I'll apologise to them in full, don't worry. I'll fill the jacuzzi with J and B to compensate. And I'll tell you about Kev (in full) some other time.

As for the million dollars we were meant to get out of it. Henno bought a second-hand Jag, which got rid of him, and Ou Sara'll get her pension; after that there won't be much left, I assure you.

Certainly no compensation for our world collapsing, people can't even say a decent good day any more, the rand's to shit, moffies don't talk for the condoms over their heads they're playing it so safe . . . You know, I don't even *kiss* Jannie any more; when he kisses me it's a dry one here on my cheekbone. Like cold-germs, now we carry the plague. Lovelessness nearly done me in.

FOKOFF KLAUS YOU DESERTER – JUST JOKING. HE'S GOT TO HAVE HIS MELES ON TIME. LOVE TO PAUL. JANNIE.

P.S. I SUPPOSE YOUR SWISS DOCTORS ARE FURIOUS WE DID IT FIRST. MEDICAL WONDERS AREN'T MADE IN NEUTRALITY BUT IN WAR. ANYWAY, YOU JUST CAME HERE TO MAKE YOUR ILLGOTTEN GAINS AND PAUL IS ONE OF THEM. THIS IS MY COUNTRY AND MY

NURSERY. WHEN THE BOMB REALLY DROPS BOYS, GUESS WHO'LL STILL BE HERE TO SEND YOU FRESH-CUT FLOWERS.

Bairnsford Nurseries, P. O. Box 21, Mooinooi, Transvaal. Champion, quick-flowering crysanthemums. Noble variety – yellow. R1,95 plus GST.

The main thing is never to get stressed again. But if you could see what I had for lunch you'd know how difficult that is: boiled chicken (200 gms on the little scale), one boiled potato with jacket and carrots and peas. Mind you, anything more ambitious Belinda can't cook. And still water, with ice cubes in it. Loss of weight and tranquillity. Actually, I quite enjoy typing on this thing.

You want medical wonders?

There weren't any of those available when Belinda got in trouble. She's the last child of Ou Sara, Sara who came with the farm. Occasionally one of her sons comes in a bakkie from Impala Platinum where they work, with a crate of you know what under a sack, and the nursery staff's out for the count till the Monday, and you don't give even Sara, who's not quite so teetotal as Kev, a plate to clear until at least Tuesday.

The drums start up at the kraal with Saturday lunch-break. We can hear Timothy's stereo on batteries now. He hires it like a jukebox until it mercifully conks out. But that's not before four in the morning. After that it's screams and broken glass, and at dawn Jannie has to load the whole shebang in the truck off to Richie's clinic up the pass.

Richie is Richard, son of the Cape Judge, and Alfie the surgeon's piece. Just finished his housemanship at Baragwanath, and still a real idealist – he does medicine for the poor at Alfie's expense on *their* tax-loss plot. Being the celeb surgeon of the moment, Alfie can carry it, as you may imagine. What Richie has to say about lack of rural medicine would make your hair stand on end, assuming you've got any left . . . so be prepared to be shocked out of your welfare state.

Belinda who was only fifteen at the time you left . . . these really were the bad old days and I must say Timothy has been a *good thing*, really getting the farm on its feet. He's organised the physically able into a high-stakes team and they go to play Brits police tomorrow. Last week they beat our dreaded rivals, Kierieklapper! Soccer's a year-round obsession in the Valley. Suits me.

We don't know which one, or if it was a visitor, obviously had a go at Belinda. She didn't say a word until long afterwards to Kev. She said that there was *more* than one. (Three.)

First thing I know about it was, you know, the tractor shed at the back here with the stores, and beyond the native shop is the clump of eucalyptus – well, there's a pit-latrine for them. So here I am, counting the paraffin to see it's all there, and I hear this baby crying.

Remember Paul said for every newborn infant's cry, that's twenty years of a man's life gone. Well, no one is around, unlike when it's payday or Jannie has the shop open just after. Funnily enough, though we had no evidence that any single one on the farm was pregnant at that time, I thought for winter, when there'd be a new crop, we'd better lay in a stock of woollies, you know, and mothball them.

So to me the newborn cry meant it was just as well we had first-size jumpers and bonnets and such. Not that we knew what was fashionable, but Mrs Leibnitz at the Co-op is very helpful. Remember when we went there and you had sachertorte and real German coffee, and she said never underestimate German-speakers abroad. And you said Africa was so insanitary it would even get the finest German-speakers down.

I could not locate this cry, right there in broad daylight with the eucalyptus shimmering in the bit of breeze. Never occurred to me it was shut in the latrine. So I went up to the potters in the nursery to find if any one of them was maybe babysitting for next door. Because they do that, in a big circle, gupping all day and the babies crawling over the potting-soil, and there's something very age-old about it and pleasant and efficient. Anyway, at the end of the day you get from piles of plastic bags and seedlings a half-acre of healthy brown pots like a massed parade ready for market. That's a damn side better for them than working in a factory, don't you think? Belinda's right among them, her legs spread out, bending to put this plant in the right way up.

And I say, just generally, hasn't someone left one of the Whole Earth Ceramics children down in the tractor shed, and I don't want it there because it could get run over? There's the usual general round of denials, before the group will forces the individual confession. I just left it at that. I thought if the staff was contented to let a baby cry ... well, that's Jannie's responsibility, not mine.

He came in to lunch late. He had a whole consignment to send off to Wakkerstroom – he's done really good work opening up to local nurseries, because going into Joburg is really too expensive now, and the truck always breaks down at some shebeen. Better not allow for that temptation too often.

I can hear the cry intermittently and it's weakening; he says it must be a piet-my-vrou as there just *aren't* any babies on the farm. You know how they cry at the same pitch and when they're really horny and aggressive it lasts all night? Often the birds do the talking for us in this house!

It was not a piet-my-vrou, couldn't he hear the difference?

Ou Sara came in and confirmed it was a piet-my-vrou, so that was that.

Everybody on this place was just knowingly and willingly collaborating on a murder-in-action; call it infanticide. Can you believe such a thing, when the breeze was blowing the eucalyptus so romantically, and you've never seen so many jolly pots lined up with blossoms zinging about like flags, and the heavy sound of trucks pulling out and cash pouring in.

But can you credit it, an actual death occurring in the pit-latrine? The baby wasn't just stuck behind the door, or bundled up on the planks which you sit on, but was *in* the drop which is a bloody deep one . . . we want no overflows in that quarter, thank you very much. I tell you, Klaus, did I feel sick. That's where it was – every time I went *coo* through my handkerchief it gave a little response. It was not on the floor or on the planks which are quite hygienic, but *down* the thing.

It's not exactly my scene to descend to such depths after any little mite. As you know in those days I was over 200 lbs. The drop is filled *with lime*, anyway, and I suppose you know what a few brushes with that do for your skin. Never mind the half-digested shit down there, frankly. I had a few little half-digested vomits of my own, let me tell you.

Sorry to give you the lurid details. But what do you do? *What do you do?* You used to get so morally revulsed about South Africa, you just rolled the windows up tight and turned on the air-conditioning in your BMW . . . yes, you did. So did I, and so did Jannie with me in the Merc. Getting involved with this farming lark is a moral issue everywhere you turn. Richie is admirable in that respect and he's taught me a lot; he just digs his big hands right in, even if it is a suppurating boil under some labourer's armpit.

Turn a deaf ear, I suppose, like everyone else. *That* I will never forgive, the conspiracy throughout this haven. *Everyone knew*. Why weren't they, sitting under the tree only 20

11

yards away, using the latrine as they normally would? The men came down for lunch; *they heard*. Suddenly they're all holding it in till they get right to the other side of the farm, which is *three-quarters of a mile away*.

Call the cops. Well, you can imagine what that would mean. I don't want *them* having tea with lemon in *our* poofta parlour, thank you very much. Besides the fact that you can never get them when you need them. *Besides the fact* that if they sniffed what those bastards call a bunch of Kaffirs committing a murder, how many staff would we have left?

A group decision had been taken. Ou Sara wasn't talking, even though it was her grandchild. Belinda was fifteen, for goodness sake, and thin as a rake. When she had the smallest swelling Jannie actually got her worm pills from Mrs Leibnitz. She was meant to be in school, not even working here in the first place. Later it transpired that was why Ou Sara was keeping her home, and when her time came she just went to the loo and had it like a yoyo on a string ... and wiped herself off with a piece of *Farmer's Weekly*.

I just knew that I had no choice: get a torch and a large piece of canvas so that I didn't make contact with the quicklime, and wrap it in that and get it to hospital p. d. q. (English expression, meaning if you don't you are as criminal as the criminal who did the deed). A live baby, Klaus ... apparently not destined to wear many of the pink and white knitted booties in the shop, with drawstrings so you don't stop the circulation at the ankles. None of that for this little one.

I won't put you off your apfelstrudel by telling you what your old friend looked like after an afternoon in the family pit. It was caught on the ledge. Nor what a totally newborn babe with attachment looks like after landing on lime.

I got it out and into the sunlight. Its dimpled black fist clocks me on the nose. It was a real champion, that one. Would make fourteen rounds in any gym with fists like that, and already a broken-nosed effect. Agile little feller, too.

But by then it was dead, you see. So even if I had cleaned up those terrible, terrible burns ... what good would it do? I suppose I should admit I was besides myself, but I wasn't ... I suppose I was a bit out of breath, and I just sat there under the eucalyptus with this ... thing ... in the canvas.

All the way down I talked to it – I know it couldn't understand and would grow up, I don't know, talking Tswana, I suppose, and Afrikaans as they all do. So I kept on talking in friendly English ... I had quite a repertoire by then, 'My little Fighter ... ' 'Look at the Manchild Granny found in the poofie cabbages,' 'Wriggled so much in the Stork's Nappy, fell out in the shithouse, hey?' and I don't know what all. Really my worst, when my head was echoing from those cries, was 'Not quite the Nursery you thought it was, Battler my Babe!' Would you have thought there was so much distress in me, dreary old queen covered in shit and *burning*. That stuff irritates if you so much as get it near a soft part – a slow inflammation I felt on my skin for weeks afterwards. When it's powder you can't wash it or it digests you. You have to brush it and let it grow out with your skin. I couldn't go to my office sixteen floors up and open a window – a pall of pong would've polluted the Central Business District.

As no one was claiming the late Lil Champ, the rest was then just between the two of us. We talked this out at great length, oh yes. We agreed the options were limited. If Timothy came past, I'd have handed it over and let him deal with it; they are all wary of Timothy because he's not from the Valley – but that's exactly why he's the best foreman we could have. If Jannie came past, a few piet-my-vrou calls . . . and that'd be enough.

The women kept sitting there, sticking an odd finger in the soil. Not talking; seeing me peripherally. They were braced for me to march into them and demand an explanation.

But I made my decision. I placed Baby Superbrat in another hole, not ten yards from the one he first fell in. At least this time he was comfortably in the canvas. If anyone saw me with a spade, they never commented on it. It's nicer round that side of the eucalyptus grove, out of sight of the house and the sheds, and it's raised with a view over the mustard field to the riverbed and up into the hills.

And that's the story of Belinda's baby and how I got involved. You must grasp it all if you're to have any idea about Kev. If you don't, you won't understand a thing.

I used to go round the eucalyptus with the dogs and throw branches across the mustard and watch them carve into it. Their barking covered the words I was saying to myself.

That's the worst of us dismal queens, you know – talk for ever about things that never matter, and never talk about what does. I miss you a lot, you know . . . YES, YOU KNOW – you always were a good LISTENER.

I could see your ears go limp and you sag on the couch and, when you unplugged the phone, you knew you were in for it. You should have been a shrink! I just want you to know I appreciated it.

So, get another drink and wait for this one. How long does a disc last on this thing? I can just send you the floppy disc and you print it out. Oops, Jannie wants to search for his labels. Love from us both. Actually I'm getting the hang of this, and you know what: it's fun. When I get back that new ratbag secretary of mine SHE'S FIRED.

Jannie just wants to say hello.

HELLO KLAUS I HEAR YOU SWISS ARE HEAVILY INTO PRANGING APPLES ONLY JOKING ACTUALLY ITS GOOD FOR HIM YOU SHOULD SEE HOW HE SWEATS HES GOING TO MISS XMAS

We have friends you don't know for Christmas, so can New Year hold off much longer? A blissful 1988 to you! If we look as if we'll tell, they want a personally guided tour. Jannie does the quick one for straights and I do the slow one for gays, with chalk and cheese commentaries. You're getting the cheese, naturally.

I'll have a terminal installed in my same flat opposite the office, so I can continue with this in the evenings when I can't drink. This is becoming more than a letter – it's a bloody sober man's diary.

That's if they keep me on much longer. Martie and Danny will have told you . . . I got *demoted* on top of it all. The shame of it! These young upwardly-mobiles have everything going for them but mercy. It was all David Bennington's doing, and wasn't he such an innocent bliss number to begin with? Sheerest bliss. Danny and Martie brought him out here last New Year – I suppose they told you – the shaggy male who's into babymaking. Treachery wears such classical features.

I guess they'll bring back a little something from you to us. This is my present in return, so I better move it.

The amazing Kev should be next, and this is really dredging into the muck Danny and Martie are too brittle to comprehend. Yes, our sweet Kev, who's never been known to say a word. Remember how he used to be such a *wallflower* – if you didn't have your glasses on you'd hardly *notice* him. They tracked down his pathetic mother afterwards, and that's exactly what she said: Kevin was always a self-absorbed child. Mind you, she hadn't seen him since he left them. He could hardly go back with ear-rings on and a blow-cut, and a salmon-pink tracksuit.

But he was essentially not very flamboyant, a quiet boy . . . and you never knew if it was because he was shy, or a bit dumb; nagging him did no good. You just knew that he had to tag along. While everyone else was measuring out cock and tot, and all pairing off for life . . . there was Kev dreaming away. He was planning a quite different future.

I didn't even know what he *did* (window-dressing for Edgars – not Edgars, but that other chain). Did you realise that? He was accepted for their trainee course, everything . . . and was very good at his job. They put him on the real country-town circuit, but on Saturday nights did *you* know he'd been out all week? Crimplene they're still into in those places, I ask you – and blue Sunday bolero hats! Danny and Martie who collected all the clippings gave us one from your paper. It says he was a fashion *designer*, born in *Paris* – Mrs Leibnitz's translation. Mind you, the way you have to winkle things out of Kev I'm not surprised. But it was *Parys*, on the banks of the bloody Vaal, not *Gay Paree*!!

One day of course he chuffs into his ghastly Calvinist backwater-on-Vaal, and he has to decide – does he visit his mother, saying nothing as usual . . . and go to work before she asks if he's got a girlfriend in Joburg yet, and where's the wedding. But the train was late, so he went straight to their branch, right on the main street. And then it happens, down the pavement comes his mother and his sisters with their shopping bags, and they stand outside the same window to *see* what the chappie from Joburg's arranging for the new season.

Kev's such a clot – he said he had his mouth full of pins and he couldn't talk. But he could have *waved*. No, he just continues rucking up this prewar abomination on one of those horrible models. All they see is the mode, not the moffie; they don't even *recognise* him. I said to Kev why didn't you bang on the glass? No, he said, he didn't want to leave marks on the pane.

Sure enough, an hour later when he's hanging one of those real dopper suits, fitting the detachable arm up the sleeve, hoping pinstripes on black will really *catch on* now in the Free State, and waistcoats . . . pulls up his father in a bakkie and puts money in the meter. It's a pity you don't know Afrikaans because the few words Kev *does* use are so apt. That *papbroek*, referring to his khaki shorts dangling off his arse; that *bierpens*, meaning his beer-belly, but an animal's not a human's. And what an old dried piece of doggy-doo he turns out to be. You know, he forbade Kev's mother and the sisters to talk to the press – they were quite in favour, actually – and said his sum total was NO COMMENT beyond he'd thrown his darling son out ten years before and wasn't going to start missing him now! The women in that family used to dress Kev up and put rouge on his cheeks, that was the trouble. They let him be the fashionable troll they weren't *allowed* to be, can you believe it? – at least this is my interpretation.

I suppose it went from playing dollies with his sisters to slipping into their unused high-heels for a little trot after school to the corner café, and while the sisters grew vaster and more ugly, Kev was ever more Miss Parys. The dominie had words to his father and his father had words to his mother and she went back to the dominie and by this time Kev was into floral nighties.

His first moffie friend was a coloured guy on the border of the location, which I suppose really did it. This coloured guy was studying hairdressing by correspondence from his mother's sewing room, and wanted someone to practise on. I guess heated tongs weren't doing too well on the local raw material, so there's our Kev with a Toni perm and a hairnet with spangles, sipping a milk-shake on the barstool. In comes the high-school rugby team after a heavy practice, and well, they're not going to mooch around for long listening to boopidoopidoo from the princess of Standard Eight. He was so fucked up the coloured boy had to fetch him from the gutter and wheel him home over the crossbar.

So the mother protests to the dominie who protests to the father . . . and Kevin learns to suck more quietly on his straw and wear his Marcel wave under his schoolcap and, when outnumbered, to shut up. Kev learned other ways to talk, though. I cannot give you all the details, but even in Parys accommodations can be made. I do know this – they found a job for him in the cadet armoury and eventually there was not one moffiebasher in that school who would go out in his uniform before Kev had given him the thumbs up. Kev there in the reviewing stand, so proud of them as they marched past, waving at the eyes right, his charm bracelet jingling. You can't keep the lid on bottled peaches for long, can you?

I suppose all these painful memories flashed through the so-called mind of his father as he contemplated his only son and heir through the display window, smiling at him. This time recognition ensued: Kev raises the model's arm to salute his old man. He drops his six-pack in horror.

When the old man's found what is evidently more important to him, Kev's got a strip of pink crepe arranged around his lovely bod and is slowly peeling it down, which gesture goes to the zip of his track-top. By this stage father is standing four-square against the window, hoping to hell no one else has noticed. Kev's signalling he should come back after the show and all.

Altogether father is beyond speech and fumbles open a beer right in the street and half drains it, when somebody *does* walk round the corner. He has a split-second for one little gesture, before he's into the bakkie and tears off. Know what it was? One Castle beer bottle aimed straight at Kev. It didn't break the window, but it sure exploded.

Such provocation, in the sleepiest dorp you've ever seen! Such passionate responses! Kev had known for years that dumbshows speak more than words. Really, I don't think he gave a damn.

Lunch. It's quite a lovely day, balmy. I don't know why I slang the platteland when it can be so beautiful, after rain. We live in it too, after all. We've had over a hundred millimetres this month already and the drought is giving way to floods. If this carries on we'll be an island next year!

But when all this was happening to Kev it was as dry as an ox's jawbone, there along the Vaal. I'll tell you more about that day in Parys in 1986, just as the state of emergency was being declared.

Kev couldn't revisit that adolescent fantasy room of his in his family home, as he'd had a longing to – heart-shaped pillows and the Marlene posters and fishnet stockings draped around the body-length mirror. This *was* kept as it used to be, as we saw when the *Sunday Times* got in – but it was also kept firmly locked. He had a collage of about sixty Liz Taylors with the violet eyes contemplating him, and all the rejected cosmetics samples that never sold in the Parys pharmacy, a rack of artificial nails and lipsticks and a wardrobe of the cutest casual numbers for a quick stroll down to the trucker's strip for a hotdog. I suppose, now, they'll turn it into a paying museum! What other famous sons has Parys produced?

Parys didn't have a bypass in those days (like me!), and, like all those towns, lived off the through trade from the highway. The whole life of a community depended on who might be in town, if only for the duration of a fuel-stop.

So Kev could not go for the night to his own room and wash and stretch out a bit, and his train wasn't leaving till the next morning. So when he's changed the windows in Voortrekker Street and it's early still, off he goes with his travelling bag to the main drag – his old standby, the Shell garage. Shell's in a lot of trouble now for supporting apartheid; they'll have to change their name like Caltex.

Remember the Caltex circles with the flying Pegasus? – well, it's Zenex now, no frills. It'll be sad when those yellow abelones slip from the sky.

You've guessed it: first encounter with the dreaded Henno. Down the main drag he steams on his Japanese huge bloody machine, all chrome and oily casing and exhausts, for a quick top-up under the golden Shell. Peels off his crash-helmet and ruffles his blond hair with his glove . . . stretches his jeans down his thighs and pinches his crotch . . . goes for a satisfying slash. Comes out and pinches his best asset again . . . Puts his keys in the petrol cap and forks out two rand.

Kev, standing off the apron, just knew where his future lay. He'd been through all this so many times before, but the last time he'd left Parys for Joburg to seek his fortune. This time he wanted the other way, deep into the heart of Boerdom, to beat his train.

'Vredefort?' said Kev.

'Viljoenskroon,' said Henno.

'Bothaville?' said Kev.

'Bothaville,' said Henno.

'Odendaalsrus?' said Kev.

'En Welkom,' said Henno. 'What, your Porsche broke down?'

'I don't drive,' said Kev. 'And two rand won't get you to the other side of town.'

'Not with you on the back. Can you passenger on a pillion and all?'

'You just sway your hips,' said Kev.

'I haven' got a extra helmet,' said Henno.

'I'll buy one,' said Kev, 'to keep my hair in place.'

But for the meanwhile he handed over a five-rand note, and the attendant filled her right up.

'But I want you to know that if I accept your kind offer, this is for keeps,' said Kev.

'Put it there, my buddy,' said the man in his life, and they shook on it.

Henno showed him his saddlebags, full of free samples. He took orders for those addictive headache powders in sachets that fix your aches and pains and then give you a hangover, so you have to have more. Not hard to sell, if you think about it. Never fall in love with a travelling salesman. But still, he did have a job and his own bike, and who was Kev to argue with days of railways cut short. Kev would have to strap his travelling bag behind.

I suppose Kev had some regrets, streaking through Parys

for the last time. I'm sure he had a lot more when Henno didn't take the Vredefort turn off, but zoomed down the dirt track towards the banks of the Vaal – to the traditional bathing hole where you can't see the river for condoms hanging out to dry.

Now Kev, who had been down that track with just about every hungry male in Parys in the early years, was being very careful not to blow this one – at least, not in that sense. He'd kept his hands in the right place, and never once squeezed that nature's own arse between his thighs – just in case.

Henno dismounted. 'Overheating,' he said, adjusting his jeans.

'Where?' said Kev, remaining seated, his toes on the ground.

'Where d'you think? – in the radiator,' said Henno.

'This model's air-cooled,' said Kev, 'and it's cool enough for me.'

'All right then, *I* want a drink, so mind,' said Henno. He unstrapped one of the pockets under Kev and rootled for a plastic cup. There was a halfjack of brandy, but he didn't touch that. The back of Henno's palm touched Kev's calf, but it could have been accidental.

Henno stood up, the streak of dirt and sunburn down his open shirt glittering like a snake. 'I drive, you fetch water, man,' he said.

Kev dismounted, taking the cup. 'Come down with me,' he said, 'I know a nice place.'

'I mus' jus' fix this,' said Henno.

Kev sashayed along the path, and halfway down he was stopped in his tracks.

'Hey, you,' Henno called, 'is it you a moffie, hey?'

Kev did a turn from the hips. 'Yes,' he said, cool as can be, 'so what's that to you?'

Henno's face creased up. 'Hell, if there's one thing I hate it's blerrie moffies,' he said.

'As Delilah said to Samson,' Kev remarked.

'Jus' don' you try anything with me,' said Henno.

'As the actress said to the bishop,' Kev concluded, giving the slightest moue.

'Listen, don' you fool with me. I eat moffies for breakfast, I'm telling you,' and he plunged his screwdriver into the nether parts.

Kev went down to the river, which was only a few terrapins and baked mud where the cattle trod deeper and deeper in. When he found a puddle that was passably clear, he skimmed the dust off and filled the cup without getting sediment in it. Then, because his heart was beating, he splashed his face again and again. And that's when he heard Henno start up and drive off.

He ran up to where the bike had been. He gathered his things from all over the veld and packed them tidily and sat down, thinking this was going to be a troublesome and protracted affair. Anyone else but Kev would have walked back to town and started again. But he couldn't return there now, he was stuck.

Presently, as one of those beautiful, slow sunsets was mellowing out, if there'd been anyone on the Viljoenskroon highway they'd have seen this roaring leather monster coming down the blue tar and – for no explicable reason – throttle down, and stop, and do a U-turn to retrace his trajectory, going even faster than he came.

A while later he's on the track to the trysting place. There are cows standing in the way, because he hoots impatiently. But he's travelling slowly now, swinging his headlight from side to side, apparently looking for something. He comes nearer to where he stopped in the afternoon, takes a wrong turn. In the grass he makes a wide circle and eventually bounces down to the clearing. He stops, swinging the light into the thornbushes. The engine purs between his legs.

He switches off. It's the last heavy red flush before pitch dark. He says out loud, 'Hey man, I was only joking . . . Carn' you even take a joke?'

Kevin has perfect timing on these things and, like I said: no words.

'Come on now, I mus' get on. It's late.'

Kevin stays hidden, his tracksuit zipped up tight.

'Listen, I know you there. I saw your footprints and they not on the track. You behind that bush. So don' try and fool me with moffie shit, man.'

Kevin emerges . . . so I said, Why didn't you just go up and spit on him? Tell him to fok off man . . . leaving you in the pitch dark and unprotected? – with your things chucked out and all. No, I wouldn't put up with it. That's malicious damage to property . . . and desertion.

Know what Kevin said? Well, he didn't say anything to that right bastard. He just gave him back his filthy plastic cup.

And so it goes, the odyssey of Kevin and Henno – or at least as far as I can tell. When did they start bonking one another, I want to know? Jannie and I couldn't even make our first date for that. You were even quicker on the draw with Paul, as I remember. But I suppose it is different for a flimsy drag-queen who'd met God's gift, or that's what he thinks. And he's got the bike and you've missed your train.

But he did come back, didn't he? Yes, he did.

I wonder how Kev knew he would. He won't say, of course. I suppose he has more experience of playing that field. Having to wear lipstick so that you get rings on their cocks, because they can't face the fact that that throat down there may be a man's.

That night the most incredible charade starts up. Kevin books them in some boarding house with two single beds and a shower; he's paying for this, mind you. They've been to the roadhouse, so they don't have to go out and eat. Kevin's exhausted, but his lord and master doesn't even ask if he'd like to shower first. And in he goes fully-dressed and closes the door and starts singing Bobbejaan klim die berg. Hey you can do footnotes.[1] And Sarie Marais.[2]

When he comes out, treading on his pants and in the tightest towel you've ever seen – you know how economical those Free State towels are? – and threadbare, Kevin nearly faints. He nearly faints again when he turns back to what he's doing, which is washing the skidmarks off Henno's briefs in the handbasin with his little packet of Lux.

So what were the first words said on the wedding night? There was Kev bent over, up to his elbows in suds, and Henno dripping excess water down his shoulders.

They were Henno's. 'You got a comb?'

Gasping, fainting, Kev crosses to his side and fetches his.

'Thanks, man,' says Henno, turning to the mirror. And Kev gets a shot of the muscles up his backbone and the patch of golden fur above the cleavage of his buttocks.

This is too much for Kev, and he slides to his bed.

From the mirror Henno says, 'What's your name again? Sorry, I forgot.'

'It's Kevin,' says Kev, gulping, 'and you never have to say sorry.'

Henno finishes stacking round the wet hay on his head which has proliferated since his army days and places the comb on the dressing-table. Then he climbs onto his bed, occupying the whole of it, sprawled out on his back.

Kevin coughs a bit, because Henno undressed is quite a

---

1. Baboon climbs the mountain to you.
2. That stays the same. A song of heimvee, my dear, for a little Dutch person left behind, and there's no way Sarie Marais was a man.

spectacle, I must admit. He's all loose jointed and very well developed. His limbs just swing like broken branches. Display him on a slab like that at the Health Baths, and fifty minor queens'd go gas themselves in the shower!

But anyway, the point is our Kev had a pretty mean little bod too, and he wasn't about not to use it. He picks Henno's splashed garments off the tiles and hangs the briefs to dry over the bath and, half in the doorway, peels off his track-top, and then the pants, letting a bit of leg show past the door. Thinks twice about a flash of pink panties, old Kev, which can stay unrevealed for the while, and plunges under one of those measly slops of brown water that constitute hygiene in those parts – no wonder Free Staters look so tanned.

Old Kev sure must have taken his time in there provoking Henno, for when he emerges with the other threadbare towel draped about him like the Venus de Milo . . . Henno's disappeared. Dressed and pissed off. (Not with the bike this time. That was on its stand right outside the window.)

So Kev, one rather let down lady, does his usual toilette, climbs into bed and reads a bit. Clutching the pillow in his arms, he falls asleep, staring at the dents in the bed opposite, if that's possible.

Later, after closing time, Henno returns, stiff-drunk and throwing his kit off. He does notice Kev's lovely liquid eyes are following him, and he comes round to Kev's side. The breath is the smell of a wooden vat when the harvest's rotted.

'Know what?' says Henno. 'I been to every dorp, and every dorp's got a poepgat floosie, and old poepgat Henno, he's had every one. Ja man, they mad for my body.'

With that he pats Kev on the cheek. His fingers smell of chalk, and Kev knows it's snooker was all, and Autumn Harvest.

'Ja, they mad for me,' says Henno and as he turns he begins to snore.

The next town it's the same, only this time Kevin sees to it they're in a room as far from the bar as possible. The shower is out in a tin shed through the garden. Pelargoniums!

'It's too far,' says Henno.

'But you must cool down,' says Kev.

'I haven' got a dressing gown. They all sitting out on the back stoep, admiring the flowers.'

'Wear my track suit. I'll wash your shirt meanwhile.'

'Thanks.'

So when he's back and climbs out of the tracksuit, assumes another threadbare towel and hurls himself on the bed again,

Kev figures he better get into action *before* traipsing out for a wash.

'Jus, it's hot,' says Henno, exhaling sportily.

Kev looks across at this and swears blind the bugger's showing what they call a premonitory twitch. He takes the comb out of Kev's spongebag and wipes it on the pillow. Passes it back: 'Thanks, ou pal.'

'Kevin.'

'Kevin.'

With all the courage in the world, Kev says: 'You're terribly windburnt. There, in front.'

Henno pats his chest, signals it's nothing.

But Kevin moves about to intrigue him. Oh, he's already in his towel to sweat off a bit, and has the electric fan on to stir the tense air . . . and he produces from his spongebag a dinky jar of Vaseline (I mean, how *obvious can you get?*). He sidles round for a hand towel and, like any masseur, dips in a finger for a spot of petroleum jelly, sniffing it to see it's still clean.

He perches alongside Henno, bumping his hip ever so delicately, and anoints the first bit of charred flesh.

Henno winces.

But without saying anything Kev takes another dab and strokes it over the collarbone.

'Ouch,' says Henno, 'it's raw, man.'

'Is it sore?' says Kev.

'Not so bad,' says Henno.

Emboldened, Kev takes a larger dab and progresses down the sternum. Henno closes his eyes tight. Kev can feel his heart beat and the hairs on his red flesh rise up. He smoothes across the little cluster there to the one nipple and it stiffens into a thimble.

Henno wrenches his head round, without opening his eyes, and his teeth are showing. Heavy breathing. Kev thinks this must all now signify something – the guy's getting aroused, maybe? *He* was getting aroused. He shifted around his towel, but one look at Henno's fist opening and closing on the counterpane said, Be careful, boetie, one wrong move and I crush you.

But the sore strip continued down the bulge of muscle below his chest. The fan swung, lifting up the scent of jelly and sweat. Henno's heart beating, the shiny cross of viscid fingerprints and the incredible sensation of touching something cool where it hurts . . . Kev gentle as a fly landing and taking off, his fingers going plop and the fan catching the drying strands of Henno's blond hair . . .

Well, all it needed was to bend forward and gently kiss that bristly neck. Do I have to explain? Actually, I get quite horny just thinking about it – *don't you*? This bypass so quickens up my reactions – my *natural* reactions. Remind me, I must tell you about coming round in the hospital, all right?

Ah, Klaus . . . I suppose that's all we want – a bit of loving care. I mean, who can resist it? Let your fingers do the walking and the fan going round faster and faster and that *smell*, for God's sake! Like the whole world's one huge big sweating shiny pubic zone and don't touch that, boys, be careful, it's going to explode. Know what I mean?? I can think of nothing more tense . . . except disposing of a Russian limpet-mine during rush-hour at Checkers. Yes, we have those too, bomb-scares, I mean. Sex is far less anti-social, don't you find?

You want to know if Kevin made some progress there – with Henno's head going back and forth and a total circus tent below. There could be *no doubt* about arousal. And Henno doesn't have a cock; he has a *fifth limb*, I assure you. Kevin with his fingers squelching in the belly button, slowly . . . and the fan sweeping up the fold in the towel.

He must have heard those jokes about greasing up the cat, damn it. All Henno needed to do was plash his big fingers in the jar and – fuck the boy to within an inch of his life!

I said to him, Why didn't you just say, 'Henno, now listen. I know you want it. Your body wants it, even if you don't. You don't have to go out and spend money on a floosie. Maybe I'm next best, but I'm sure I'll do. Touch my lips and see, sink your teeth in my tits. Don't just lie there *groaning* . . .'

But *that* is the entire point. Kevin was not made like you and me. He'd been so slapped around, I think, by other dudes who stole his virtue and his purse as well, just for good measure, I suppose he couldn't be like us anymore.

How I wish old Henno'd just buggered him up, right there and then, and left it at that. Kev would have hurt a lot for a few days, maybe a month . . . and then it'd all've been over. A lot better for poor old Kev, and for all of us as well, frankly. You can't imagine how tetchy we get if Henno's within a mile of here. He knows exactly where we're vulnerable, and homes right in. In your *Zeitung* they say he is 'genial' (Mrs Leibnitz) – I suppose all ball-bearing cock-teasers in Switzerland are described as 'genial'. What, for their sunny temperaments? Under this particular healthy exterior walks poisonous shit, I'm afraid. Bad news is Henno, indeed. And they've got his name wrong, too: it's Wasse*naar*, not

Wasser*man*.

But *what am I trying to tell you?*

The fan's going round and Henno raises his paw, not to stroke Kevin's cheek, but to press the button off. He looks at Kev.

'Let's go sink a few beers.'

Kevin blinks. 'I haven't showered yet,' he says. He trails his finger down from Henno's throat.

'Yes, well I'm thirsty,' says Henno.

'It won't sting so much,' says Kev.

And it's the same again. Kev comes back from the shower, and Henno sinks his floosie (though this point is in doubt), and the breath is malted spirit. Kev doesn't even open his eyes, because he's quite snug in the tracksuit smelling of Henno, which is probably as close to an embrace from him as he'll ever get.

The next night there's an agricultural fair on – which, incidentally, means good business for both fashions and headache powders. All they can get is the last room in the hotel and, you guessed it, it's a ricketty double-bed. Down the passage are two shower cubicles, so this time there's no way Henno can slip out. They both shower together, I mean separately but at the same time. Kev has bought a real shower kit for Henno – that soap that hangs like a slice of melon on a string, and some French shampoo.

All he didn't buy was the comb, because once they're changing again in the bedroom Henno looks across at Kev with that romping mop of his. Kev sits him down on the chair under the light and, with an expression of Ah, now *this* is the way to do it, begins the most elaborate procedures of coiffeur. Singing a little tune the while.

Henno's fists are balling and unballing on his knees as if it's sissy to look refined. When Kev applies a little dab of fastener behind the ears, *pst*, *pst*, Henno completely squirms. He brushes at the air to get rid of the smell. There now, they are ready for the descent to the ladies bar.

The place was packed out, so it wasn't going to be as if they were perching there like a washed-up couple. The ladies at the store immediately grabbed Kev, who'd been doing such nice new windows all day, and he asked Henno just to get him a Coke. In the crowd Henno made for the poolroom and was not again seen to be associated with Kev.

When the women had finished their sweet sherries, Kev went to get another round for them and a Coke for himself. With great good spirits they solidly advised him on how *next* season's fashions should go . . . off the neck a *little* bit, and absolutely more *flowing* at the waist. Because he takes their needs seriously, Kev is hugely popular with them. They tell him at length about the appalling defects of their husbands in plain and humorous ways, and they roar with laughter, Kev quite included in the circle. He is the only out-of-towner they can *talk* to, somehow, without said husbands being jealous.

'Know how much we took today because of the show,' says one. 'No, just at the millinery and modes till. Go on, guess.'

Kev can see the results all about him: gloves, now with sparkling wine stains on them; lacey ruffs around sunburnt necks, still stiff from the factory.

'I must do my washing,' he says at last.

He sidles out through the mass of people so heavily drunk they'll not go home now, past the poolroom swing doors. A stud-farmer is charged through, carried shoulder high by a scrum of men in khaki, a silver trophy in his muttonchop hands. He has won the beef-producers' floating cup for the third year. Through the clapping of the doors Kev sees Henno *has* found the town floosie. She has arranged herself over his back and shoulders, two of her red fingers inside the belt of his jeans. Henno leans forward under her weight, egging the pool-players on.

Demure and dutiful upstairs, Kev does their laundry and hangs it out on the string in the window. The town square is as yet untarred, so the dust shines silver with tyre treads of cattle-trucks. The neat line of Henno's bike, unbelievably still a novelty in those parts, heads for the garage and doesn't re-emerge.

Rucked on his side of the bed, he could not sleep for the crashing of glass and the thuds of furniture in the bar below. Still, it was a lot better than travelling by empty second-class carriages or connecting with railway buses, always late – streaking along on the back of that silver machine, arms round Henno's chest . . .

The bars finally close, though it sounds as if they're being pulled down . . . At about two o'clock Kev thinks he hears Henno's boots approaching across the square and the duck-boards to the hotel door. It is locked and he hasn't taken the keys. Kev wonders if he shouldn't float down in the dark and release the Yale.

But from the grunts and clatters, it is clear Henno has another route of entry – up the guttering onto the corrugated roof of the balcony. So pitch-drunk is he, he weaves like King Kong in the moonlight. Kev whips up the sash window and signals palely and, when Henno latches onto his hand, reels him in. Over the sill he thunders, puking as he hits the floor. Kev gets the potty and holds his forehead. The vomit shoots out of him like soda from a siphon. 'Thanks, hey,' says Henno. Another heave of creme-de-menthe, and he subsides.

Kev has only his facecloth and cleans up. Then comes the unenviable task of getting this unco-ordinated hulk stripped and into bed. This he manages to do with great dignity. Apart from creme-de-menthe, the wretch stinks with the red-fingered girl's perfume. 'Help me, man,' says Kev, half-lugging Henno in his briefs across the carpet. He manages to lumber him into the waiting sheets.

This was only the third night – downhill all the way. It could only get worse. (Break time.)

Mustn't spill tea on this keyboard. Trouble is the screen's top has a slope.

Can you see the pattern emerging? I won't go on and on about it. I haven't sorted it all out myself, but of one thing I'm totally sure: we got it all wrong then. We just assumed old Kev was willing to put up with the social stigma for the wonderful screws he was getting and, like most men, Henno couldn't acknowledge in public, and not yet in private, that that thing he schlepped around was his. So what? – many a lively match is made of worse.

From the outside they were a good team, Kev redecorating the windows on schedule and Henno signing up substantial orders from his drinking buddies. I suppose he was genial on the surface... he was getting his lust satisfied by shameless women who knew how not to hang on – can you believe so many one-night stands are available in places like that? Kev, well Kev, like all of us, had to learn to have no sexuality at all.

But still there are so many elements I cannot reconcile. Kev's not telling is part of the problem; maybe he *can't* tell, cause he really doesn't know. Why, when he has a father like that, who could only throw beer-bottles at him, should he go directly for that same type? Why, when his mother and sisters didn't even see him – or were *not allowed to see him* – should he spend his life drinking Coke with women as repressed as them?

Know what Kev replies? – you can't leave a man when he's down. (Isn't *that* the cry of all South Africa's wives?)

But why, when you have the richest queens in Joburg tripping over themselves for you – you can have a sportscar and tennis and swimming pools and constant patting and petting and a very good life . . . *and* an allowance for clothes, for goodness sake?

Because this is for keeps is for keeps, says Kev.

Next day they were zooming on and the bike broke down. Nothing serious, but it needed a new part. So Henno leaves Kev out there in the middle of nowhere to look after the bike, while he hitches back into town.

And exactly what I say happens: a great polished Maserati slows down and turns back, and out gets a real smoothie, who obviously knows nothing about bikes, and asks if he can help. He was doing the Casino Route and had lots of time on his hands. All Kev had to do was pick up his bag and before nightfall it'd be the luxury suite at the Mmabatho Sun. You know what a Maserati costs these days.

No, says Kev, he's going the other way and must wait for his friend.

Hours later Henno gets a lift back in a clapped-out Volkswagen, with the replacement part in his greasy hands. Know what time it is before they get mobile again? – *twenty past four*.

So they get to town when everything's closed. This dump is so dry there isn't even a bar, let alone a take-away at a café. They book a room with an old widow; she's *very* suspicious of two men wanting to share. But not to worry, the beds are *ten yards* apart. They wash up in a basin with a jug and she gets the maid to serve them some dinner. There's a wind and it is right down to near freezing, so they eat heartily. Thanks to this gnarled old presence, they say nothing. There's no TV, no radio, not even a magazine with colour pictures. The light's flickering from her generator and that's going to be switched off. One candle with a box of matches for emergencies. A night of penance for sins past it is to be, for on each bed is only one blanket.

'Shit, it's freezing,' says Henno, planning to tuck in fully dressed.

Kev thinks to go and ask the old witch for an eiderdown or two. That's right – he puts his hand on the doorknob, opens it and there she is scuttling off from the keyhole with a lantern and her grey plait down her back. Henno stands on the stone, clutching his balls. They wait for a moment and, sure enough, the lights go out. And all is silence and wind. Henno climbs into his bed, his teeth chattering. Kev feels his way along the washing line to his. And they lie like that, curled up with cold.

An hour passes.

Then Henno gets out of bed and fumbles around along the wall. Kev holds his breath, knowing Henno has been thinking a lot to himself. He quickly relives Henno returning in the Volksie, striding with the spare part in his mits, giving it to Kev like a token. Could that be the behaviour, not of a home mechanic, but of a shy lover?

'What, for me!' Kev nearly said, as if it were a bunch of wild flowers.

Was he now pretending to sleepwalk so that in the morning he wouldn't have to remember? He expected a pat on the cheek and breath of – what? Coffee and toothpaste?

Henno was stumbling around for the wash-stand and found the jug underneath. Presently the jet of his piss hit the enamel, but in fits and starts because he was frozen. He finished with a few squirts, then replaced the jug.

Kev said into the silence: 'Are you all right?'

'Jus' had to have a slash,' Henno paused. 'Did I wake you?'

'No, I'm awake,' said Kev. Long pause.

'Did I wake you?' Henno repeated.

'No,' said Kev, holding his breath.

'Shit, it's bloody cold, hey?' said Henno.

Kev shifted. 'You can say that again.' But he wasn't going to make the invitation.

Next thing Henno was at the edge of Kev's bed, saying make room, make room.

Kev pressed against the wall and Henno climbed in – a solid lump of ice. He stretched down inside the bed until their bare feet collided, then he moved away from Kev as close to the edge as possible. 'Good night, sleep tight,' he said. 'Maybe now we can get a bit warm.'

He gave a paroxysm of shivers.

Kev bided his time. When he could feel the warmth slide out of him towards Henno, he placed his arm round Henno's waist. The gesture was familiar enough from motorcycle riding.

Henno brought his hand over Kev's rather reassuringly and Kev, though his heart was going pitter-patter, thought they would now fall asleep.

Occasionally Henno's toe would twitch and Kev twitched back, just to indicate.

Even though there was six inches between them, the equalising warmth was so reassuring Kev was really dropping off . . . when he heard Henno whisper something.

This was hardly the time for the big scene, but he pulled himself awake and said: 'Sh . . . it's all right.'

Henno whispered back: 'No, it's not all right.'

'Um, I don't mind if you climb into bed with me, Henno – just to get warm.'

'That's not what I mean,' said Henno, obviously in total, confidential agony.

Kev risked a reassuring pat on the stomach.

'Don' do that, man, it just makes it worse,' said Henno. He lunged around, elbowing Kev's arm away from him.

Kev counted five. Quietly he said: 'Makes what worse?'

Henno put all his courage into one breath: 'I carn' get it up . . . for *them*.'

Six, seven, eight . . . '*Who?*'

Nine, ten. 'Girls.'

'What girls?'

'You know, floosies.' Henno breathed as if his life depended on it. 'It just . . . stays pap dead . . . and then I get drunk.'

'Oh,' said Kev sympathetically, 'but that isn't the end of the world.' He waited to hear if there was more. 'I thought you're crazy for girls,' he added.

'I am, ever since I been in Standard Six,' said Henno. 'But I carn' get it up anymore . . . even when I got her stripped . . . and she's lying there wide open for it . . . just *waiting* for it . . . nee, that slap thing's going to go in no pink . . . you know.'

'What?'

'Twat, man.'

Kev felt very moved by this and, not thinking, reached for Henno's neck in sympathy.

Henno intercepted his hand and led it down his body. 'But for you . . . you see, it's action stations.'

'Well, I'm very flattered,' said Kev.

'I'm not a moffie, but –'

'I had noticed I turn you on,' said Kev.

Kev withdrew his hand and wiped the slight dampness of urine on the sheet.

'See if you can do something with it, or if it goes pap.'

Kev pulled himself up on his elbow. 'Now that is the meanest, sneakiest way I've ever been approached,' he said in a huff.

'I am not gay,' said Henno. 'But you get me up, I carn' help it, man.'

'Keep your voice down,' said Kev.

Henno whispered urgently. 'You must bring me off or I'll go completely mad.'

Kev bundled the one pillow under his arms. 'And what makes you think I could save your sanity?'

'How'm I supposed to know what you must do?'

'Just because you can't find a spread twat tonight . . .' said Kev. With that he picked up the pillow, squirmed his way over Henno and folded himself with dignity in the other bed. Face to the wall.

'Why did you do that? – just to make him even hotter?'

'No, when it happens,' says Kev, 'it has to be exactly right.'

'So did you get it right?' says Jannie, who never failed to mouth a gift horse in his youth.

Kev stared lugubriously at both of us as if we had very low standards.

We all know what it's like when this desperate impulse is on you and you just *have* to. I'll tell you the hospital story (which I *haven't* told Jannie) . . .

When I was coming round with a lot of whimpering and very confused. I don't know, the stuff they pump you full of. Dead of night it was, and me in my private ward. I suppose I was rising from unconscious to semi-, propped up on pillows, long drip coming out of my arm. I was in an erotic dream like I hadn't had in years. I don't know, I was muzzy . . . All I could think of is if I can find my glasses I'm not dead yet. My chest was so bandaged I could hardly stretch.

So I sank back a bit, my head was full of the smell of chemicals and flowers. I continued to have this wonderful sensation – well, frankly, from my cock. Absolutely wonderful, washing up me as if I was sixteen once more.

I thought, but this is incredible; already I am a new man.

In sheer relief I put my free hand down there, and what did I feel? Well, can you imagine?

It was a very woolly hairdo.

I shook my head insofar as I could.

But no, the blanket and sheet was drawn down to my knees, the flaps of my pyjamas were apart and there, when I could offer no resistance at all, was someone having a go at me. Such bliss!

Such total bliss . . . maybe I *was* dead, and all they say about paradise is true!! In that case, I assure you, I rather rejoiced. Give me more, give me more, I said.

Who wants to reach consciousness in Parktown East after that?

But then I thought, a *woolly* head. That seems very out of Africa to me.

So I rejoiced that I was *alive*, after all, with the biggest fountain of come choking, *spurting* out of me – as I say, like the very first time. And I was totally *shaken. This* is what it's all about. O sweetness and light! I hadn't felt so completely joyous since my youth.

Well, it was Parktown East, all right. The person responsible takes a towel with the hospital crest on it and wipes me down, and does up my jamas, and neatly pulls up the bedding.

'Hey, whoever you are . . .' I say, 'thanks a million.'

Out he slinks with a little wave at the door.

Only then did I realise my new heart had passed its first test . . . with *flying* colours, I assure you.

Next morning I couldn't wait to find out who it was. My managing director came in personally with his wife for the usual pleasantries, as if it hadn't been touch-and-go. This was very good of them, considering the circumstances. David Bennington, the bastard, came in with a huge antherium and looked contrite; I stared at that gross speckled shaft with its label around: With love from David.

Jannie came and sat with me and we talked about the nursery – all progress and planning. Decisions: change over to succulents because people wanted drought-resistant gardens. In his every gesture and phrase was such relief. Once when the sister entered he was about to say something, but he held back until she'd gone.

He clasped my hand under the bedding and was going to go all mushy. The simplest things are the hardest to say. He said: 'I don't know how I would have been able to do without you.'

He must have thought me a callous brute, because I could not help shaking with laughter. 'Me too,' I said (laugh, laugh, laugh) and all I really wanted to admit was *there's somebody loose in this madhouse who gives the most divine . . .*

'Never mind,' said Jannie. 'We're finished with hospitals now, aren't we? I'll pop in tomorrow and you'll be fit and well.'

'Sure will,' I replied, and I forced myself not to giggle; he was getting really pissed off.

When everyone's gone, thank God, in comes this cleaner with a bucket and mop, back on shift.

'Was it Dr Alpheus sent you,' I said, 'last night?'

'No,' he says, with a bit of a smile. He's quite a becoming lad with a big frizz. Unassuming, I would say. Surely Kev's friend in Parys was like that.

'Do you know Danny and Martie?' I said. 'That's just the kind of welcome back present they'd arrange.'

He looks thoughtful. 'Danny and Martie?' he says.

'They live two blocks away.' I didn't want to add they're into odd types and it seems most likely.

'No, I don't know them,' says this lad.

'Who was it then?' I ask, bursting with curiosity.

He makes a few more swabs. 'I wasn't *sent* to you by anybody, sir.'

'Except by God, I suppose.'

He swabs around briskly, and then he stops and gives it to me. 'It's like this, sir. I was in the operating theatre when they brings you in.' He makes a few strokes to show what he was doing there. 'Nobody listens when a patient's going down, but they talk talk talk like you got no idea. And I thought –' he poses on his mop, 'that one, sir . . . *he's* going to need something really special he hasn't had in a long time. Or he won't come right at all.'

That put me in my place.

There are night-time encounters and night-time encounters. You of all people I should be telling. By contrast with mine, Kev was having the other kind. You'd have spotted it coming a mile off.

I suppose that's really why you left. South Africa always breeds this incredible violence. You used to say you could *smell* it in the air. If your nosebuds are that sensitive I suppose you had to go – back to your hygiene and your gemütlichkeit. Just right for you, Klaus – and I'm really pleased for you . . . While we sit in this rising stench! The state of emergency just legalises violence (you're perfectly right).

Here, then, is something you'll really deplore. *Deploring* is what you do at a distance without getting involved, by the way. We didn't want to get involved either, of course.

But what would you or we have done if we had *had* to be there . . . in that forlorn, wind-stricken room with floors like a morgue and no electricity at midnight zero? What would you or we have done to intervene for Kev, beyond the reach of civilization, such a sweet, quiet, unprotesting fellow (one of ours – and at times of threat the queens' union should stand together most)?

Well, we'd have done a lot more than the Free State police did, *that's* for sure.

We've been over this I don't know how many times. Jannie *still* says it was that hex at the keyhole who was involved. Bursting through the door with her burning broomstick and hissing cat . . . and a red-hot cross to fasten to Kev's flesh, and beat him down with a Bible. Certainly he was tied to the bedposts with her washing-line, as if for an exorcism.

That would account for her wanting to have nothing to do with it in the morning. She never went into the room, but left the maid to find him. And the police came, not because she called them, as you would expect ... but the maid did through a neighbour. Then, when they eventually pitched, that old crone wouldn't let them in (because she didn't want her secrets to be seen, says Jannie).

She didn't want the scandal to spread and spoil her business. I can understand that, and I don't blame her. She wanted just to bury it all, like I buried that baby. Kev's right; some things are better left unexposed.

Poor Kev. So at last two policemen burst in and this is the evidence they find. I suppose you've heard differently from Danny and Martie – that there was blood on the walls, semen-stains like saltpans in the veld, and every other sign of a battle nobly fought and terribly lost.

There was exactly this: Kev tied upside down to the bed as you know, naked but thawing out cause it was quite a nice day. He couldn't call for help – his panties had been taken from the same line that tied his wrists, and jammed down his throat. His jaw was tied shut with a strip of sheet. Somebody'd smashed a half-jack and written with the broken edge – moffie – on his back. Only Kev's quite tiny and the letters started too big, so it was M-O-F-F. This had taken a long time because candlewax was dripped all over him. Kev had shat himself a little, and who could blame him?

Oh yes, and he'd been doused in a jug of urine. This they spent a long time trying to figure out, sniffing the bed and sniffing the jug that was thrown across the floor.

So the case is before you. Pretty clear who did it.

They are a white constable and a black one, and while the black one unties Kev the maid brings in tea for three. I suppose the white one didn't want to get his hands dirty, but didn't mind pouring the milk.

The woman who runs the place wants compensation for the torn sheet and for the mattress.

The white constable throws Kev a towel to cover himself. Kev crawls to a sitting position with his back to them, says won't they just also sit down.

So the maid fetches chairs and the white constable sits with his teacup and the black one stations himself outside the door, in case the criminal comes back to the scene of the crime.

'So what happened?' says the constable, playing it as if

he's seen far worse – a young guy, newly married, obviously scared out of his wits.

Kev sips and replaces his cup. And what does he say? Kev says, 'It's nothing.'

'Was it that ou on the motorbike? What's his registration?' Henno was half-way back to Bellville by then; that's where he lived. 'We seen him chasing down to Brandfort at sunrise.'

'It doesn't matter,' says Kev.

'Don' you wan' to press a charge?' says the constable.

Kev says: 'No.'

'Well, I got to take your particulars,' says the constable.

'Can I wash up first?' says Kev.

'Yes,' says the constable, and he goes to call the maid for a bowl of hot water.

Kev cleans himself, though how he managed without help I don't know. He also tidies the room as best he can. Half an hour later a dab behind the ears and he emerges in his tracksuit.

The old woman presents him with the extra bill. He has just enough cash to cover it. So he wasn't robbed, and he had everything he owned safely in his little zip-up bag. Particulars are taken.

'You mus' press charges,' says the constable. 'We jus' radio through to Bloemfontein and they got him for questioning. Once he's past Bloemfontein, he can go ten ways.'

'Who?' says Kev.

'The person who did this to you.'

'What?'

'Well,' said the constable, 'we call it assault with intent to do grievous bodily harm. Ten years minimum. For attempted murder – twenty.'

'No,' says Kev.

With that the black constable opens the door of the van for Kev, and they give him a lift to the shop in the next town where he's due and where they were going, anyway. The constable shakes his head all the way.

'Thank you,' says Kev as he alights.

'Hey listen,' says the constable, taking off his hat and fanning himself. 'Are you really a – you know . . .?'

'Yes,' says Kev.

'Then jus' keep your shirt on at all times. That's my advice.'

Kev thanks him and the black constable and goes to work.

'That's exactly where you made your mistake,' said Jannie. 'You *should* have pressed charges. If you didn't, you know what it looked like? You two got in the room of this poor woman's house. She didn't want to take you in anyway. No one's going to believe the keyhole business . . .'

'She was watching all the time,' said Kev.

'What d'you mean,' I said.

'When Henno was doing it. I could hear her in the passage. She could see because the candle was lit inside.'

'Oh my God,' said Jannie.

We just sat there glum. My thoughts were racing. 'My God, Kev,' I said, and went for a top-up. One for Jannie, too.

'But then,' said Jannie, 'why didn't you charge him with violation of your own person? You even had her as a witness. She'd be forced to testify.'

'None of us love the police, Kev – but there is a law and if you go on pushing hard enough they have to serve it.'

'You were too taken with the constable, you dilly queen, so you played your usual tactic – passive resistance,' I said.

'He was very afraid of sexual matters. He was only eighteen,' said Kev.

'But in *his* eyes, assuming he could think that far,' said Jannie, quite exasperated, 'look what it looked like. You are anyway suspect – all the defence had to do was phone up your pa. Both of you get to that bedroom and naturally *you're* the one makes the indecent proposal. In *their* eyes Henno's the one who acts correctly. He's never been so insulted in his life; he's outraged and provoked; he reacts exactly as any man would. He ties you up to keep you off him, you lascivious bitch. He scratches what you are on your back, so that everyone else finds out what he has and can stay clear. She's *never* going to tell she's seen him have congress with you . . . most probably had her hand under her nightie all the time as well . . .'

Jannie lost the thread as his sister came in. She never had a sense of when we wanted to be private.

'Fiona, kom sit by my,' said Kev, moving along the sofa.

She went to fetch a drink.

Jannie whispered quickly: 'You see, if you didn't press, *you* were the one destined for jail.'

'No,' said Kev.

'Yes,' said Jannie.

'For what?' said I in a fuddle.

'You do know by now,' said Jannie to me with patience, 'it is against the law to proclaim you're gay.'

'So now he tells me,' I snapped in irritation.

In comes Fiona with her fourth double . . . she should be in clover. Jannie tracked her down to one desperate room in

Berea. At least with us she could get no more than scotch. Kev was the only one who actually liked Fiona.

He pats the sofa and they both sit, wiggling their bottoms to get comfy, as well they might.

'And so,' said Fiona, looking around. 'How's sales in the flower business?'

'Not as good as the liquor business,' I said.

'Fine, fine, my skat,' said Jannie.

I could see the rest of the evening was shot, just when we were getting somewhere.

Fiona swung her eyes round.

'Sorry,' I said to her, 'we were gupping . . . you know. Not strictly *your* subject.'

'Oh, don't mind me,' she said, and thought better of it: 'I'll just get my knitting.'

'You do that,' said Jannie, and the moment her bare heels were round the door added: 'But Kev – quickly man – what I still don't understand – did he want to and have to – just screw you to prove he could – or was it? – you know, really rape?'

Surely Kev knew the difference.

I shot across: 'Was it he fucked you . . . or, you know, he fucked you up? Sorry to put it so baldly.'

'He didn't use some soap or the Vaseline?' said Jannie.

'No, no,' said Kev.

'Then it *was* rape,' I said, sitting back and looking for the video control.

'No,' said Kev softly. 'You don't understand a thing.'

'At least that was the end of it, and I'm glad for your sake,' Jannie whispered, 'and you're rid of the rubbish. You did the right thing not giving his registration number. Otherwise you'd have to face him again in court.'

'It's for the best,' I said. 'You're shot of him, so choose better next time. And choose in Johannesburg where you've got masses of friends, and thank God meanwhile you're alive . . .'

'. . . to tell the tale,' Jannie concluded. 'End of story.'

Kev was not satisfied with that, but Fiona came in. 'What are we seeing?' she said.

'*Witness*,' I said.

'Is that *Witness* with Harrison Ford or *Eyewitness* with William Hurt?' she said.

'We'll soon see,' said Jannie.

'What's the difference?' I said, and flicked it on before she could explain.

'No, it's just *Witness*,' she explained to Kev even before the credits were underway, 'where he punches the tourist because he's laughing at the religious people.' She arranged Kev's balled fists and draped a hank of wool on them.

'It's not the one about the murder in the office,' said Jannie.

'That's *Eyewitness*,' said Fiona.

'This one's where she strips off in the attic to have her bath and he sees her,' said Jannie.

'I prefer William Hurt,' said Fiona.

From Kevin: 'You mean this is the one where he dresses up for dinner in jail?'

'*No*,' we both shouted at him.

'That's *Spider's Kiss*,' said Jannie.

'*Kiss of the Woman's Spider*,' I said.

Well, you try and say it fast when you're past it.

'It's *Kiss of the Spider Woman*, for Christ sake,' said Fiona.

'No, it's *Witness*. Look, it says,' Jannie pointed at the screen.

Whichever it was I slept through most of it. Fiona'd gone to bed because she'd seen it before. Jannie woke and brought me a nightcap and went off to bed himself.

Kev looked completely relaxed and had enjoyed it.

We talked a bit, insofar as you can call it talk, and then he helped me up. The advantages of restraint – he was fresh as a daisy.

'I'll take you, just put the one foot forward,' he said. 'Any one.'

'Piss off, Kev,' I said, but I accepted his shoulder.

Halfway down the passage some nagging thought surfaced, and I stopped for a breather. 'I just want you to know, Kev... Any time... you're in trouble... you know you're... more than welcome. Treat you like blood-family. You're much more welcome than bloody Fiona, as a matter of fact.'

'Fiona's fine,' he said, egging me on.

''Cept she never knows when she isn't wanted.'

Kevin stood in front of me to coax me on. Then it struck me what I had to know. I said I wouldn't go to bed ever again if he didn't tell me.

He said he'd let me know in the morning.

I put my hands on his shoulders. I said: 'When he bore down on you did he hate you or did he love you? That's all I want to know.'

Kevin turned around to lure me forward.

I took a few steps.

'All right, I'll rephrase the question,' I said. 'When he

imposed himself upon you, did he do it . . . to make you feel lekker or make you feel sore?'

Kev was signalling like a traffic cop at the intersection of the passage. My right of way, then left.

I grabbed the china cupboard and could hear a plate slide.

'If you don't tell me, Kev, I'll sleep in the hothouse just to spite you and catch pneumonia.'

'I *wanted* it to hurt,' said Kev.

'What?' I said, trying to adjust the plate, but he steered me the shortest route to my bed.

'*Why* did you want it to *hurt*?' I said.

'Ah fokoff, man, both of you,' said Jannie, waking up.

'I . . . can't . . . explain,' said Kev, 'I . . . wanted it . . . to be sore.'

'You will be sore in a minute if you don't shut up,' Jannie threatened.

I beached myself in the pillows. 'Ah Kev,' I mumbled, 'be an absolute angel and switch the lights off.'

That's how it went. It's much better now we don't drink so much.

More flashes from the neon-light of memory. I'm in the freezing flat. This terminal seems to be fine.

Why am I going on like this? Because the only part of me still drunk is my hands on the keyboard – like two crabs trying to mate.

As you must know, when you're a reformed liquor-head . . . your social life is finito, as Gino would say. I miss melting into an armchair at the Pink Flamingo and an evening of merry backchat. It's hopeless to go now, just because the top of a bottle connects with the bottom . . . and when the others are tick-tight and oblivious, how can I still have my memory glowing like neon?

I use a very weak tot beside me, with soda to the brim. This must last me till the hour. Drinking to get warm never worked anyway.

I'm not making all this up, you know. I can relive things I thought I'd long buried. Dialogue is the most difficult. (I do those bits again and again!) But Klaus, can you see how I actually hear how people *actually talk*? Good, I hope so! I want to get it – *exactly* – right for you.

I'm doing this bit in town as I don't want Jannie to see. I may say, with the new regimen I'm *so* pleased to be with him every Friday night – so it's not bad relationship making me secretive. But you know what, I'm quite enjoying this. (It's got a bit beyond a letter, hey?) Oops . . .

Guess who's on the phone? *David Bennington*. He has a nerve. I must tell you how Jannie and I tried to find out if he had a piece or not. Excuse me, can he take me to Stacks and Flywheels tomorrow? But my boy, how *kind* of you to keep asking . . .

Right. The return of Henno.

One sultry evening, when we were all depletedly sitting on the balcony of the Flamingo Lounge (you knew so well . . .) and the stars were twinkling on the surface of the pool below, the crickets stridulating (beat that!), the fireflies . . . and it was Paul's turn for a round of doubles, this being his farewell do, and Kev was backed invisibly into a potted palm with his Coke can . . . It was crowded, *crowded*. I always preferred the balcony – from there you could inspect the talent without getting trodden down.

You know what I'm talking about. So I can skip this bit. All right, so I'll skip it.

You should have heard your Paul give a real low-class blast of the Alpenhorn he calls his throat, as we see this leather number throttle down pure steaming steel and draw to a halt in the street. Paul'd been practising for that moment all right. Everyone else of who's left's drooling over the railings like it's feeding time at the zoo.

'Hm, hm, Cape numberplate – Bellville breeds 'em roff,' says Danny. It was one of those chance observations.

Also it was chance I saw Kev stiffen up. He leapt to the rail . . . but the bike was already underneath.

Kev says nothing, indicates nothing. But *he knew*. Wish to God *we'd* known (about the rape and all). Then, in our right minds, we could have smuggled him into the john, let him down the creepers on a rope of our handkerchiefs . . .

Do you see how ghastly ironic it was? Paul comes with the tray of refills and says anyone know a Kevin Vermaak round here, and of course he was just teasing him and we're immediately alert. (Check the details with Paul.) Cause there's Rambo in chains at the door and he's not trying to rent his jockstrap for the floorshow! Could Kevin Vermaak *please identify* him at the door.

And Kev, who's blushing at this chorus of we told him so, his hand to his breast as if to say . . . *ME*??

Of course, drunken farts, that's what we should have done. Sent Kev to a neutral country. Like Switzerland. Immediately.

Kev's blushing redder than Coke and minces off to the

door. We thought it was at last his great and secret assignation and, kind of, toasted him, 'Good luck, Kev.'

But you see now what it was: the *sacrificial lamb going to the butcher*. And proud of it.

If only he'd stood there in the door in the pink light and just, all at once, spat at him. Had Henno struck back at Kev, I promise you, two hundred screaming faggots like a flock of furious gulls would have pecked him to death! He'd've been dismembered on the spot! He'd have been mixmastered! His cock'd be stuffed and mounted above the bar, with a sign saying: NOW DON'T YOU EVER EVER GO FOR SUCH A JERK AGAIN! We'd have used his BALLS for PUNCHBAGS!

Paul didn't know; we didn't know. All we thought five minutes later when we saw the bike emerge was: Now there's a news item for *Exit*, so keep drinking till it's off the press.

David Bennington really doesn't show. A little light-wristed on the gearshift, maybe. Stacks and Flywheels is coming up nicely since we took it over.

But hell, it's amazing, I was thinking all day, the devious ways relationships work. And here I'm not going to be so harsh on Henno because, believe me, I can see what it's like – unemployment. We've put 50,000 people off. Mostly it's coal that's hit. In many ways you and Paul wouldn't recognise South Africa after the slippery slide – you can't go through a door without someone accosting you for work, or get to a stop-street without a request for money for bread.

Mind you, that isn't to say the economic crunch isn't changing other habits as well. Know what I saw the other day when I went to Pick 'n Pay? A *black* Father Christmas! Know what was sitting expectantly on his knee? – *white* kids.

Anyway, so a few months later Henno had lost his job. I don't know if he wasn't selling enough or his expenses turned out to be phoney or what. But he was fired. Now how can a twenty-six year old, with no education and training – but he knows every pharmacy in the country districts – who can hardly sign his name, get another job? Folk medicine is dying a death; they're into prescription drugs now, even on the platteland. What must he go and sell – bionic ears, for God's sake? (Oh yes, I was going to tell you about our medical miracles. That's one of them: the deaf can hear and, you know what? – apartheid's *defeated death*. Fat lot of good that does if an able-bodied man can't get a job.)

Henno's out of one, and I don't know what kind of

41

erosions this set up in his personality. He tried everything, but many blacks are far more skilled than him. Being a bricky. Manual labour. His drinking habit couldn't've helped, not to mention a floosie a night – I suppose he maintained that routine, or he'd like us to think he did. But your virility's the first thing to go when you're insecure. Although that was maybe a good thing, frankly, I won't be too hard on him.

So he's driven to the lowest he can go. In this case it's find his mom, which is better than Mother Army. Unlike the defence force, she's chucked him out years ago. She chucks him out once again, but this time with a difference: fifty rand.

All this I got from Kevin later – actually when he was hiding permanently with us and we had more than enough time to talk. That's when I was in trouble, too. So I *do* understand what it's like.

Fifty rand is not enough to get to Pretoria from Cape Town on a bike, but he can just make Joburg. The needle is on red.

So how did their reunion dialogue at the door go? You borrow me five and I take you for a ride.

Work it out – the pattern holds good for a long time. That was the deal, and Kevin went for it. He had his very nice flat, remember – more than he could afford and the furnishings not half paid for, but the bike could be safe in the stairwell. In the lounge there was a place to sleep, on the sofa.

First we know of the details was when Kev invited Jannie and me to one of his perfect little dinners (just after Paul'd gone). I thought it would be a homely foursome, but Henno didn't pitch on time. You know the way Kev keeps it so spick and span you wouldn't know if an ant had passed through, let alone an out of work bike-boy on the bum. But when I went to the toilet (he served only a little Boschendal Grand Cru, and Jannie was going to have to go back to the farm, so we weren't going to get that plastered) ... there in the broom-cupboard was the evidence: not one, but two, crash-helmets hanging neatly on hooks. Also, Kev's face and his hands looked as if he'd put in a lot of open-air miles in the last few weeks. He looked fabulous.

At table Jannie said: 'So what happened between you and that guy in chainmail?'

I gave him a shove with my knee under the table.

Kev faltered with his soup-spoon in the air. 'Which?'

'The one who fetched you at the floppy Flamingo,' Jannie persisted. 'I heard about it from everybody. He showed me the bike in question's still downstairs.'

I gave Jannie a clip on the shin.

He turned to me. 'It's no use kicking me, you shit. I'm sure Kev has absolutely nothing to hide.'

'It's none of our business,' I said, planning to get him back later.

But Kev said, to my relief: 'Um, he takes me when I'm on circuit. That's much quicker. I'm back for the weekend.'

Kev took the soup-plates to the kitchen. I scowled at Jannie.

Putting his hand on the fourth soup-plate, Jannie whispered: 'Well, he's obviously not going to join us.'

I opened another bottle and talked through the gap; it was too small for me to get in there and help Kev. 'So you use him to race the public transport?' I said.

'Yes,' Kev said, letting the oven door go.

'Well, as long as you keep wearing your helmet,' I said.

'And use it as a condom at night, Kev – you never know where he's been,' said Jannie.

'Oh, we've got lots of real condoms,' said Kev.

'You see, she's bragging already,' said Jannie to me.

'Know what they call a place where they sell pre-stuffed condoms?' I said.

'A creperie,' said Jannie. 'You told it before.'

'Well, I'm glad you've settled down into something, Kev,' I said, with no clue how he was covering up.

He served mutton chops with mint and there was more than enough with the extra portion to share.

Actually Kev had bought the place under sectional title, not rented, and could get something back if he sold. I used to handle his affairs for him and it was quite a good deal. The value of property was shooting up as fast as the bottles emptied.

'In effect you employ him. Pity it's not tax deductible,' I said.

'So do you give him pocket money as well? Must be nice to keep a man,' said Jannie.

'Twelve rand a day, absolute maximum,' said Kev.

'Twelve rand a day . . .' said Jannie in admiration. 'That's not too bad if the benefits are good.'

'They are,' said Kev.

What he meant us to infer was that he had never believed life could be so great. It didn't need quick calculations to see Kev was living beyond his budget.

Kev served strawberries and cream.

'How's the nursery business?' he asked. 'I saw some of your cuttings out in Delareyville – Bairnsford Nurseries on the label.'

Jannie was so pleased. 'Strelitzias,' he said.

'No poinsettias,' said Kev.

'Not in *Delareyville*,' said Jannie.

'Maybe it was Sannieshof. No it *was* Delareyville. They planted a hedge – to keep the dust out of the post office.'

'The strelitzias were Sannieshof. See, I told you we're going to beautify the Transvaal, if they water them.' Jannie raised his glass and, as Kev didn't have one, tapped mine.

'Sounds like a tongue-twister,' I said, 'strelitzias in Sannieshof . . .' Well, you try saying that when you're deep in.

'Better than Physostegia virginiana in Sendelingsfontein,' said Jannie.

'That wouldn't last very long,' said Kev.

We looked at him. I believe that's the only time Kevin has been known to crack a joke. Like most of the things he did, it had the opposite effect to the one intended.

'A virgin among the missionaries. Wouldn't last so long. That's all I said,' said Kev.

'What d'you mean, our plants *are guaranteed*,' said Jannie.

'It was only a witticism,' said Kev.

'Yes, and I want to know why when you do talk you *always* say the *wrong* thing,' said Jannie.

'Leave it,' I said quietly.

'Don't you dare insult my Physostegia virginianas!'

'Jannie!' I said.

'They the best in the bloody Transvaal. Ask Kierieklapper, ask even Floribunda, they'd have to admit. Why do you think we're getting so many orders for them?'

'Jannie,' I said, 'watch your manners.'

'Manners!' he exploded. He raised his head and his beard seemed curled with ferocity. His great blue eyes took in none of the white furnishings or the wall-hangings. His anger generated phlegm in his throat and he swallowed. He swallowed again. There are times I love Jannie so much I just stop functioning. But that's between us.

He hadn't flown right off the handle. 'Well,' he said, all subdued, 'that's good news about the strelitz . . .' His tongue, like a delivery van going into mud, slewed to a halt. 'No, I'm really glad,' he said. 'I better eat my sht . . .'

'Cor, they do breed these things so vast today,' I said.

Kev passed Jannie the sugar for them.

His hand shaking, Jannie took some.

Kev wanted to get a cloth to clean up the excess Jannie had broadcast, but I restrained him. 'It's all right,' I said. 'We're going just now. Sorry.'

Kev indicated his feelings were not hurt.

I contemplated a strawberry so large it could hardly fit in my jaw. I suppose that's all a man wants, really; gross fruit to suck, with a bit of economic security as back up. The trouble with Calvinists like Jannie and Kev is they can't *enjoy* themselves unless they're rich.

Kev clears up and puts the coffee on. Who lets himself in with his own keys – but Henno. Well now.

I stand up out of politeness. This is my first sight of him – at close up, I mean. Overfirm handshake, familiar only to drunks. He's most probably sunk vodka, cause he doesn't smell of anything. He has that deferential way of inferiors, or at least those who think they're inferior . . . looking you in the chest while you look them in the eye. His own chest is worn like biltong; he couldn't cover that with his shirt or it'd catch fire. What a lunchbox, as they say.

'Good evening,' he says, in a brisk, clipped accent. 'No, don't get up,' he says to Jannie who's struggling in the chair legs.

They shake across the table.

'What did you say your name was, sorry?' says Jannie.

'Sorry, Wassenaar,' says Henno.

'Is jy van die Louis Wassenaars of die Kaapse Wassenaars?'[1]

'Nee, van Bellville af. I was working there by Grandpa.'

'For your grandpa?' says Jannie.

'No man, the powders.'

'Oh, Grandpa Headaches, you mean.'

'They very good for hangovers,' I say.

'You can say that again,' says Henno.

Kev comes in a bit late for introductions – you can see he's flustered. No 'Where have *you* been?' or anything like that. He just gives half a smile and gestures to Henno's seat at the table.

'We already been introduced,' says Henno. 'No, don't let me disturb you. I'll just –' He clomps into the living room.

'Actually we must go now, Kev,' I say. 'It's late.'

'Yes, we must go. Shit, look at the time,' says Jannie.

I don't want it to seem as if we're walking out. Kev has the coffee ready, and stares at us. Something in him is saying: 'Help me.'

---

1. Afrikaner tribal custom. I suppose it helps to know if you have domestica or a hybrid in hand.

In the lounge you got some idea of what old Kev was having to put up with. In three seconds that lout had his greasy jacket here, his boots up on the glass table, socks all over the Rorke's Drift carpet. Like a Bez Valley husband coming home, punching the wife and screaming at the kids. Jannie's own father was like that; that's why, after years of it, we had to accommodate Fiona. Yet such goodness can come out of filth and deprivation – witness Jannie.

Henno wants to sleep, but now we're sitting on his bed, waiting for coffee. He just curls up in the single armchair at the end, and I know, even if the flat is serviced, Kev's going to have to clean it down in the morning.

'O die *Kaapse* Wassenaars,' says Jannie, just to make conversation. 'Is dit die Wassenaar-Browns of net die gewone?'

'No, it's plain without filter,' says Henno. His point.

Kev brings in the silver tray and I leap up to take the boots off the table. He goes out to get the Cointreau.

Seeing his opportunity, Henno is quick as a flash beside me. 'Listen,' he says, 'I mus' borrow back Kev some bucks. You got twenty to spare? He treads from one foot to the other, as if he's squeezing grapes.

'No,' I say, 'not on me.' I suppose he thought he'd spotted a soft touch. See how economic necessity takes precedence over sexual prejudice?

But Jannie is the one who's like steel on cashflow. 'Neither a borrower nor a lender be,' he says.

Kev comes in and Henno circles about a bit, banging his fists. He's a feisty type, a real battler. You'll never breed that out of them. He's not as big as you think he is, but he takes up space. Kev, meanwhile, you could fold into a shoebox!

Henno now has some party questions. 'Hey,' he says, 'how do you prevent yourself getting AIDS?'

I don't know; I stare at my quivering liqueur. 'Use a waistcoat, I suppose.'

'No,' says Henno . . . 'don't *bend* for a *friend*!'

Well, that didn't get a chuckle.

'How do you . . . get four moffies on one barstool?' he says all in a rush.

Jannie also has his Cointreau ready for absorption. 'I don't know. One on the north, one on the south . . . but there must be a catch.'

'Yes, no,' says Henno, slapping both arms of the chair. 'Turn it upside down.'

Well, no response from us.

'Hey Kev, Kev, how do you . . . get them off again?'

'Get what off again?' he says brittly.

'The moffies, man, that's stuck with their arses on the legs.'

Kev has his coffee cup to his lips. 'I haven't a clue,' he says.

'Run in shouting AIDS, AIDS . . .' goes Henno, and he absolutely pisses himself. Rather characteristic, I'd say.

Presently he gets bored at the women's gossip, and goes to the jazz.

Kev looks up at us both as if he wants to know what we think.

We listen to the prodigious stream hitting the porcelain.

'Well, if you want to know,' says Jannie, 'you get out of this *right now*. I mean *tonight*, Kev.'

I agree exactly. 'He's got a very good bod and all. But he's basically hostile to gays. He won't make you happy, Kev.'

Henno flushes.

'I can't,' says Kev. 'He needs me.'

'It's not him we're worrying about,' I come back instantly. '*You* don't need *him*.'

'Out,' says Jannie. 'You know what to do with rubbish? Dispose of it.'

Henno comes back in. I suppose what we were meaning to do – and too pissed to do – was grab him from behind and shove him out the door, with his boots and socks and helmet after him. And keep Kev's keys. They were right next to his coffee cup by the single armchair.

Henno glances at Jannie. Guiltily Jannie says: 'You want to sleep here now?'

'No, it's all right,' says Henno.

As if he has been reading our innermost thoughts, he takes those very keys, puts them tight in his pocket, and goes off to *Kev's* bed next door.

'What you going to do *now*?' says Jannie.

'I don't know,' says Kev. 'Sleep in here.'

Pretty hopeless, our Kev.

And that's Henno for you. The type of guy who spends his childhood pulling the wings off flies, and his adulthood ripping off gays. That's genial Henno for you. Fade to black on this one.

Funny to think that he became the father of our child.

The conception of our child took place under circumstances so different from what Beta Agency put out, I don't know where I'm even going to begin.

The time and place was New Year's Eve, 1986-87. The rutted road to Bairnsford Nurseries was worth all that drive; we'd had a little rain and, believe me, it sparkled.

The parking area was solid with jacaranda above and below. Dimorphoteca and sparaxis by the million in waves down to even the Busy Lizzie; heavy, unbelievable hydrangeas and the Pride of India was magnificent. Jannie had every plant that performs in December active around the patio. You couldn't get to the drinks without clawing your way through blossom. We tried to get people to come while it was still daylight. Some of them were working late; Alfie and Richie pitched only at about *one minute* to midnight, so they missed the dinner and floorshow, but they didn't miss the *best part*.

Kev was invited as usual and he said could be bring Henno. Jannie said no; it was strictly family. I said if he could have *Fiona* (who was family of a different sort), Kev *could* have Henno. He said couldn't I see Fiona knew the scene by now and would be the last to make trouble, poor thing. (Fiona was so advanced by then we couldn't in all honesty leave her in town ... anyway, she'd be drowned out by exuberant queens.)

I said if Henno didn't know the scene by now after living with one for over six months, well then, I was Cleopatra; anyway, he could play Antony to me any time he wanted. So they could both come, even if that would change the *tone* of the thing.

But the main item on the guest list, remember, was David Bennington and his mystery 'friend'. Unfortunately it was practical for Danny and Martie to fetch them, as they must have told you ... but they had *strict instructions* not to camp it up and make it unpleasant for them if the 'friend' turned out to be technically female; she'd get depressed enough having Fiona to swop clothing hints and dirges with. It turns out Danny and Martie also had two numbers they may not have mentioned, picked up in Fontana and not invited by us ... (my dear, the sveltest disco-kids you've ever seen, claiming to be Malawians, but at the end, when all was revealed, of course they came from *Standerton*). Which made *six* in Danny's padded old Rolls.

My dear, so out step these two has-beens with their footmen ... Jannie's panting to see Bliss Bennington and I give him a friendly handshake, and I'm panting to see Bennington's other half ... And out comes this ... well. All I can say is that if Dave Bennington gave me the heart flutters, this one was the *direct cause* of my bypass.

'A very different boy, none of that flash-trash,' says Martie.

'He's deep into discipline and short back and sides,' says Danny behind his hand, which could you not but tell.

A very cleancut and upright boy, who wasn't going to give away one thing, my dear. Later in the jacuzzi I said what did he do to get a body like that. He was evasive. Of course he *couldn't* tell, nor could David Bennington – if he had we'd have all fled screaming into the undergrowth. But at least the 'mystery' was a man, a real one, and I had Dave Bennington out in the open.

The two 'Malawians' told us their names and we immediately forget them; clearly Martie and Danny would keep charge of them and that was that.

'Welcome to the Country Club,' says Jannie.

'Changing room's that way,' I say.

In steams Kev and Henno, looking as if they'd had a few rolls in the dirt on the way, but the costumes were okay – Kev borrowed them from his chain for the night, for him and for me. Henno looked so pleased to be invited I almost began to like him. I suppose without us he'd have been smashing bottles on people's cars in Kotze Street as the clock struck. Still, nothing was going to turn that brute male rapist into anybody's simpering fairy . . . as you'll see.

We put Kev and Henno in the rondavel, which got rid of them. Where you and Paul stayed the year before, not that I mean we wanted to get rid of *you*. I mean there *they* could sort out their own thing, as you did, *not so*? The best bedroom inside had David Bennington and Mr X, and the one next to ours was reserved for Alfie and Richie, and Danny and Martie with their lot to sort out camp beds in the dining room. All the eating things were outside amidst the floral display.

That's about it and for a while it was getting acquainted with the new, improved bar area. Val was there, too, of course. I can take old Val only in small doses – in fact, annually. He's taken to lurking in the shadows and then if something struts past he sidles up, saying 'Hello, dearie . . .' and slides his hand straight in. Well, some people let him and others are affronted, so the best thing these days is to get him seated in a low chair he can't get out of. Fiona sat next to him on the couch and Henno on the other side, so you know what he does? – stretches right over her and goes for a grope. Jannie says: 'Val!' like you would for the dogs to come to heel. So he transfers his attention to one of the so-called Malawi boys on the other side and does that one just give a polite look of puzzlement.

So those who are not in the bar are stripped for the jacuzzi or strolling down the lawn to the garden – we've got it floodlit now, down to the eucalyptus grove, which is an incredibly restful effect. Jannie was in the kitchen and I was dispensing, so when the actual dogs were going crazy around the jacuzzi I went to call them off. Poor David Bennington's trying to have a quiet moment with his piece and is being barked to death. He pulls one in, and then the whole pack piles after it, and you've never seen such a mass of yelps and shrieks in soda-water. Then the whole pack climbs out and over the newly ploughed turf, and so that's it to clean clothes for the rest of the night.

When it's muddy paws and wet arses at the banquet, benches and garden chairs outside have to do. I'll give you another party rule: don't have strings of *coloured lights* over everything, because it makes the most beautiful food in the world look gross. Jannie from the one end, when everyone had a place, was going up and down with a flashlight to show them what delicacies they were actually eating. Stick to lanterns and old-fashioned candles.

We didn't have a seating plan so I inevitably got the drinking circle of sodden old pisscats my end. Val was on my right and we isolated him with two chairs for Alfie and Richie, and Martie and Danny on my left, undivided and undiluted. Beyond that there was an increasing gradation of merriment. Ou Sara, and we had Belinda on for her first big do, served from my end down. It was hell of a nice.

Inevitably Val starts on the annual stocktaking. Figures may be my world, but honestly – he is into demographic gay statistics of the most specialised variety. Who's died, who's gone straight, who's come gay, who's emigrated. As I remember we drank quite a few toasts to you, and to Paul as well, on your first anniversary.

'Remember that wasp-waisted number at Pete's place? The one who ended up with Willem?'

'And then Jensie at Pelindaba,' said Martie.

'Yes, that one,' said Val.

Danny remembered. 'Then he ups and offs to wasn't it Henk?'

'Which Henk?' from Val.

'Henk, you know, who runs 24-Hour Trucks,' from Martie.

'Yes, that one. He's gone,' Val confirmed.

'What, big A?' I said.

'No, A for Australia,' said Val, ticking off.

We all followed up his route to see if he could possibly have made a mistake. 'Yes, that's right, that's right,' we said.

'And that gorgeous Roddie, he went big C,' Val continued.

'What, to Canada?' said Martie. 'How utterly mean not to say goodbye.'

'But surely . . .' said Danny, chewing. 'Klaus's friend.'

'Yes,' said Val dolefully. 'In his case the C stands for cirrhosis of the liver, I fear.' (But you knew that.)

'What happened to . . .'

And so it plodded on. All our gruesome losses. In due course the younger ones down the table would move up and know how we felt. Val makes me constitutionally *depressed*, you know. I tried not to wonder who'd be gone by the next year. Of course it was going to be Fiona, from an ordinary thing without a fancy name (and I'll never ever be harsh about her). But she was twenty-two and we didn't suspect ordinary people also had such afflictions. We just thought it was a lump removed from her left breast. For Val she didn't qualify that year or any year. When you get a purist gay like Val, you've really had it, haven't you?

'Victor,' said Val.

'Back to Venezuela,' said Martie.

'Never made it to the Vatican,' said Danny, and I filled up: we had Boschendal Blanc de Noir 85. Not good for dieting.

On came the Christmas pudding – we had overstocked; not *left over*, but unopened, you know what I mean. I signalled to Kev it was going to be late, and we left them haggling over a churnful of brandy butter.

As ever Kev had done the perfect job. But when he zipped out of his track-top in the bedroom – suddenly I saw his back.

I said, 'Kev, what is that on your fair skin?'

I could see the scars.

'That's why I didn't get low-cut backs,' he said.

'But Kev, you're marked for life. You're *branded*. That's . . . terrible. You'll never be able to swim in public again. Who . . . did this to you? Kev?'

He turned and held up the larger frock to check the fit.

'Never mind, at least this is perfect,' he said with pins in his mouth.

'But Kev,' I said, feeling distinctly sick. I sat on the bed, clutching the material. I thought, I'm not going to perform happy love songs when this kind of thing happens in the world. I am not. (Usual nerves, of course.)

Kev led the way, wriggling into his frock, identical but a quarter the bulk – they stock the whole range from anorexic to outsize. He backs up to be zipped and I have to touch those awful marks. At least they're on his *back* where he doesn't have to see them all the time.

'But Kev,' I say, all wretched.

He hauls out my old blonde wig and chucks it at me. He

pulls on his own, which as you know matches perfectly. Then he busies himself with the make-up tray, applying it to my twitching face.

'Oh God, Kev,' I say.

'Sing middle C,' he says, and goes aaaa... 'Come on, they're clearing up the coffee cups.'

I go aaa... like a dying bagpipe.

Kev's made-up in two ticks and as you know a fabulous natural beaut.

'Let's cut the can-can tonight,' I say.

'With these dresses we'll have to,' he says.

In a flat panic I make myself right. Kev checks me out; I check him out. A little more powder on his shadow. We can hear the chairs scraping together towards the stage area.

You know how it is. When our two faces come together in the mirror – the last surviving Andrews Sisters – and the tape starts blasting out, and they're screaming and cheering even before you fling open the double-doors and step down in your sequined heels... well, a girl's heart leaps into the right place at a moment like that. *Er-one, er-two, oopedoopedoo* and away we go. You just get... carried away... I tell you, you can make the whole of the Magaliesberg *ring out with joy*!

Ah well... Kev was perfectly fabulous and, if you don't mind my saying so, so was old wheezing, grunting pre-operative me!

You've seen it all before, I know. But that's what a drag show's all about, isn't it? Saying you're going to win, *yet again*.

There was one lovely moment at the end, when we had them hysterical – literally rolling on the tiles – which I will always cherish till my dying day. Ou Sara charges up to me with this enormous tray of champagne glasses and I say: 'Not yet, Sara, not yet,' shooing her away. She looks me straight in the face, stricken, and does a bob and says: 'Ja miesies.'[1] With that there were *contortions and fits*!

God knows what those brown old eyes had seen. Did she really think we had imported Juliette Greco for the night? Or that I had been metamorphosed? Shame, she was just being polite and didn't want to spoil the show. That's loyalty for you.

She and Belinda were missing the alternative show outside Timothy's kraal; God knows the hullabaloo that was going

---

1. Even you know that means 'Yes madam.'

on *there*. With a lot more stamina than us, that's for sure. They carried on until *January the Third*.

Well, it wasn't even midnight yet. Time to get slobbery over the old year and wait, as in all things, for it to pass. I was in love with our place, then, with guests scattered all over the lawn and the faintest, diamond-point drizzle in the floodlights. The wild banana giving a little rustle and the bloody dogs charging out of the lamium maculatum and dancing round each other, sniff sniff sniff. Kev and I just stood there, and I felt so close to him – it took me a lot longer to stop panting. Kev wiped his mouth with Kleenex.

Jannie came up with two doubles and Kev tactfully went off to change.

'How did it go?' I said, not really needing a reply.

'Well, if you ask me,' he said, 'a whole lot better than when Klaus and Paul were here. Sorry about the volume. We must get that speaker fixed.' Then he backed up against me.

I sighed, finally catching my breath. And we both took sips.

'I just want you to know,' I said, 'you've really made an Eden out of the desert. The way I feel now I'll resign from work tomorrow.'

'We can't afford it, least for another five years. I'm meant to be *losing* you money, remember.'

'I mean to fix speakers and things.' Perhaps David Bennington coming into view with his beau had something to do with it. They had both been wearing whites. 'He can take over in turn. That's what he's after. As long as there's one of the two of us in my position.'

'For Christ sake, you're only forty-two,' said Jannie. 'Don't give it all away.'

'I can rather turn this place into a paying proposition,' I said.

Bennington and Mr X came under the trellis, not exactly holding hands, but nearly.

'Help yourself,' said Jannie.

'Better take those trousers off or Martie won't let you back in the Rolls,' I said.

David did take his off and drape them in the vine, and then Mr X too, and eventually they were just in their delectable briefs. So were the reputed Malawians, but they wore different colours, so when the mudwrestling really started at least they were coded.

Jannie went to get the champagne out of the fridge.

I was thinking how everyone was drifting around, sometimes in different combinations – which is a sign of a *good* party – biding the time, when Kev came back, still in his outfit.

'What's wrong?' I said, for he was giving a hint of the maiden in distress.

You know Kev; he merely asked me to follow him.

I suppose if I'd got my thoughts together I'd have worked out what it was.

Anyway, down to the rondavel we go, picking our way over the clods. Have you ever seen anything like it? Kev's heels were already ruined. I'd be lucky if mine lasted another glutinous yard.

Kev goes ssh and, without creaking it, pushes the top of the stable door open. I haven't got my glasses on so all I see is what looks like a pale Gothic arch in the air, there on the other side of the doublebed.

'Fiona . . .' whispers Kev, '*your* sister-in-law.'

I can slowly make out it's the back of her legs, with her big toes crossed. I thought she was doing exercises, though admittedly in an uncomfortable place. Clearly it was Fiona; she was going gasp, gasp, gasp, like a little girl.

It dawned on me what was causing this.

Kev tried to dissuade me, but I pushed open the bottom door. I wrenched the bed aside. Ha! Caught in the act!

'*No man, Kev,*' Henno gave a heartfelt yell.

'Man, fok off, fok off,' said Fiona.

'It's not Kev, it's me,' I strode towards them. 'What d'you mean, behaving like this on my property?'

'You fok off too,' said Henno with a groan.

'Fok off, fok off,' said Fiona, her legs subsiding round Henno's back.

Kev slipped alongside me.

'You think you a woman. *This* is a real woman, so fok off, Kev,' said Henno.

'Fiona, you are a naughty girl. You know you're meant to be taking it easy,' I said.

'Fok off,' she said, putting her thumb back in her mouth. She kicked Henno's back, as you do a horse.

'Hey, Kev, Kev,' said Henno. 'Don' be mad at me. I got it up, hey?'

'Seems more like you got it *in*,' I said.

Kev flounced down on the floor, not to watch them; just to recover.

'We got every right,' said Fiona past her thumb.

Henno gave some pumps.

'You mean, you missed our concert for this? Henno, that's

very impolite,' I said, tetchy as hell.

'Shut the door and fok off you both,' said Fiona, gargling.

'It's very impolite to stare,' said Henno.

'Yes, I know,' I said.

'No, we saw your show and you know what –' said Henno.

Fiona takes out her thumb and completes the sentence; '– it was a lot better than Judy Garland and Liza Minnelli.'

'Oh, thanks,' I said, patting my cheek.

'It was you two turned me on,' said Henno.

Kev makes a wriggle of appreciation. 'Thanks, Henno,' he said.

That eases things up a lot.

'Hey, you want to see what I got to show?' says Henno.

'Who, me?' I say.

Fiona slaps him cause he's going to pull out.

'No, Kev,' says Henno.

'I've seen it,' says Kev. 'And it isn't the crown jewels, you know.'

That was his exit line, conveying more from Kev than I've ever heard before. He's into the flowerbeds, tearing up St John's Worts and all. You can understand why the destruction – I've fed him, I've housed him, I've dressed him, I've paid him, I even comb his hair – oh the no-good goddamn downright louse! Bang goes the climbing rose in the gazebo.

I thought I'd better go pacify my sweet sister in song. But there they were, fucking away indifferently, and Henno's hand pulls mine, wrenching me to my knees.

'Take a dekko, just go on, man,' he says. He raises his hip a bit without coming out.

Well, I don't know if that sort of thing turns him on, additionally I mean – if that's possible – but it certainly turns me on. I saw a Japanese photo once of two guys in the same hole; how they get the camera right for a shot like that I just don't know.

Slowly I moved my hand over the back of Henno's stiff thigh. I didn't want to go between the two of them. I reached the hairy patch between his legs and sort of pinged his balls with my thumb. Now he's thrusting like mad and it's hard to know where to get a grip in there. Fiona's heel is hitting my head and she's gargling much better.

I took his cock at the base and you know it really was the biggest bloody shaft. Like a fencepost! I tell you not a lie. Sticky with creosote which I suppose naturally came from poor Fiona.

Well, I see this is working them up to great heights, so I won't let go and I just squeeze as hard as I can. She's getting the kick out of it, not him. 'Yes, yes, yes,' she goes till I'm sick of it and when she's done, Henno stops bracing himself and relaxes a bit, saying, 'Not yet,' so I pull out my hand and give him a break.

He's sweating and panting like a bloody mule, so I go round on my knees to his face and wipe his forehead with the dress. I had not really thought of it, but since I was right in position it was silly to miss the chance. I took Henno by the ears. Of course Fiona was underneath all this and I don't know what she thought. Maybe she liked to be smothered in male bodies.

Then I heard Jannie on his way. Quickly I pulled down the hem.

Jannie threw the light on. 'What's this, what's this?' said he.

'Oh no,' said Fiona, and she gave Henno a huge kick to get on with it.

'Fiona,' he said dryly to his sister, 'you're meant to be in bed!'

'Fok off!' she said, sticking her thumb down her throat.

Jannie was so enraged, I've never seen him like that. Off comes his leather belt and next thing he's going to tan Henno to within an inch of his life.

'I wouldn't if I were you,' I said, composing myself. 'It might egg him on.'

'*As for you*,' Jannie turns on me, and I get such a fright. 'Kindly tell your friend Kevin Vermaak he is *not* qualified to landscape Bairnsford Nurseries.'

I scuttle out of there, thinking Jannie would follow, but what do I hear? – Henno say, 'Hey, Jannie . . . you want to see what I got?'

Following the trail of wreckage, I teeter off after Kev. This is when the mud business was underway, and I'm just in time to see the Malawian in blue, who wasn't a Malawian, sling Mr X in white right over his shoulder and into the muck. The other Malawian in red has his muddy paw round David Bennington's shoulder, and they disengage for a polite round of applause. I hope they knew what they were doing. Of course the other moffies were screaming for blood from the rockery.

Val comes out of the shadows and gooses me.

'Fok off, you old pervert,' I say, and go in quest of Kev.

'See you bring him in alive,' says Val.

Kev's down at the sheds, trying to pull off the Virginia creeper. I grabbed him from behind. I hit him so hard his wig shot into the magnolias.

'Take that, you stupid bitch,' I screamed.

'Well, well, well,' said a voice, 'what *do* we have here?'

It was Alfie who'd arrived, and Richie who invariably sided with the underdog. Richie dragged Kev forth.

'Take him to casualty for all I care,' I said. 'No really . . . he was overreacting.'

'Look who's talking,' said Alfie. He took my arm and helped me untwist my knickers.

We limped back to the house.

'Hope it isn't midnight yet,' said Richie. 'We did it in an hour, you know.'

'Sorry you missed the concert,' said Kev.

'We've still got athletics finals in the rose garden and a live sex show in the rondavel. Never mind they've missed little old us,' I said to Kev. He was covered in scratches, as if he'd been mauled by a tomcat. 'Ag, I'm so sorry, man,' I said, and gave him a big kiss.

'While you two make it up, where shall we put our things?' said Alfie, eyes glowing deliciously.

Richie had Kev's hand. 'It's just a cut, put TCP on it.'

Of course Alfie wouldn't condescend to examine a little wound like that.

'In the usual,' I said, thinking I'd better get back to the rondavel before Jannie had his finger up Henno's arse.

Now *everyone* was in there, with the bed pulled right into the next room, the lights full on – climbing muddily over the dogs to get to the front. But they weren't going to see where it counted, because Jannie had taken it into his head (I suppose to defend the last of his family's honour) to hold up that big picture-book – you know, the Michelangelo we bought by the Duomo in Florence.

'Spoil sport! Censor!' they were going.

'Fok off, fok off,' both Fiona and Henno were moaning with increasing desperation.

I could foresee it. Jannie stands, down come his pants, and did *he* have something to hide. So had everyone.

That's when Ou Sara comes in with the champagne glasses again and everyone shouts: 'FOK OFF SARA!'

I was at the switch, plunged the scene into blackout.

Old Val had the champagne lined up and was screaming, 'You're going to miss it, you're going to miss it!' So we all trudged off to the patio.

Soon enough there was a volley of corks, and dogs running for cover. Just in time we gulped down a glassful and hugged and kissed somebody, and you didn't always get the right person. I got Val. Then we all joined hands and sang, 'Should old acquaintance . . .' etc., and I suppose you and Paul were doing much the same, you dreary sluts, under the lee of a glacier.

There's an ad on the radio now by Swissair before they bring us what (censored) news there is: *Pamper yourself with a little class . . . three flights from Joburg to Zurich a week, and when you arrive in Zurich they know you mean business. And from Zurich the world's your oyster.* See, I know it by heart. I swear I'll come and do business with you one day. Bloody cowards, why did you pack up and leave? I hope everything's subzero for you! Put that in your rösti and swallow it.

Goodbye to one wretched year; welcome another.

Relations with David Bennington: well, they are improving, though I do find it difficult to take. We went out to Magnum Magnesium to catch up on the books.

I didn't know until that evening he and his Mr X's secret vice was carpet wrestling. If that's what they did in public, imagine what they must have done in private. You know what his buddy's name was: Stefanus van der Merwe, I swear – Steffie for short (but hardly to his face). Another mixed marriage like ours (Afrikaans and English). These low-class Boer boys really seem to have something to offer. They were both married as well – wives and children, I mean. They hadn't divorced or anything (their wives, I mean), just avoided them two nights a week for a bolt-hole in Kensington. Welcome to the wonderful world of the bisexual.

Stefanus had no scruples about who kissed him, let me tell you, when he was off-duty. The one Malawian (blue) had his tongue half down his throat on the couch. Obviously there were no safe sex practices wherever he came from.

The other (red) Malawian, so called, was in the flowerbed nursing his collarbone – he thought he broke it, but Richie assured him no.

Val fell asleep where he was and I got Martie and Danny settled in to their first movie feature of the year, *Gallipoli*. (Have you seen it? – you must.)

Jannie was in the jacuzzi with David Bennington, cooling off.

'Who hasn't had any champagne?' I said, totting up.

'I'll have some more,' gasped Stefanus, coming out of his clinch, and I tottered over with two glasses, but spilled them. Have you ever seen champagne go down a Malawian-who-isn't-a-Malawian's back?

'I'm *terribly* sorry,' I said, 'I'll get a cloth.'

'Don't worry, I'll lick it,' said Stefanus.

'Sis,' I said. Don't tell me he hasn't come out, that one. The other Malawian joins in, giggling like mad; I think they were all a little pissed. I just gave them the bottle to pour over themselves.

Of course, Henno and Fiona. I took them well-charged glasses. I knocked on the rondavel door and said could I come in? Jeepers creepers, keep your ski-ing marathons . . . that fuck was into its *second year*.

With their permission I switched on the light. 'Folks, don't you want a pillow or something? You don't have to hide anymore. Look, I brought you some champagne.'

'Thanks, hey,' said Henno, his back giving in a bit, ungluing himself.

He took the one glass and gave it to Fiona, who sat up. He crawled on the bed and I gave him the other glass. He played with that dong of his like an expiring fish.

Fiona pulled a pillow towards her and climbed up with it, covering herself. I could see her skinny twat; it was totally pink round about, as though it had been pulped.

'Well, I leave you to it,' I said. 'Have a very Happy New Year.'

'Just wait for the glasses,' said Fiona.

They toasted and drank.

Somehow Henno playing with himself irked me. 'Christ, Henno, haven't you even come yet?'

Fiona said: 'He's come twice . . . and I've lost count, so just piss off now, hey.'

'That's right,' said Henno, getting his legs right to work it up again.

She handed me her glass, and took his from him and gave it to me.

'Would you like me to bring you a refill?' I said.

Henno had his face all contorted: 'Bring the bottle,' he said.

'Well, please have a breather till I come back. I don't want to intrude again.'

'I . . . can' . . . man . . .' said Henno, and a little pearly jet shot between his fingers.

'*Ag no sis man*,' Fiona, who was the recipient of this, brushed her neck.

'I mus' love you,' said Henno goofily. 'Hey, did you hear me? I said I love you . . . what's your name?'

'So what?' said Fiona. 'It's Fiona.'

'And I'm Henno,' he stuck forth his hand.

Fiona hit him with the pillow.

I put the glasses on the dressing table and went for the nearest bottle. I got back to the rondavel as quickly as I could. I'd had enough of this now. Clunk, clunk, clunk, there they were at it again, she riding him against the cupboard.

Ah well, if they needed it that much.

Thought I'd join Jannie in the jacuzzi and cool off a bit on more familiar ground. At least get out of that wretched *dress*, which was split at the seams and in tatters, you should know.

Jannie was in the bedroom, having a heart to heart with Kev. They sat opposite one another, elbows on knees, a few inches apart. 'But Kev,' Jannie was saying – not irritably, but nevertheless firmly, 'that's what I meant – he only does it to provoke you, to make you feel mad. It's not because he prefers women to you.'

Jannie winked at me over Kev's shoulder.

Kev turned round.

'Sorry, there'll be no sneaking this back to the factory like you thought,' I said, wriggling out of it. 'I'll give you cash for it.'

'It doesn't matter,' said Kev . . . 'nothing matters any more.'

'Of course it matters,' said Jannie, winking at me again. 'Kev, jus' listen here . . . No, jus' listen.'

I tiptoed out and let myself into the soothing bubbles between Alfie and Richie. 'Sis, the dogs have been in here,' I said.

'So's a lot more besides,' said Richie.

We bobbed there with our arms out on the tiles, our feet crisscrossed over the light. Richie pushed along a bottle and a glass.

'No, I was saying to Richie,' Alfie continued, 'medical technology is never as complicated as you think. It's made like that to mystify the layman.'

That's actually how we got onto that topic, so I might as well give you a run down here.

'That Mozambiquan comes in with his white wife and he's been in agony for years on end –' says Richie.

'You mean the tallest man in the world?' I said.

'Tallest, smallest, what does it matter? That's only the press aspect of it, like sideshows in the old days,' said Alfie. 'But from the *medical* point of view, they engineer the guy a new hip. So what – what's so difficult about that?'

'You're completely forgetting the patient's faith, Alfie,' said Richie. 'If he hadn't had his wife, whatever colour she was, beside him and all the fuss about his specially constructed bed –'

'Gabriel Monjane,' I said, 'and he was 2,42 metres high.'

'He's even taller now,' said Alfie.

'Yes, but without the public's goodwill and everyone praying for him like good Catholics, and him *knowing* that, he'd never have got through,' says Richie.

'Bullshit,' says Alfie, 'plain bullshit.'

'Well, if I had a life and death operation,' I said (*not knowing*, of course), 'I'd sure like to know I'm not alone in the thing.'

'You would be,' said Alfie. 'Who else's body would I be cutting into?'

'It takes goodwill, it takes goodwill,' said Richie. 'That cures more than any technology, ever since Hippocrates.'

'Maybe in your rural areas, but I'm talking about civilization,' said Alfie.

'What about that Jorge business up in Tzaneen just the other day? The *whole world* was watching that. That was a first. The first time a grandmother bore her own daughter's children for her. I mean, isn't that a first for the *whole human race*?' I said.

'Yes, I admit,' said Alfie, 'but the only thing to comment there is *why* didn't it happen before? When Chris Barnard first gave Washkansky his heart, *twenty years ago*, why didn't transplant surgery develop faster? I mean, other countries have got a million times the resources we have.'

'At least it put us on the map,' I said.

'And the way they're handling apartheid's put us right off again. Haven't you been reading the papers recently – what's left of them?' said Alfie.

'It's not like servicing a car,' said Richie.

'I hope if I serviced your car I'd make a better job of it than most mechanics,' said Alfie.

'I'm sure you would,' I said, taking a gulp of champagne. I passed it back to Richie.

'But that's exactly it,' he was saying. 'Your goodwill would see you, your team and your equipment do the best. Thanks,' he took the glass.

'I'd do it for my fee, and so as not to get sued for negligence, that's all,' Alfie replied.

'Oh Alfie,' I prodded his knee. We relaxed in the bubbles.

In one direction we could hear the Gallipoli landing. In the other a squeal from Fiona. Even further, the other party down at the kraal.

'Christ, are those two still at it?' said Alfie, reaching for his glass.

Richie gave one of his famous grins, which lit from beneath is quite something.

He passed me his glass. 'You can't catch AIDS from sharing champagne. Specially not from me.' Shit, he's a lovely boy – Richie, the judge's son.

One of the Malawians came haring round and I jumped up: 'No, you can't come in here!'

Instantly he looked caught out and apologetic. 'Sorry, baas, sorry, baas,' he backed away.

'No, no, no,' I said. 'I meant you can't come in *like that*. Just please have a shower first – over there, over there!'

He looked incredibly relieved. He strode to the cubicle, summoning the other three after him.

'He thought it was because he's black,' said Alfie.

'I know,' I said, deeply ashamed.

'He's not from the Malawi if that's his reaction,' said Richie.

'I know,' I said. 'But he's welcome nevertheless . . . as long as he doesn't have AIDS.'

'Even if he has you won't catch it,' said Alfie.

'How do you know?' I said, all paranoid.

'For Christ's sake, didn't you put *chlorine* in this passion pit?' said Alfie.

So with lots of 'Hello, hellos' from us, in glided on their naked bottoms four of the most beautiful men on the subcontinent, and just to complicate matters seven bloody dogs.

By the time we'd thrown the dogs out a glass was broken, *in* the water. So I had a wonderful time as the perfect host, ordering everyone to sit quietly till I'd fumbled round for every last chip.

Anything you want to know? I'll be happy to tell you . . .

So I end up on the ledge between the one Malawian (without the briefs you couldn't tell which) and Stefanus van der Merwe. To make conversation I say what does he do? David Bennington eyes me.

'I'm afraid I carn' say,' says he.

'Why not?' I say. 'We have no secrets here. He's the best surgeon in the country, 'cept he hasn't had the chance to prove himself yet. He's finishing his housemanship at Baragwanath, David you know, and I'm his financial manager.' I turn to the lad from Standerton. 'What do you do?'

'Ah . . .' he says. 'Fontana . . . He too,' he points.

'Ah delicatessen salesman,' says the other, 'that's right.'

'No really I carn' say,' says Stefanus van der Merwe.

'Let me guess,' I say.

'Please just leave it,' says David Bennington.

'No no no,' I say, 'I'll get it in time.'

'That's what I'm afraid of,' says David.

Stefanus van der Merwe looks across at him in what – could it be panic? He hurls water in David's face – to sober him up, or create a diversion?

If we'd really known we'd have been out of that pool so fast you couldn't have counted us, putting a thousand miles between him and us. (Of course he was S. A. P. I should have known from that moustache – to make him look more brutal. Admittedly not one who goes around shooting black kids in the townships for breakfast. We should have lined up to be arrested. David Bennington sure liked playing with fire.)

Maybe I should draw a veil over the rest of the proceedings. There, I've decided. Love to you both.

That's all you need to know.

II

FOLLOWING MODERN BUSINESS PRACTICE BAIRNSFORD NURSERIES ISSUES NO RECEIPTS FOR ACCOUNTS PAID BY CHECK.

Me to Klaus. Letter continues.

My new secretary sent off Disc 1 – she knows how to pack it. Looking forward *eagerly* to your response. You can show Paul, but nobody else. Love from both of us to both of you.

KNOW THAT HARRY BELAFONTE SONG IF YOU HAVEN' GOT A PENNY A HAPENNY WILL DO IF YOU HAVEN' GOT A HAPENNY THEN GOD BLESS YOU. I'VE GOT ANOTHER LINE:– THEN FUCK YOU TOO. (ONLY JOKING) LOVE JANNIE.
P.S. HE CAN PLAY ON THIS AS LONG AS HE DOESN'T SEND OUR *ACCOUNTS* TO YOU LIKE HE DID THE *LABELS*. PRINT OUT AND SEND BACK *PORNTO*. JANNIE.

Honestly, if we had a spelling cheque on this thing, half of Jannie's stuff would get thrown out! No wonder nobody pays their bills.

Clearing accounts is a bit of a sore point recently. You know what Fiona's bills came to, and Jannie her sole traceable relative? – seventeen thousand four hundred and fifty-four rands and twenty-seven cents! She had absolutely no medical benefit. Cancer's not a cheap way to go. My by-pass was cut-rate by comparison (Alfie put in only a minimum claim and the insurance covered most of it).

But that's not the point. Don't think like most people that just because I'm an accountant all I can rate life by is money! On the contrary, I can see how money can be used to people's advantage ... *and* how frightened or mastered the average bloke is by it! The truth is I feel very bad when I see how life and money interact. Flip a coin: heads you're alive, tails you're not. She's dead, I'm alive ... all within less than a year.

How you have to work at living, too: I go round the

rondavel and through the peaches to the pump at the river, up past the eucalyptus to the nursery, not once but three times a day – after breakfast, after lunch, and before supper. As Alfie says, you've got to make an effort to live, even harder than Fiona did.

This letter is part of my labour, so here goes. (Stirs his lemon tea.)

Kev was the shining example, I suppose. But Kev fucked off with Henno to town and we didn't see him again till (like most people) he needed us!

So we were left with *this dying woman* in our lives. Wish to God it had been someone a trifle more cheerful, if we *had* to have a woman at all – like dear Mrs Leibnitz at the Co-op or, heaven forbid, even my old secretary. Do you think Bairnsford Nursery would be in the mess it is if we had one of them half-days? But Fiona, poor thing . . . all she could do was cry, and knit herself out of it. Sit and knit. The Magaliesberg's sub-tropical, remember, so there's not exactly an urgent necessity for a sodden *woolly wardrobe*! That was the childhood she never had and the lack of parental care coming out in her.

After New Year her situation became clear. She had the biopsy on her shrunken left breast, about half an inch underneath. In some cases they try not to do a mastectomy. Stupid girl, she didn't tell anyone and didn't have the money to remain under supervision. She kept up the chemotherapy erratically. But even if Fiona could think, she was far too buggered to think clearly by then. Jannie took her over, put it all on some systematic basis. He got her pathetic amount of things and installed her in the rondavel, and when she was due for treatment (the nearest is Pretoria) delivered orders in the area, and brought her home afterwards.

For about three days after those things, she'd just lie there and vomit . . . and her fair fell out, all that. When I returned for weekends she was cheered up, and we got used to this stalking death in our corridor and at our table and knitting at the TV. We couldn't have guests out during that, it would be too distressing for them. Meanwhile Jannie found a whole new meaning to life: nursing his long-lost sister. And I helped, too, when I could. With a situation like that in your lives there is *no room* for anything else. I was mighty relieved to set off for the office on Monday mornings, I admit.

You can say as much as you like – it was not her fault, it was the *disease's* fault – but that doesn't stop *your* marriage going all tight-lipped, tense and precarious. I don't want

Jannie to see this, shit. (That's why I sent Disc 1 with the labels!!! Just hurry up and return, please – then I can erase *everything but* the bloody labels. I know there's nothing worse than a middle-aged queen moaning about his marriage behind his partner's back... when he should be talking to his partner, that's who! Just understand I'm not *asking for advice*. I'd phone you for that! It's hardly practical by word processor and when there's all of Africa between us, and time-lag.)

Now wait: back to Position A. Correct all selective and distorted press reports like the one you have in the *Zeitung*. 'Genial' is our example... Now I see they call Fiona Henno's *wife* (how respectable and middle-class, N.B.), who fought such a *plucky battle*. So she was aided by her trusty brother, was she? – but note how they will have nothing to do with gay affairs. Who is her brother meant to be?: *Kevin Vermaak* (not poor Jannie, of course...) Take my word for it – it'll appear in the *Guinness Book of Records* like that, too!

Position A also includes me jabbing at this keyboard. And you know what? Increasingly I feel I will not be able to correct the world this way!

Well, we know the signs well enough, don't we? Tight-lipped, even tighter when boozed. Standing with his feet apart, because otherwise he'd fall over. When he's basically unhappy he gets so seedy-looking – dry skin, only talks in the imperative, beard all scraggly, eyes going round like roulette wheels. You hope that some day you'll strike the lucky number and he'll light up and say, Hey, I see it all clearly now, I do love you. Having Fiona here was difficult, forever knitting – tick, tick, tick.

Anyway, Jannie phones me at work, which he's never done before and instructed never to do. My old secretary puts him through: 'It's a medium-distance call. Bairnsford Nurseries on line 2.'

I never realised the old Valley party line could stretch up into that skyscraper. Sounds like my beloved is talking into a tin, and I'm at the other end of the piece of string.

I stage-whisper back: 'Don't phone here, no matter how urgent it is. Switchboard listens in. She listens in. They're trying to get me!'

'I don't care how embarrassed you are by me,' says he. 'Just get Alfie to come here on Friday night.'

'He won't do any favours for your sister,' I say.

'Well, get Richie then. I don't care how you do it, even if you have to pay him, but *get* him,' says Jannie.

'So you didn't just phone for a rush of long-forgotten

endearments?'

At that moment in walks said secretary with a pile of ledgers, and I clapped my hand over the receiver.

Jannie had his say, and it wasn't about living and loving under a cloudless sky.

Know what I said back? 'Well, in that case I'll have the bouquets only. Thank you, much obliged.' I put down the receiver.

The next call came through on the direct line. 'Bennington,' he said.

'Yes, *Bennington*, what've you been up to?'

'Only a little fives; wear a glove and beat the ball against a wall. Wrestling's too public, if you know what I mean.'

'Well, that must be nice for the kids,' I said. The secretary was still fussing around.

'Not kids, man. Steffie's free tonight. Dinner at my place in Kensington? I'll fetch you at seven.'

'That'll be lovely. I'm dying to meet your wife,' I said. Moffie's are quick-witted, hey?

'Not Bedfordview, Kensington,' he says.

'All right, Bennington, I'm very busy now with you know what,' and I put the phone down.

Secretary did a quite extraordinary turn about the carpet and wrung her jersey. 'Please, please . . . I must tell you I'd *never* do a thing like that.'

'What?'

'Listen to other people's conversations!'

'Oh, eavesdrop,' I said.

She fell right into it, didn't she?

Now do I give you Fiona's extraordinary feat or Bennington's little love-nest? Which comes first? I know which you'd prefer. How Bennington gets into this story in the first place I really don't know. Except he's such a bliss number with such rocks to get off. They're always welcome to weave in and out of one's life. Except that this one was trying to *dispossess* me. Not that I had proof, but I had a shrewd idea. How else could he get where he wanted to go? All with impeccable style, let me tell you. Nothing Bennington ever did appeared less than cool . . . except opening up to me. I'll tell you about Bennington cause that'll really work you up! Ah, to act like a twenty-eight year old again.

So he fetches me in his more modest car and we go, not to Bedfordview where he does indeed have a wife and three kids, swimming pool . . . the complete aspiring exec's happy family property, even with a granny cottage! And a granny! But we go to the south side of the Reef, of course . . . up a side street off a side street to the flank of darkest Kensington on the hillside opposite. I am the only one of his business circle (or his family, for that matter) to be so honoured. We go into this 1916-style upright, tin-roofed one-bedroom bungalow and what do I see? – orange wall-to-wall six inches deep, the lounge full of work-out equipment, a fridge of diet drinks, and some superb wines on the side, the bathroom he's converted into an intimate shower and shit-stall, and the sauna, if you don't mind, where the loo used to be. An immense double bed with a closet, into which he shoves his pieces if anyone straight happens to call. The thickest of curtains and a tapedeck with Mozart and disco, anything a hunk for the night might find conducive. The hedges are so tall there aren't even neighbours.

Oh yes, and a phone on the floor (unlisted number). A shelf of those rousing Alternative Books. *And that's it*.

'What do you do for food?' I say, seeing no signs of even a stove.

'Take-aways,' and he gives me a Chateauneuf du Plastic Bag and a paper cup.

'No, I'll have a bottle of Bull's Blood and a corkscrew, if you don't mind,' I say, and he passes me those and a glass.

He phones for three pizzas.

'I like the big one with everything on it,' I say.

'Steffie's mad for calzone,' he says, and places the order.

I don't mind sitting on the carpet – I'm damned if I'm going to risk it in an electric chair with weights or damage my cleavage on the saddle of a bike bolted to the floor!

We talked of this and that. I didn't really know what to say. I mean, how could he lead such a daring *double life*? And take it all so solemnly. All I could think of saying was: 'No wonder you look such a picture of health.'

'Thanks,' he said, putting on the Mozart clarinet.

I stared across at glum Bez Valley, where Fiona and Jannie had such a putrid upbringing – or part of it, cause they moved from pillar to post, evading drunken father and the landlords. You know, houses like this with seventeen people in them. You could hear kids screaming even now, down in the urban hell. In South Africa poverty's black; no journalist writes of *white* poverty, but we can offer that, too.

Over to the west the sparkling towers of downtown. Our own vast Cincinnati, dumped in the veld. Southern Sun and the Carlton twinkling against a magnificent sky, as though the light bursts upwards to frazzle the ozone layer. You could see our building with the green top floor; where my flat is, behind Fox Street.

Someone was intruding, so I drew the curtain. Not Stefanus van der Merwe, though it looked quite as active as him, bounding up the steps. It was the pizzas: Gino's, I saw, from the white paperhat.

The doorbell went and I waited out of view. He was very suave and efficient, the pizza-man. Wouldn't mind biting into any crust of his. Obviously David Bennington knew him only too well. Gino remarked he was lucky to have *two* guests.

David paid and hustled him out.

I stepped forth. Gracelessly I said: 'I'll have the calzone if Steffie doesn't come.'

'*Don't* call him that to his face,' said David. 'He'll bust your teeth in.'

'Oh so butch,' I said. 'Don't you and Steffie waste time on sweet words at all?'

'We don't waste time talking; we just do it,' said David, fetching from next door a fat pillow which was more suitable for me. I couldn't make out if he wanted to repay the hospitality of New Year, or it was confession time. I settled back against the wallpaper and said: 'So how did you two meet up?'

David sat cross-legged against thin air. So athletic. This is what he said: 'I just had a breakdown in my car . . . and he followed me home to see that I was all right.'

'I see. That's quite lekker,' I said.

'It was a trick to make a trick. It wasn't broken down, really.'

'You like your pick-ups to come in their own trucks.'

'Yes. That way you can be a bit selective.'

I said, 'I suppose you've had a lot of AA men?'

'No, they actually fix up what's meant to be wrong and send you on your way,' he said with a little grin.

'I suppose it works if you look like you, and stand helplessly in the headlights,' I said.

'That way you also get somebody who can drive themselves home afterwards.' So cold-blooded, so calculated. He added: 'You must understand I have limited time.'

'Yes, well,' I said, 'I think we should maybe start on our pizzas.'

'Obviously he's delayed, poor guy,' said David, going to fetch two of the boxes. But the phone rang.

So I got the boxes, sorting out which was which and looking for implements. It was useless to expect a table, as I say. I placed a cloth and the exposed clockface where he'd sat, and pulled mine to between my knees. I started at the olive end.

'He isn't coming,' said David rather flatly. 'His wife is . . . having a miscarriage.'

'Oh shit,' I said, licking my fingers.

He brought the calzone and put it beside me.

'Sorry, I'll get you a serviette,' he said, meaning a paper napkin. When he settled down, he looked at me as if to apologise.

'Eat it before it gets cold,' I said, spitting pips.

'Sorry to disappoint you,' he said.

'That's all right,' I said. 'He can hardly stand up his – real wife – at a time like that.'

David pulled a bit up like the tongue of a shoe. 'Bisexual's very different from gay, you know,' he said.

'I can see that,' I said. 'Your pure gay doesn't have to drag his arse out to the freeway in secret – for willing home mechanics, for fuck sake. Behind his wife's back!'

'You can't have children,' he said.

'Maybe,' I said. 'There's something in that.'

'Bi's can,' he said.

'I see,' I said. 'I've always felt there are quite enough children in this world, and most of them are starving to death, anyway. Gay's quite nice from that point of view.'

'You don't know how it is to have children till you have them.'

'Till your regular wife has them.'

'My three climb over me when I come home.'

'When you go home to Bedfordview.'

'Yes, but you can't imagine how nice that is,' he said. 'Gay can never participate in that experience. Gay's quite sweet, but not everything the world can offer.'

'Well, if gay's *sweet*, you know what bi is? – *deceitful*. I've never heard of such double standards. What does your wife think you're doing now?'

'Out with you.'

I ripped apart the last piece of pizza with my fingers. 'No, David, no,' I said. I chewed. 'What was your poor wife doing on New Year's Eve, while you were dandling some – black delicatessen number – on your knee in the jacuzzi?'

'Probably dandling my little one if he woke up in the dead of night.'

'David, no,' I said. 'And that Steffie, what if his wife miscarried – and she just hadn't a clue where he was? What if she'd miscarried on New Year's Eve? While he was also in the jacuzzi, dandling a –'

'Black delicatessen.'

'Yes. What if she knew? If I had an affair I'd at least tell Jannie. You should be ashamed of yourself.' I was getting quite angry. I pushed aside the empty box and opened the calzone; offered him a share.

He declined.

The calzone was all curled around in self-protection. 'Look, could you just get me a fork?' I said.

He brought me one.

'It's not what you think. I just need a place where I can be myself once in a while,' he sighed.

'*No*, David,' I said. I plunged in the thing's spine and split it. 'You can't have it both ways. Which do you like sex with – your wife, or numbers with spanners in their pockets . . . and make no mistake, after working out on that – treadmill – and pulling a few weights, one of them, one day, if you so much as flutter your eyelid'll be turned on by no less than doing you in. That's what rough trade's all about – so don't come to me with a dumbbell sticking out of your skull.' I really gave it to him. 'That'll be an end to one promising career, and make no mistake. Take it from me, cause I've been through most of those decisions myself. Even if I had only one way to decide and did end up with food and drink!'

'I won't be done in,' said David. 'I've got protection.'

'What protection?' I said. 'You should know you're even more vulnerable than I am. What's your wife going to say when you pitch up with stripes on your arse or like Kev?' (By then I knew all about what Henno'd done to Kev.) 'Or the board of directors? – please, sir I got beaten in a clinch with a bloody sumo wrestler, while wifey and granny were missing me.' I speared out some bits of ham.

'Wrong,' he said. 'Steffie's a policeman. He knows how to fix things.'

I could see those cubes of ham shoot across the carpet. 'What! What did you say?'

'That's why he could not tell you his profession.'

'What!' I said. 'A fucking cop, and he knows how to fix things!'

David went to change the tape. Mozart piano. He poured more wine.

'If he's a cop then he's got the whole lot of us,' I said, my mind shooting into reverse.

'*No he hasn't*,' said David. 'He has his allegiances, too. Where do you think he learned wrestling? In police college, where else? Except he developed a taste for a bit more. It's quite normal for a healthy young recruit. I should know – I got a scholarship to my school as a boxer. Then he was expected like everyone else to marry, and he found the right match. They were happy for a long time. Then with the first kid she wasn't turned on by him anymore. He wasn't turned on by her new fear of him. He hankered a bit after the old easier ways. She wasn't going to gym every night with him – how could she? So he decided to . . . catch up on what he enjoyed most. Feel a man again.'

'Is that his story, or yours?' I said.

David smirked. 'What difference does it make?'

'Well . . . there you've taught me something,' I said. I got some ham out and in my mouth.

'So were the Malawi boys, for that matter.'

'Bisexual?'

'And cops,' he said.

'What,' I said, and I swear I spattered him with shock. 'Sorry.'

'It's all right,' he said, picking up a piece out of the pile. 'Next thing you'll tell me they have wives and children too.'

'Well,' he looked apologetic, 'yes, they do. They keep them out at Standerton Barracks. Working in Fontana is only a cover. Couldn't you *see* that? They couldn't tell the difference between pickles and paté.'

'But can spot a homosexual a mile away.'

'All they're really trained to do is trap drug-dealers, and you're not one, so I knew it was perfectly safe.'

'Fiona's on grass. Couldn't you see she was smoked up to the eyeballs that night?'

'I said drug-*dealers*, not users. She's just small fry.'

'But still, David,' I said. 'Touch any of that and you're on the slippery slide right into the underworld. Give me more to drink and then I'm going to my flat!'

'Living with a policeman means I'm safe, don't you see?' he said. 'Besides, if it doesn't sound awfully coy and that – we're actually – very well suited to one another.'

'No,' I said, 'plain no.'

'Look, if you go on saying no I'll take you home right away.'

I was out of my depth. All I could say was, 'Well, that does put some of the *police* in a new light.' And as he filled my glass, lamely, 'Well, I hope you're both very happy together.'

'Thanks,' he said, which made a sort of détente. 'I'm sure we will continue to be.'

I couldn't make out if he was a fatal optimist, or really had blended everything and come out on top. Best of both –

several worlds. I sort of backtracked to familiar ground.

'Pity you can't turn this hideyhole into a very exclusive private gym, and write it off against tax, like we do the nursery.'

'I don't need to,' he said.

'Must be very expensive, running two places. You've put a lot of money into this. You can't pay for two properties and three kids on your salary. You've got to have capital to social climb. No wonder your car keeps breaking down!'

'I don't need to pay for this,' he said. 'Only rates and they very low. My father left it to me when he died.'

'Oh I see,' I said. 'Well, you have done well for yourself. Not many make it from Kensington to Bedfordview.'

'Sky's the limit,' he said, drinking deep. 'Funny thing, you remind me a bit of my father.'

'Oh, please . . .'

'No, he was gay, too, fundamentally. Lived through his marriage for my sake. Taught me really to fend for myself. Loved me to bits. Ah, what the hell . . .'

'What the hell,' I said. 'Cheers.'

Well, that didn't come out so light, did it? It's going to be even harder to make Fiona funny. I'm going to have some real supper.

Why I hesitate about the Fiona scene is (a) you must have figured out the general outline, anyway, and (b) I know such pure moffie highlivers like you – who have found your special world is as real as anybody else's in a haven like Switzerland – probably get all squeamish when I venture into the realm of bibs and nappies, all that. To me too kids were other people's, to give presents at Christmas, and for the rest of the year strictly – go out of one's way to – ignore. I don't think – like David Bennington – I *could* have kids clambering all over me. Ear-splitting monsters! To be avoided at all times! (Do you notice how few of us ever talk about our childhoods. I only found out about Jannie's through Fiona.)

I suppose with all that bedlam – savagery unleashed – David Bennington had to have his fantasy palace as a retreat. If he felt his cock ruled at home, he had to have another place where the rest of him could be a man. Leather and sweat! – not my scene. But so macho, such contest, what shiny muscles, as true as the mirror above his tumble-in bed. All this activity did keep him fit as hell. (You see, you do like that stuff!)

Cut to Fiona. You're going to hate it all, and skip like crazy. Well, don't. Otherwise you'll never keep track.

It wasn't hard to get Alfie and Richie out that night, cause by then they had the idea to purchase that plot up the Nek, and we were obviously able to help them. Lots of wild chat about the prospect. (That's where Richie has his weekend clinic now, and is far happier, trying to raise the health of the Valley from the grassroots.) Lots more, well . . . instantly firm friendship.

Since Alfie was so specialised with his time and money, while Richie still toiled in the wreckage of a casualty ward . . . Jannie took Richie aside and asked him just to check Fiona out. We thought she'd been sicking not so much from chemotherapy, but maybe something else.

'No, that will not happen,' Alfie overheard, 'it's not possible. I told you if you've got complaints, go to her specialist. He's the one.'

'That costs money she hasn't got. We don't charge you for advice about plants or property, do we? Just let Richie have a look at her,' I said.

'Richie doesn't know the difference between a kneecap and an ovarian cyst,' said Alfie.

'That's not a very nice thing to say,' I remarked.

'Medics aren't meant to say nice things,' said Alfie. Now I could see *he* was miffed at not having been asked to favour us with his decisive wisdom.

So I made conversation with prickly Alfie while ever-sweet Richie inspected Fiona on her sickbed in the rondavel and Jannie held the flashlight for extra illumination.

When they came back and sat with their drinks, Alfie took his time, but their silence finally wore him down. 'Well?' he turned in the middle of a sentence.

'She is,' said Richie.

'I *knew* it,' said Jannie, 'I *told* you!'

'Oh, don't be silly,' said Alfie, 'what do you know about symptoms of pregnancy?'

'Nothing, but I believe her when she says she is,' said Jannie. 'She's been pregnant before.'

'And what came of it then? If a baby was born every time a girl misses a period, there'd be standing-room only on this planet!'

'She knew enough about her own body to have an illegal abortion,' said Jannie.

'She is pregnant and that's that, Alfie,' said Richie.

I said, 'I'm not sure if we're geared up to have a baby here, you know.'

'You won't,' said Alfie. 'Her treatment'll knock it out long before you have to worry.'

The dogs came through.

We settled down again, and Richie said, just generally: 'Well, whose is it?'

'What?' said Alfie.

'The *baby*,' said Richie.

'I told you, there is not going to be one,' said Alfie.

'Fiona's, I suppose,' said Jannie. 'She wants to keep it this time.'

'I meant who's the father,' said Richie.

'Who else but Henno,' I said. 'We saw that with our very own eyes, if you remember.'

'What, that biker number who didn't even wish us Happy New Year?' said Alfie.

'That's the one. Who else?' said Jannie. 'You actually saw his schlong go right into my sister, presumably just so that he could deposit his trouble in there. That is how it works, you know.'

'I meant has anyone else been doing that to her?' said Richie.

'There was someone else, more than one, in fact,' said Jannie. 'She says the treatment made her horny. But she had her last period on Christmas Day and there's only been Henno since. We won't let her forget that, and not many heterosexuals get down to the rondavel.'

'Jesus,' said Alfie.

'Don't swear,' said Richie.

I said, 'That'll only rub it in with poor old Kev.'

'In addition,' said Jannie, 'she hasn't felt horny since.'

'Oh, you dreadful old queens!' Alfie struck the arm of his chair. 'Don't you know *anything* about women? Just because she isn't *horny* as you so quaintly call it does *not* mean what you think. In her advanced case it means she is a *very sick* little girl. It's a phantom pregnancy, you farts – all it means is that is what she'd *like* to be. She's telling us her body isn't rotting away to death; it's *worth something*. God, you creeps!'

'Just stop insulting middle-aged queens, Alfie,' said Jannie. 'You are one yourself.'

'And a creep and a fart like the rest of us,' said Richie.

'Maybe, maybe,' said Alfie with hubris, 'but *not* when it comes to *basic* psychology.'

'All right, all right,' I said, 'we all know you're the finest surgeon in the country.'

'I'm sorry, Alfie, but she is pregnant,' said Richie.

'Says you, who doesn't know the difference between a

twat and an arsehole yet,' said Alfie. 'I've been capitalising on your inexperience for four years now, not so?'

'I made the choice to live with you, and you *are* one,' said Richie, cheesed off.

'What?' said Alfie, equally cheesed.

'Well, you're *not a twat*,' said Richie.

Alfie groaned, and I went to get them refills. When I got back it was obsessional insults.

'You're the pretty one with the twat!'

'If ever I've seen a pregnant woman!'

'She's *my* sister, and *she* can decide ... oh thanks.'

'Thanks a lot.'

'Thanks.'

Alfie and Richie being so in love and Alfie having helped Richie so through his medical studies (Richie's father wouldn't pay beyond the third year) – and even though we were rapidly becoming their best friends ever – they still have confidences to hide. Alfie doesn't want it seen that there could be anything but sweet serenity between them. I thought I should pick a fight with Jannie, just to demonstrate it was all right for them to disagree!

'Jannie, just go and tell your sister to stop turning our household upside down,' I started.

'Household! My sister,' Jannie took the bait. 'This isn't our household; it's everyone's madhouse!'

'Well, we can't have a pregnant woman running round Bairnsford Nurseries when perfectly respectable customers come on perfectly respectable business! You don't think Henno's going to pitch up and make an honest woman of *your* sister, do you?'

Jannie smiled awkwardly across at Alfie and Richie, as if to say what does *that* have to do with *them*?

Alfie and Richie exchanged the quickest glances.

'Well, all I know is I feel blood is thicker than water at the moment,' said Jannie. 'She *is* pregnant and there's no point in sitting around saying she isn't.'

So Alfie and Richie saw that, if we could racket on, tearing ourselves apart in company, they had not made a spectacle of themselves. And notice how adroitly Jannie had thrown the appeal for expert advice back into their court. Those are the incredibly fine moments of a marriage, and we had only to test the firmness of theirs. Fiona had precipitated a very remarkable advance in all our lives: into bare, daredevil trusting.

Jannie says it was something else made Alfie pick up the torch and go with him; he wasn't used to Richie graduating and becoming a challenge to his authority.

Once they were gone Richie revealed he, too, had a fantasy palace. 'Know what I'm going to do? Use that old derelict shed if we get the place, as a clinic.'

'Steal from the rich and give to the poor,' I said.

'Yes,' he said. 'Well, it isn't so much that. Rural medicine is making a comeback. Your infant mortality rate needn't be so high.'

'You can say that again,' I said. I almost opened out about the dead baby under the eucalyptus.

'And it's sick to have any malnutrition when this is one of the richest food-growing areas in the country. It's a disgrace,' he said, 'that South Africa should look like Mozambique.'

'That'll go down well at the next HNP rally,' I said.

'Someone should explain to them they'll make greater profits if *no one* is starved.'

If David Bennington's fantasy was the all-round Renaissance man, Richie's was – Livingstone in Darkest Africa.

'Thank God we only grow flowers,' I said, somewhat flippantly.

'I suppose your dream is the Garden of Eden?' he said.

'Only if everyone in it is nude – and eighteen . . .'

'And male, and well hung . . .'

'Of all colours, serving delicacies!'

'Yes . . .' sighed Richie.

'But the HNP and the CP won't let you improve *their* labour. They'll have you die young first.'

'Well, there's no harm in pricking an abscess under somebody's armpit.'

'As long as that's where it is,' I said. 'And not in some handsome black arse.'

'Forget it,' he said. 'You've obviously got no code of conduct in accountancy.'

'But I can tell you about my speciality – tax write-offs, hey,' I said. 'But these locals are into lynchings, Richie – not love. We should know that, we live in the Valley. This isn't called typically South African for nothing. Haven't you read the papers recently, what's left of them?'

'You don't need the press when you work at Baragwanath. I could turn out far better unrest reports than they do. That's what I say to Alfie: we wouldn't have two people in a bed and ten on the floor between if they stopped riot control. You know what I've become a specialist in? – gunshot wounds. I guess I'm just heartily, totally sick of it.'

'At the weekends why don't you put your feet up and relax?' I said. 'At least till the rings have gone from under your eyes.'

'Don't think about it,' he said. 'Don't worry, we'll give your staff special rates you've been so helpful to us.'

Alfie came back with the torch and Jannie. 'Well, I don't know how anyone can watch Bop-TV and knit at the same time,' he said.

'I'll get you a top-up,' I said, because he looked really bushed.

'And did you see what she's knitting? – baby clothes,' said Jannie.

'When we have a whole shop full of them already,' I said.

'I'll get the drinks,' said Jannie, collecting the glasses and going off.

'So, what's the verdict?' said Richie. 'Don't please keep us in suspense, you dreadful old middle-aged queen.'

'Creep,' said Alfie.

'Fart,' said Richie.

Alfie resumed his armchair. 'Well, I hate to say that – it nearly kills me to say this,' he said. 'But I have to admit Richie's perfectly right.'

Richie clapped his hands together and cheered. 'Miracle! And you, dreck, don't believe in them!'

Well . . . I'd hate to tell you what my fantasy was. But I can certainly inform you it wasn't about to be a creche with Mickey Mouse to teeth on in the living room. And plastic ducks in the bath.

We were heading for bed when the dogs went berserk. I suppose our heads were full of the sobering thought that we'd have to make it clear to Fiona over breakfast that, if she wanted to have the child, she'd have to get that turban off her head and her hair growing normally again. That is, make it clear to her that the baby's health depended on hers. For a normal woman, it was no smoking, no drinking . . . for her a frightful choice: keep on the chemotherapy and certainly kill the child, but live herself to see another day, or come off the chemotherapy and die, but not before giving the child a chance to live. Only a very malign universe could have devised such a dilemma – don't you agree? This was all muddled in with Alfie and Richie having decided to go for the plot up the Nek – which at least was a dead cinch. So we were anxious and joyful all together; just a group of friends deciding to go to sleep. I thought it was Timothy down at the kraal with a party, which usually incited the dogs.

Jannie turned on the floodlights. There was Kev, with his overnight case. We ran out and called the dogs off. We walked him in. He'd been on circuit in our area. 'I tried to phone,' he said.

'What, did you miss the railway bus back to town?' Jannie said.

Yes, and he got a lift quite by chance with Mrs Leibnitz to the crossroads.

'What's happened to Henno?' I said, suspecting something. 'Come in, come in.'

'Sorry to arrive so late,' said Kev.

'But the crossroads is miles away,' said Jannie.

We hauled him in and started up again. When Alfie and Richie were sure everything was fine and tiptoeing away to their favourite bed, Jannie said tomorrow they were going to make an offer no one could refuse for the plot.

'That's nice,' said Kev.

He never comes out with it, does he?

Jannie tiptoed off and I thought I'd better get Kev settled in the other room. He set off for the rondavel, but I said Fiona was installed there with the TV and all, and by the way expecting.

'That's nice,' he said.

I got Kev unpacking and said, 'So, out with it. Where's Henno? I thought you employed him to transport you so you don't have to traipse through the Valley alone at night.'

'He's invading Angola,' he said in a hurt way.

'Oh I see,' I said. 'You mean he's got camp.' That's become such a part of our lives you can never make up a decent guestlist in advance for the call-up. Well, that's why Paul joined you, isn't it? (You know, they spare only male ballet-dancers now; parades ruin their pliés, my dear. Just wait until it's Grandad's Army; I'll have to shape up, won't I?)

'I suppose you waved him off in gloves at Park Station?' I said.

'No, he just went when I was broke,' said Kev.

'That must be quite a relief, I should think.'

Kev put his toilet kit on the dresser, hanged his head. 'We were going for a holiday together. Tomorrow, for two whole weeks. To the sea.' This was wrenched out of him.

'To the sea,' I said, 'My, wouldn't that have been lovely.'

'I haven't seen the sea before,' said Kev.

'Well . . . you'll just have to change your leave and go when he comes back.'

'What if he's in a bodybag?' said Kev.

'Oh Kev . . .' I said. Kev's fantasy, I suppose, was sneaking bloody Henno a kiss inside the sharknets at Margate Sands!

And being rescued from a swoon by sixteen lifesavers!

'Kev,' I said, 'I know what you must be going through. You can't face the prospect of arriving at an empty flat. Tell you what . . . we'll get dressed up and give them a live TV show over breakfast.'

'I sold the flat,' said Kev.

I figured that one out. 'Well, you know what,' I said, 'you, my boy, are an A1 bloody doos.'[1]

When I told Jannie in bed, all he said was: 'Pity we drained the jacuzzi for winter. He could have paddled in that to console himself. You know what?' he said, adjusting the pillow.

'No, what?'

'That Kev is an absolute A1 doos.'

'Well, he's got a fortnight to decide if he was right or not,' I said, pounding my pillow into shape.

'You know what?' said Jannie, taking my glasses off and putting them on my side table. 'We're becoming a home for any drop-outs and derelicts who care to drop in when they please.'

'You can say that again,' I said.

'Maybe that's what old age is like,' he said.

'Yes,' I said.

Ou Sara bounced us out onto the patio, ready for breakfast and anything else. She'd done us proud. The usual for six, plus kidneys and sausages and fried tomatoes. 'You know what?' said Richie, 'I could eat a horse.'

'Me too,' said Alfie, and they looked at one another longingly.

It was a beautiful autumn day.

Fiona and Kev had beaten us to it, and were waiting.

Fiona who I must say had grown quite accustomed to gays, and we to her, without any scruples lifted her nightie right up to show Kevin where. 'Right there,' she pressed her middle finger an inch below her naval.

'Fiona, you have the most devastating pair of panties!' said Richie.

'I'm supposed to have,' she said.

'Kev'd kill for a pair like those,' said Alfie.

'I would not,' said Kev, and he put his finger exactly where hers had been. He listened very carefully, as if his hand were a stethoscope. He absolutely beamed. 'My God,' he said.

---

1. Which for your information means an ace prick.

'So what's the matter now?' said Jannie with the tongs in his hand.

'It's – it's *Henno's baby*,' he said. His world had gone rainbow-coloured.

'Now sit down Kev,' I said. 'You too, Fiona, cause we've got something very important to say to you. And the first thing is you're going to eat properly, starting from now.'

Fiona wasn't listening. 'Wie's *Henno*, for Gor's sake?' she whispered to Kev.

Kev did a double take. 'He's – you know, Mister Muscles who got you like this.'

'Oh was that's what his name was,' said Fiona. 'I was so stoned, man.'

'Fiona,' said Jannie sternly, 'can you for once behave yourself, especially when we have important guests who have your interests at heart? Just sit . . .' he said, 'eat and shut up.'

She and Kev sat and received their plates, but that didn't stop them giggling like schoolkids.

'Fiona,' I said, 'wait while I say grace.' I've never said grace before, but at least it compels discipline.

Evidently they couldn't suppress themselves. Three minutes later she blurted out: 'I though his name was *Blammo!*'

'*Whammo!*' said Kev, and he laughed so much he had to ask to leave the table.

'Do you really think they'll go for a hundred grand down?' said Alfie.

'We'll know soon enough,' said Richie. 'Bacon?'

We put every detail of the choice before Fiona. That rather congealed her plate for her. Kevin came and sat beside her and listened.

When it was all laid out, she said quite sensibly: 'I'll have to think about it.' She pushed her chair back and went to the sanctuary of the rondavel.

Kev wanted to take her plate to her.

'Leave her,' said Jannie. 'For once let her make a decision that involves her own body, fully informed and on her own. She's had quite enough interference to cope with in her life, thank you very much.'

'I was just going to help her,' said Kev. 'And as a matter of *fact*, part of – part of her body isn't hers. It's Henno's!'

'Henno,' said Jannie, 'that piece of shit!'

'There were *witnesses*. That's quite unusual in a paternity case,' said Kev.

'Don't get nasty now,' said Alfie, 'or we'll phone your boss and tell her whose dress *you* were wearing on New Year's

Eve.'

'Just because Henno got one squirt right that didn't go over the duvet, Kev . . .' said Jannie.

'. . . doesn't mean he has any moral claim on her,' I completed the thought.

'Legally he has,' said Alfie. 'Kev's right. Only he and Fiona should be on the inside of the decision.'

'That wouldn't wash in a court of law,' said Richie. 'The biological father has no stake unless he does the right thing by her – marry and support her, you know that.'

'And that's not going to happen,' said Jannie.

'Imagine the face of his c.o. in Cabinda. Come back, Blammo my boy, and pay for your fuck. All is forgiven. Love Fiona,' I said.

'Sex-show can't go on without you. Love Richie.'

Alfie's turn: 'Hey listen here, major. That private there's gone public, you know. He's got a damn side more dangerous duties at home.'

Jannie: 'Hey, battalion commander. Just put that bloody cock in front, hey. Nobody wants an offensive weapon like that behind.'

'That's not funny,' said Kev. 'And if I have to make the choice, I'd be fair to the baby before Henno.'

'Sorry, Kev, but let's see what she says first.'

'Sorry, man.'

'Sorry.'

'Kevin, come on. Stop having dramas every five minutes.'

'But it *is* partly his child,' he said.

Fiona came back, fully dressed, looking nervous but firm. 'Hey, Jannie,' she said, 'jus' – jus' take me to Pretoria, all right?'

'But your appointment's not till Monday, my skat,' said Jannie.

'I know,' she said. 'What do you think I am – a total idiot?'

'No, of course not,' said Jannie.

One of the dogs licked her and she stroked its nose. 'I jus' want to tell the doctor,' she said, 'I'm not coming any more.'

Glances all round at her courage . . .

'But my skattebol, all we have to do is phone him. It's as easy as that,' said Jannie.

'If the phone's working,' said Kev. It was too much for him; he jumped up and embraced her. So did all the dogs. From then on Kev and Fiona lived like sisters together, and I am not kidding. Kev became the woman in her life; they were inseparable.

'That's very brave of you,' said Jannie. 'Now Fiona . . .

come and eat your food for once. You have to.'

'Yes, I will,' she said, Kev tucking her into her seat.

She looked at all of us. 'Sorry, chaps, for the disturbance,' she said.

Kev was all busy-busy. 'Haven't you got – some *warm eggs?*'

And so we go through the days when Alfie and Richie moved some of their stuff to their plot, so we had neighbours (well, near-neighbours), and I went back and forth, having the occasional dinner with Dave Bennington (he took me to his Bedfordview home and, delightfully, it was as he said it was – lovely wife and kids for real, very special), and Jannie cleared out stocks ready for Easter, and Kev moved into a residential block in Berea near the Flamingo.

Life went on for a week or two more . . . until on March 1st it was clear Fiona wasn't going to make it. Already she was like a corpse . . . a corpse with a foetus one inch long.

She was dying all the faster, Klaus, because of her brave decision. It was in her lymph-system, her joints, rotting her apace.

'Call for you on Line 2. Middle distance.'

The tin and the string.

'I don't care if the Tricameral Parliament is listening in. Get Alfie and or Richie, get them now. Not tomorrow or the next day. I mean this instant.' He rang off.

I put the phone down. 'Love you,' I said.

I picked it up.

'Sir?'

'Get me –'

'– Dr Alpheus, I have his number right here.'

'No, you old bag. Aren't you incorrigible? Detective Sergeant Stefanus van der Merwe. He's at Brixton Murder and Robbery. And hurry.'

'Yes, sir. Sorry, sir,' she said.

I shoved the cashbooks I was working on towards my briefcase, then thought twice. Picked up the internal phone. 'Bennington,' I said, 'oh Bennington. The Free Gold I'm in the middle of. Finish for me tonight. They're on my desk. *Don't* ask one question – I am your boss.'

'Call on Line 1.'

'Thank you. Now get me Dr Alpheus.'

'Right.'

'Ah, Detective Sergeant van der Merwe. Stefanus.'

'Yes, who's speaking?'

'Steffie for short . . .'

'Er...'

'Now this may come as a surprise to you, but I am your genial host of New Year's. Instead of phoning your wife to ask how she is, etc., I phoned you... I need some crucial advice. Where can we meet – say, in fifteen minutes? I'm in Fox Street, travelling your way.'

'Er, is this official or unofficial, Mr er –'

'Which do you *think*?'

'Corner of Bree and Burgersdorp, past the Market and north of the Oriental Plaza, where the old Pass Offices used to be.'

'Thanks.'

'Dr Alpheus has gone home, sir.'

'Shit,' I said, 'I mean *blow*. Now... phone Victoria Mansions, Berea. If he's not there try the Pink Flamingo. The name is Kevin Vermaak. Tell him he is under no circumstances to have dinner, got that? He doesn't drink, so we're spared that problem. He is to check in at the Trescott in Parktown East at eight o'clock. He can walk there. All he needs is his overnight bag. Got that? Yes, Pink Flamingo – P.I.N.K.'

I slammed down the phone, tore through her office. 'Thanks a span,' I said.

'Good luck,' she said.

In the lift who's there? – the managing director, going home early. Me with my tie at my navel.

Should have told him the one about the Schindler workman – who else could get a lift up such a greasy hole?

'Are you well?' says he.

'Perfectly,' I say.

Doors open, Mercedes, not yet rush hour.

Corner of Bree into Burgersdorp I break down out of the traffic. Try to start. Won't start. Zip outside and raise the bonnet. Peer in. Detective Sergeant Stefanus van der Merwe comes to my aid.

'The trouble appears to be inside,' I say.

I climb into the driver's seat, he the passenger's. Do a few false turns of the key. I can see he's sweating through his uniform. I roll up my window, he rolls up his.

'Look,' he says, 'once I get this thing started I can follow you home.'

'It's a hell of a long way to the Magaliesberg from here.'

'I thought you had a flat in town.'

A few kids with those knitted white caps looked into the engine. I started it, which gave them a fright. Cut it out.

Now their mother in a pink sari came to the window.

'They only trying to help,' she said.

'As long as they weren't stealing anything,' I said.

This, with Detective Sergeant van der Merwe over my knees, groping under the steering wheel.

'Ag, you bloody rich white people,' she said. 'This is *our* group area, not yours. Why don't you break down somewhere else?'

'Thanks a lot,' I said.

'Hey listen here,' said Detective Sergeant van der Merwe, 'you just go back to Purdah or Poojah, you hear.'

'Ag fok off,' she said, summoning her kids.

I pulled the ignition cable out of his teeth and plugged it back in.

'Now listen,' I said.

'Jus' don' call me Steffie,' he said.

'It's not what you think, Stefanus. I want a favour and *that's all*. Unlike your superiors, I don't care a flaming damn about your private life, as long as you don't care a damn about mine. I mean, I *do* care . . . you're a *very* nice bloke. But that's not what I came about.'

'No, fine,' he said.

'I want you to know you've got one of the finest bodies . . . and I'm very happy about you and Dave.'

'Thanks,' he said. Coy and shy.

'But – can you organise one of the tightest security operations that's ever been done in this country? You know how to, I don't. Tighter than an atomic secret?' And for a flourish I added: 'And as explosive.'

Obviously he'd had that kind of request before. Without a second's doubt he said: 'Yes.'

So I gave him the details, and added: 'Oh, and get those twin Malawi boys off Martie and Danny. They couldn't share an intravenous needle if they tried. They just look that awful naturally.'

'How do they fit into this?'

'That's the point. They don't.'

He climbed out, closed the bonnet for me. It started. He gave a thumbs-up. I waved my appreciation.

Through what's left of Pageview and past the tower to Alfie and Richie's. Up the lawn. Alfie's car's not there. Richie's parents are. Richie's parents have come up for his graduation tonight.

Richie runs me out of there. 'Alfie's sulking because he can't be included in the official celebration. We're having our KY party when they're safely in the Holiday Inn.'

'That's a bit rough, after all these years.'

'My father the judge would never approve.'

'Richie,' I said, 'congratulations and see you in hell. Where's he sulking?'

'Most probably at the Flounder in Melville.'

'It's on my way.'

He is in the Flounder, trying to make those cute waiters in red waistcoats.

I knock on the window, mime: 'Get your greasy arse out here.'

He does, cheers up immensely. We speed off into the twilight.

I've never done it to the farm in one hour seventeen before!

Jannie has Fiona wrapped up on the sofa. 'Fiona,' I say, 'it's just Dr Alpheus, don't be scared.'

She can't hear a thing. Jannie has put my Andrews Sisters wig on her, so at least she looks alluring and alive.

'Get the Trescott switchboard,' says Alfie.

Jannie cranks the phone while Alfie, Ou Sara, Belinda and I carry Fiona to the back seat of my car. Dogs, make way!

'Alfie, you're through –' Jannie shouts.

Give Jannie a pat on the shoulder. 'Shoo, I hope this is going to work,' I said.

'Shoo, I hope to God as well.'

On the way back Alfie repeated: 'I hope to God Kevin is in town. What if he's stuck out in Phalaborwa? Or Ermelo? Or Bethal?'

'I *told* you he's not on circuit this week. So quieten yourself down and get ready. Put the seat back and have a shut-eye.'

'You crazy? When Jewish boys get excited . . .'

'I thought you were quite mechanical about these things,' I said.

He stared at the white dividers flashing under the car.

'I thought you were not easily ruffled,' I said.

'The only thing that ruffles me is Richie's bloody Catholic father.'

'And when it's the first time in the history of the *world* . . .'

He reached over and tucked the blanket tighter round Fiona.

'Why are you doing it?' I glanced at him, back at the dividers.

'Fame at last, I s'pose,' he said. 'Hey, can you put a tape on or something? I'm sorry, but I don't feel like talking at a time like this.'

'Sure,' I said. Mozart horn. Imagine being blown by a horn-player.

Alfie closed his eyes, and presently opened them. 'I think I'll do this,' he said sombrely, 'not for poor Fiona or even for Kev: I mean *for* them of course. There's no option, is there? But really for *Richie*. He's a brilliant goy that, and he's going to be a brilliant g. p.'

I turned the volume down a bit. 'I feel a bit the same about Jannie. He's turning into a very good nurseryman. Well, we're not in the same field . . .'

'It feels sore. Not being invited to the graduation. That sort of prejudice. Doesn't it?'

'Tell that to Gay Lib. Why do you think they want the law changed?'

'Don't give me that,' he said, 'oh ple-ease.'

'But once you're famous, will you tell the media that you did it for Richie?'

'Of course not,' he said.

'I thought so.'

'But moffies down the ages to come. You know what they'll say? They'll whisper to one another, like frightened little mice: and Dr Alpheus, did *you* know that he *too* . . . was gay like us? And you know what, like all the greats of homosexual history, he did it to give us some self-esteem!'

In the middle of the slow movement, what do you know? We're flagged down for speeding. The cop insists on showing me the reading: 52,6 ks over.

'Medical emergency,' Alfie barks at him. 'I'm a doctor. Get out of the way.'

The speedcop slowly runs his torch over the back. Alfie lifts the wig – that's enough.

'Out of the way of progress, darling,' I say under my breath.

'Sorry, sir,' says the cop. 'If we had more staff we'd give you a escort.'

I sped off, showering them in gravel. I, too, was going quite mad with the whole idea.

One hour twenty-three; if it hadn't been for the speed-trap . . .

'Emergency ramp – no round the *back*.'

Fiona is on that trolley so fast with four male nurses (trust Alfie) in green, like lizards, spiriting her upstairs. I go and find parking. Even though Alfie's car is somewhere in Melville, I don't feel I should take his reserved place. Find a spot in the street alongside the park.

Rush inside reception in time to see Kevin. He's sitting there, knees crossed, next to a badly-lit jet of water with ferns. 'Ah, Kevin –' I cross to him. 'Kev –' I say.

He shifts up.

'Are you *sure* you want to get involved?'

The four lizard men rush through the swingdoors with another trolley.

'Do you know anyone else who doesn't drink and smoke?'

'Kev, you don't have to.' To them I say: 'This is the recipient.'

'When you gotta go you gotta go,' he says.

He won't lie on the trolley. He walks behind them with his head up nobly, like Iphigenia going to the sacrifice.[1] Or Susan Heywood off to the gas chamber.

I watch which floor they stop at, then take the visitors' lift to the same. I know this is no place for me – at least it wasn't till I took my drip for walks along those corridors more recently. I had only one green lizard wheeling me towards the theatre, the prettiest of them, and I said: 'With a nurse with a body like yours I'd go even into the jaws of hell,' and he said: 'You're right, sir, it's a real mess in there.'

Kev was on the trolley and they had his feet going down the corridor to infinity. I thought I should follow a bit. I had to make sure everything was going according to plan. I suppose I passed a dusky cleaner leaning on his mop.

Around the corner I was positively *seized* by security men lying in wait. They had that whole wing sealed off; they were everywhere. 'I'm not a journalist,' I said.

Two of them escorted me back to the lift. I thought they had an over-familiar way. Yup, those two drug-traps. At least Stefanus van der Merwe had got them off the streets. We agreed it had been a special New Year. As we went down, one of them touched me for a cigarette. 'I don't smoke,' I said. 'And I'm sure *this* is a non-smoker's.'

I shook hands with them at reception and said I was sure they'd do a wonderful job for as long as it took. Almost invited them back to the farm, but they *were* in their uniforms, they *were* cops.

So I went and sat in the car. Thank God I had the steering wheel to hold. I was trembling so much I wouldn't otherwise have kept upright. Alcoholic withdrawal? – surely not yet at my age. I hadn't had a drink since lunch. I put my forehead on the wheel.

Groped for the keys. Switched on but didn't start. That way you get music. You must be fit to blow a thing like that.

The rest you know. Or at least you know the outline.

---

[1] Greek tragedy, my dear – her father had her slit open.

Incidentally, it was *not* done by an incision through the stomach lining, but inserted through his rectum and implanted in the lower intestine. That turned out to be the correct method.

As for the donor – and they haven't stressed this at all – a lot more happened to her than removal of foetus. Alfie took off her left breast as well and right up to her lymph-nodes, and half of her jaw. There was practically nothing left of pretty Fiona. But, as you know, the cancer left wanted the remnants of her, and got them. I cannot understand how disease works: it kills what it feeds on. It races to kill its own condition of being.

If you think it was a pretty, romantic end for her, it wasn't. How anyone could convert what she went through into schmaltz I don't know. 'Died tragically young' – the phrase means one of those unavoidables, strictly not to be pondered.

After work I used to go and sit with her. Jannie couldn't because, of course, he had Kev. I grew very fond of her. As the evenings became shorter and shorter, it was just part of the daily routine: talk to Fiona. Although she was in a ward for three, there were seldom patients in the other beds. Hers faced the park. I sat and looked with her at the light going until you couldn't see who was meeting who any more. Thank the Lord we couldn't hear the maternity ward from there; that would have broken her heart.

'How's Kev?' she said.

'Fine,' I said. 'I spoke to Jannie this morning and he sends loads of love, too.'

'And Ou Sara?'

'She's fine.'

'And Belinda?'

'Also fine.'

'And the dogs?'

'Collectively them too.'

'And . . . have you heard from Blammo?'

'No we haven't heard from him. Look, are you sure you haven't got anybody in Hillbrow around where you lived I can bring to see you? Honestly, it'd be a pleasure.'

She had no one.

We fixed her up with a colour TV. Some of the others were wheeled in to watch, so she had some company.

I always felt bad deserting her at weekends; I thought I'd return on a Monday evening and her bed would be empty . . . not that they wouldn't have phoned through.

That is what happened, but not in that way. As a matter of

fact I'd just got back to my flat from seeing her, thinking nothing unusual, when they phoned me there. I returned to the Trescott and that's how it was: her bed was empty.

Jannie and I at the funeral. Kev was at work. Jannie brought two of our finest wreaths and, I don't know why, but we didn't take the Bairnsford Nursery labels off. They went quivering into the fiery doors at the crematorium. When I called for her ashes a few days later I suppose they were mixed up in them.

Who would have thought that out of those ashes should arise our joy? But let me tell you, I'd far rather have had it another way. That's for sure.

After the cremation, at which we were the *only* people . . . much mourned by her family, says your paper – *what* family, apart from the gay community? – I had the day off, so we went to my flat.

At about seven p. m. I was violently aware of the buzzer. It was Dave Bennington bringing me the work he'd done. 'Carn' offer you dzink,' I said, 'we've dzunk it all!' I must have let him in and he'd tidied up a bit.

Afterwards he said all I did was fall about in my underpants, defending Jannie, and all I said was: 'Won't you fuck off, there's a good chap?' I obviously don't know what I'm like when I'm past the point of recall.

You can see where I was headed. Everyone can tell you as much as they like, but that doesn't mean you know it for yourself. You *never* know for sure, if you ask me, until the doors open and the mechanical lift propels you and the plastic labels start wobbling. And you feel so bad cause someone else is left to pay the bills.

The next morning my secretary phoned and I said I was coming over. Actually, I was very pleased to hear her voice.

'How's everything going?' she risked asking.

'Oh fine, fine,' I said, but beyond that – like everyone else's involved – my lips, my dear, were sealed.

We none of us ever did tell anybody, not even Martie and Danny, especially them. Now we get to where they invaded us with their curiosity on Disc 1. We'd long stopped having parties, except with our fondest friends in the world (Alfie and Richie) and I'd stopped going to the Pink Flamingo, so they couldn't have imagined we were encouraging the likes of them still to drop round. You can see why. From June Kev showed, and it was a long way till expected date of birth, October 1st, all being well.

With the transplant Kev took only ten days of leave and

went back to work, of course, nobody suspected a thing. He managed to avoid getting on circuit, so that was fine, and worked at headquarters in the dressmakers', sitting most of the day and moving about when he felt like it. He'd cancelled the fortnight when he was due to go to the sea, so he had that and a lot more leave owing him from past years – he could get June, July, August and September off. I don't know; in October we'd say he'd had an accident or something. Well, he couldn't exactly apply for maternity leave, could he? (Not that he wouldn't have got it; they're a good firm and have generous conditions for their workers, unlike some sweatshops I know. Must be the American influence. Actually the garment-workers have always held out for their rights better than even the mining industry.) Having lost his flat, he wasn't going to lose his job, too, now was he?

He just inspected hems all day for quality control and laughed a lot with the mostly coloured girls, exerting every bit as much skill as them. Some were pregnant, too, so vicariously he must have picked up a lot of tips and solidarity. That was far better than sitting and brooding over it. (They only get three weeks for a delivery – who would be a woman, I ask you, for what *they* go through? Quite apart from the sheer drain and hazards.) Anyway, the point is: those girls provided a *normal environment* for Kev, he had tea with them and lunch, and it was bras and sanitary pads, incubation and women's knowledge of themselves all day long. If only he could have told them, and stayed with them, and gone through it with them. Kev was absolutely heartbroken when it was time to take his leave. *They* wouldn't have batted an eyelid. Only the rest of the world would have.

(Know what they did when the word *was* out? Threw a party for him with *mountains* of cake and lychees and jelly and custard! You couldn't see a sewing machine for tots climbing over them! That didn't get in the papers, either. Don't you tell me deep inside this country isn't an endless resource of sheer what the hell, fuck-'em-all *rejoicing*!)

'What's *she* got that *we* haven't caught?' says Danny.

You know, it would have been quite easy to tell him!

'At least in Joburg we keep our *dignity*,' said Martie, watching Kev trip through the rosebushes out of sight.

'It's so *rural*,' said Danny.

'What do you do to bona fide customers?' said Martie. 'Shake them down before they're allowed to buy? I swear we'd never have got through if the Rolls wasn't armour-plated. This place is like an armed camp.'

'What are you afraid of suddenly? Terrorists that creep into your bed? You should be so lucky.'

'Journalists,' said Jannie.

They paused, stirring. Danny said: 'And may we be so bold as to ask why?'

'No you may not,' Jannie replied.

'We've got a little secret for them,' I said, 'that's all.'

Martie said: 'Doubtless a new strain of grass you don't have to mow, and it'll take over the lawns of the world.'

'They don't want *industrial spies* –' said Danny.

'To steal a little pinch of seed and blow their almighty profits.'

'Something like that,' I said.

'So how's the gang at the Pink Flamingo?' said Jannie.

'Oh everybody left's fine,' said Danny, primping and settling in.

'Sorry to interrupt you,' said Martie, not sorry at all. 'But you do *know* who popped in the other night?'

'I'm sure you're good enough at p. r. to tell us,' said Jannie.

'Kevin's piece, back in his leather and chains,' said Danny.

I looked at Jannie, who had an oh-God expression.

All I could think to say was: 'It must be time up in Angola.'

'They've had some terrible defeats besides their victories, but never mind that now. You were there when he first appeared,' said Danny.

'Yes,' I said, 'I thought his cock should be stuffed and put above the bar as a warning to youthful maidens what to avoid. Like the posters about Russian limpet-mines and bazookas you get in every supermarket.'

'My dear,' said Martie. 'Surely it can't be that disruptive.'

'It dry-raped Kevin one windy night, that's all,' said Jannie, 'and while its owner gouged out the flesh on his back with his fingernails.'

'Oh my God,' said Martie.

'It was a broken bottle,' I said.

'You mean he – raped him with a broken bottle? Oh my God, oh my God,' said Danny. 'No wonder he can't even greet his friends.'

'It wasn't as bad as all that,' I said.

'But still,' said Martie. 'Now I know *that* I'm very glad I said what I said.'

'You know what he said?' interrupted Danny. 'This – lout – comes asking for Kevin Vermaak, anybody seen Kevin Vermaak?'

'And *he* says, Darling what's he to you? and I say, Oh Kevin Vermaak, of course –'

'– he died of Coke poisoning only last week!'

'Yes, that's what I said. Coca-Cola poisoning. Of course we really didn't have a clue where he could be. It was sheer instinct.'

'Yes,' said Jannie, looking at me. 'Now you chaps – listen, can you really keep a *secret*?'

I leaned forward, but Jannie shushed me.

'A real big secret, which is very difficult for a gossip-queen, specially when she's in her cups.'

'Oh darling,' said Danny.

'No you too, Martie,' said Jannie. 'Not even if there's an investigation and the special branch dangle you from the ceiling!'

'Oh darling,' said Martie.

'Jannie,' I said, 'that's enough now.'

Danny looked at me as if who were I to say he wasn't to be trusted. 'Promise, Jannie, cross my *heart* and swear to die in the most horrible way.'

Martie spat on his fingers and crossed his heart avidly.

'If anyone –' said Jannie, raising his fist, 'anyone ever asks *either* of you for Kevin Vermaak again, you know what you say? No wisecracks. You just say he's on holiday, perfectly naturally, and didn't you know, you'll find him on Third Beach at Margate Sands.'

'Third Beach at Margate Sands,' Danny nodded, and Martie followed suit.

'Don't *ask* people to ask you where's Kevin Vermaak. Only if, by chance, it comes up. Understand?'

They understood, and I was very relieved. For the first time I relaxed.

'You're perfectly right,' said Danny. 'Can't be too careful these days.'

'You remember those Malawian toy-boys?' said Martie.

'The ones you brought here,' said Jannie, not really concentrating.

'Well,' said Danny, 'you know what they turned out to be? We had them in the flat, oh, lots of times.'

'They weren't working in any delicatessen at all, at all,' said Martie.

I had not told Jannie this bit.

Since that's what they wanted, he said distractedly: 'I can't wait to hear.'

'Well, we weren't having any of *that stuff* in our flat, thank you very much,' Martie said. 'We're strictly alcohol's our poison.'

'Dope dealers,' said Danny. 'Trying to pass us this muck

93

and get us hooked!'

'No!' said Jannie.

'Yes,' said Martie. 'But do you *know* what we've got now?'

'Two ninjas!' said Danny.

'Indians!' said Jannie, 'cor, they get in everywhere.'

'Cutest you've ever seen,' said Martie.

To be affable Jannie said, 'Well, at least they can vote. That's one up on illegal Malawian dope-peddlers.'

'Of course they can vote; they're over age and white,' said Danny.

'*Ninjas*,' I said.

'Puts wrestling in the shade what they can do,' said Martie.

'You can say that again,' said Danny.

'Oh, I see,' said Jannie, and aside to me: 'What's a ninja when he's not at home?'

I whispered back: 'Professional killer.'

Belinda came out to clear up and they could see the drinks weren't forthcoming.

I walked them down towards the eucalyptus, suddenly thinking I wonder how *she* felt being raped by three men.

Thank goodness for the stabledoor at the rondavel. Kev stood behind the bottom half, waving distantly and smiling at them.

'Poor boy, poor boy,' they said, as I showed them off.

But I remember thinking, pray God the little champ comes out with a fighting chance this time.

Are you beginning to see how it all fits in, my friend?

Then here's the most unlikely piece. It happened like this, so brace yourself! Dave Bennington again, who like everyone else had *no clue* about any of this. But you'll shortly see how he connects. It was the blindest chance.

I was so behind in my job. I was sitting at this desk in my flat, working late. Then I discovered Dave Bennington really did have one missing cashbook I needed to finish up. It wasn't that late and I didn't feel tired.

What I swore I'd never do, I did: phoned his home in Bedfordview. I know I should never have done it, but I had socialised with his wife and I liked her very much.

'Oh hello,' I said, when she answered the phone, and I thanked her for all the trouble she'd taken over dinner for her husband's senior. 'Could I have a quick word with him? Sorry to disturb you like this.'

'Not at all,' she said. 'But I'm afraid he's not here.'

'Oh well,' I said, 'please don't bother. I'll catch him in the morning. It's not really important.'

Her line was to say it was no trouble. But she hesitated. Then: 'Could I be frank with you?'

Of course I should have said no. 'Well yes, Mrs Bennington, go ahead.'

Already my heart was going out to her.

'Well, he said –' she paused, 'he said he was finishing up late, working with you to get it done for the Friday board meeting.' She added: 'I don't know what that means.'

'Doesn't mean a thing,' I said. 'How absent-minded of me. Of course he's in his office and the switchboard's closed. I'll just nip over, it's right opposite me.'

'I'm sure that's it,' she concluded. 'I'm sure the two of you together'll get it right.'

'Don't worry about a thing,' I said, wishing her good night.

Well, he was no more in the office than I was; I'd seen him drive off. And he did have what I needed with him.

The second thing I shouldn't have done – drive to Kensington. But I did not have his unlisted number there. It was June and cold and dark. I remembered the turn off, all right. I had an increasing feeling of sympathy with his wife; I developed a peculiar notion that she was in the car with me, horrified at the surroundings. She'd probably never been that far south of the Ridge before. It's one thing to fall in love with a smoothy who's top of the class at university; another to learn of his squalid beginnings. Yet another to learn that he couldn't really leave that nocturnal life which had little to do with their marriage vows.

Had she been in the car, I'd have wrecked her life. I would also have wrecked David Bennington's. Don't get to taking sides in a bisexual set-up – it's a real strain on your natural alliances.

Then, as I figured out the turn up to the left, I thought: I'm not doing this for the company books. I'm doing it cause I'm a tad overstressed and lonely! Why not just drop in at the Pink Flamingo and see if anyone's still there. (Of course if you'd been in town I'd have given *you* a surprise.)

I crunched slowly round the next turn and knew I'd got it right. There at the end, in the driveway, was David Bennington's car. And the lights were on in the front room of his father's old house, curtains tightly drawn. I don't know why I was so apprehensive, I really don't. I was gripping the wheel, still thinking *go back to the flat now* – you have no right. Put a late night call through to Jannie and talk nonsense a bit.

(We had a kind of code, because on a party line once

you've woken the Valley they might as well listen in. 'How's the bitch coming on?' 'She's in good shape.' 'The vets say she mustn't have so little – milk – with her porridge,' etc. That bitch had been building up calcium for an unusually long time!)

But now I felt really shit-scared. You *know why*, of course. Alongside Dave's car, on its stand, was an awfully familiar motorbike. With the old kind of Cape registration: Bellville 70781. Now I knew why I was so frightened.

Then the front lights went off and the bedroom lights at the side went on.

I thought, he doesn't know who he really has in there. I thought, It's only a matter of time. If I was going to have a heart attack, I don't know why I didn't have it *then*.

I thought . . . insofar as I could think at all: Dave's big and strong, but he's not that big and strong. That's how he'll get the ultimate kick: a bigger and stronger boy back from the jungle, tanned like leather. I thought, Get Steffie van der Merwe again, *he'll* know how to deal with rampant Henno.

I reversed quietly, the tyres whispering on the tar. Down to the main road where I started cruising for a phonebooth. There wasn't a phonebooth until I got right down into Broadway.

A further rush of conscience: *what right* have I to bust up the idyll between Dave and Steffie? What is this? – when you should be into brotherly love, you're using *blackmail? Don't* tangle with the rough stuff, a man in your condition.

But all I'm trying to do is save Dave Bennington. Remember how Martie used to say 'I was *saved* by Danny'? From what we'll never know. Sliding into the lower depths on his greased arse, I guess.

'Have another djink, doll,' Martie says. I can hear him now and I could hear him then. Not that I was likely to find one there at that hour.

But *come on*, time was running dry. Fuck it, old queen – I thought – just *go* to your flat and *then* admit you're too poep-scared to save anyone. Bye bye Bennington . . . let's see how *you* explain away those ugly gouges on your gorgeous back . . .

As there was no traffic I did a U-turn with my lights scraping slowly round. It wasn't *that* late, so there should be people about. A few rather smart cars were up a side street. That was it: TAKE-AWAY PIZZAS. Some social cats were having a late-ish snack in this most deserted, forlorn commercial area. That must be from where Dave Bennington orders the four seasons, the calzone and the other one. It figured (as the Americans say, which means make sense. Figuring to me is getting the books to balance).

I couldn't see into the pizza take-away as the window was painted up with a frieze of slim and charming waiter-boys bearing all kinds of pizzas. It looked a bit as if they were going to wrap them over your face. So crudely was it painted those pizzas had acne (rather than tomato) and streaks of snot (for green pepper). The mural continued inside, for there along the wall as I shuffled in was the whole sweep of the Bay of Naples with you know what? – clumps of nude pasta-coloured youths, bathing and playing on their lutes.

Well, I wasn't going in there to have a giant margherita with ham extra, was I? In fact, I was so nervous all I wanted to do (forgive me!) was make a fart. It was accumulating inside me.

With a pizza parlour the kitchen is usually up-front, not so? At the counter three businessmen were standing (from those cars), their ties off, trying to look as if they hadn't just made a strange detour on their way from office to home. I didn't recognise them... nor they me. Their suits alone were worth a grand each.

At the other end of the counter, indeed I did recognise the guy who'd served David that night; his van was outside, too. I went straight to him, not that he'd know about me. (I was out of sight, remember, in the bedroom where David was now.)

Confidentially, urgently (and desperately wanting to fart), I put my head over the other end of the counter. His grizzly head came to meet mine. His name was on the paper hat.

'Hi,' I said. 'You must be Gino.'

'Hi,' he said. 'That's right.'

'Listen, you don't know me. I want to ask you a terrific favour and it's got to be quick.'

'You want the menu?'

'No...' I said. 'Just margherita with ham extra. Make it two.'

He wrote down 2M + ham on his order pad and skimmed the slip over to his black cook who was massaging a lump of dough next to the oven.

'Two margheritas coming up,' said the cook.

I still didn't want those business types to overhear. 'Listen,' I said to the owner.

'Won't be so long,' he said.

I got him to lean over the counter. 'You know... Dave Bennington, don't you?'

He at last looked me in the eye. This fart on board

expanded.

'Just do me a huge favour and quickly.'

He nodded curtly and backed away.

'No,' I said, but he signalled me to go round the counter and follow him through a black curtain.

I could hear the others' voices pause, then resume.

'Please,' I said, stumbling in the dark, 'it may be too late.'

He put the overhead bulb on. It was the smallest room with only a bench and with serving boxes, some flat and some folded, and it was not clean.

'Here's the menu,' he said. 'Take your pick. Take your time.'

'But I've already ordered . . .' I said. He was gone. I took out my glasses.

Well, when I flipped through the pages of the menu I had to sit down. That activated the fart, I suppose, because it squeaked out in dribs and drabs on the bench. I forced my buttocks together – no use, new washer needed.

That illustrated menu was not of course full of Polaroids of Italian specialities. It was full of Polaroids of South African boys. Each had a number and a description. The price, I suppose, was available on request.

There was No. 4: BENNIE, 22, MORE MUSCLES TO POP THAN A BATH HAS BUBBLES. Bennie looked as if he had rickets, with a washboard ribcage. A winsome smile and his cock pointing halfway north-west.

No. 9: SAMMIE THE SAILOR ON SHORELEAVE, LONGS FOR A LOVELY STRIP OF BEACH. Pic of him pulling up his T-shirt and down his pants against a sand-dune (minedump, surely, Johannesburg is inland!).

No. 14: GARY ON THE PHONE with a bulge in his pants the size of the receiver.

No. 19: The guy who put the stud back into the Student Body. Blows your mind, doesn't it?

No. 20: ACHMED THE SPICE-SELLER. Add a little tang to your tongue.

No. 21: SIPHO FROM SOWETO. It really is true what they say!

(My God!) No. 27: SPYKER. With this one you hit the nail on the head.

No. 28: Drenched with the joy of life. FERGIE THE HOT FIREMAN.

It struck me: it's fantasy-time again! Obviously none of them are otherwise employed if they're on stand-by at Gino's Take-Aways.

I snapped the album shut. I'm afraid I completed my fart!

They had a lot more style than the station boys, I'll say that. I'm sure that was entirely attributable to Gino. The Doornfontein coloured queens had more humour, though – they posed with their butts to the camera, giving toothless grins over their shoulders.

I emerged from the back room. Gino was saying to one of the expectant men of the world, 'Your order is ready, sir,' and a crisp R50,00 note slid over the counter. (We had only twenties when you were here – you can see how the currency's gone down.)

Watching him leave, the others resumed their wine. For R50,00 he didn't get a pizza thrown in, or a receipt either. He started up one of the cars.

I unfolded R20,00 and held it on the counter. The black cook, with a startling gold cross on his chest, hauled out my two margheritas and shovelled them into boxes, grinning the while. Gino made out a receipt and said nothing, took the note and passed me change. 'So you know Mr Bennington?' he muttered.

'Yes, Dave Bennington,' I said, 'lives just up the road.'

He showed no flicker of disappointment that I wasn't biting.

Then I leaned forward and his head was right by mine, confidentially.

'Look, Gino,' I whispered, 'I know it sounds funny . . .'

'It's all right, sir.'

'But . . . can I buy your *hat*?' It was one of those tall cardboard stovepipes; I suppose they wear them to keep their locks out of the lasagna. He must have thought I had some really kinky habit. 'I just want to give Dave Bennington a surprise.'

'My hat. No problem, no problem,' he said. He took it off his head and plunked it on mine. 'With compliments, with compliments of Gino,' he patted me. And with the two margheritas I was out of there. Anyone seeing me emerge would have thought I was Gino himself, making a delivery.

But that was the whole point, *wasn't it*?

I stopped beneath Dave Bennington's Kensington house. Thank God the bedroom light was still on.

I dismounted from my car, balanced the pizza box on my hand. Firmed the cook's hat on my crown. Took a deep breath. Gave last fart.

And then, as I had seen Gino himself do, with all the vim and vigour in the world, I pranced right up those steps and rapped as hard as I could on the door.

As you can imagine, there was a considerable amount of

running around inside. I suppose they thought it was a police raid!

I still had the change from R20,00 in my one hand and the base of the bottom pizza was going oily.

'Pizza, pizza,' I said in phoney Italian, 'getting-a-cold-a!'

Eventually the bedroom light went off and the lounge light on. The door opened an inch and there was David Bennington in his dressing gown, with his pants on, half undone, silly fellow.

'Two margheritas, ham-a extra,' I said loudly.

'Oh,' said David, 'clean forgot about those.' He thought I was Gino, for goodness sake.

I shoved the pizzas at him, which opened the door more: Henno's boots (unmistakable) on the vaulting horse, an empty bottle on the carpet.

'You can't come in here now,' he said.

'I don't-a want-a,' I said. 'I have to go sing at La Scala.' That must be when he twigged, for he stepped outside, looking back.

'Dave, he'll get you to want him very badly, all undeclared, and tie you down and *kill* you,' I whispered. 'He's a psycho, man.'

David heard me, but still he said: 'No he won't. He's the fellow from your party who'll fuck anything.'

'Take my advice, have *these instead*. Just let him *go*,' I said. I shoved the pizzas in his hands.

'You gave me such a fright,' he said.

'I'll tell you about it in the morning,' I whispered.

He nodded, said loudly; 'Well, how much are they?'

I gave him the receipt and the change.

'Wait a minute,' he said, rootling for twenty rand, but I was down those steps like a sprite in the night and ran to my car which was well out of view.

Next morning David was into my office first thing. 'I owe you twenty rand,' he said.

'Even the brightest accountant needs a friend to keep his own books,' I said.

He passed over the missing file.

I suppose we all spend so much of our lives acting anyway, that sort of scene comes naturally to us. You know what I mean. If you stop to think of it, I acted out someone I wasn't nine to five, Monday to Friday. When out for a boozy lunch with the top echelon, I once even shocked myself, as a waitress passed by, saying: 'Cor, wouldn't I just like to sink my teeth in that crumpet!' (*Me*, can you believe it?) Come to my flat – it was not different from any other exec's in any detail. (I kept Jannie's pic in the wardrobe, just in case.) That is the price we have to pay.

That's why when you get in the door of the Pink Flamingo and let your hair down you feel such *relief*. Bennington and I made a point of not being seen together too much in the office, *in case* the tar from one rubbed off on the other. I still feel that old inner tension when I serve perfectly nice clients up at the nursery. It's such a relief to get down to this machine again. Why am I telling you this? – *you know*. From that daily condition to impersonating Gino is an all too easy step to take. Out of sheer fear of being unmasked, you do it with ease. You even do it with style – and that's what most men don't have, let's face it.

It was getting late June and by then all of us were only too good at keeping up the deception. Think of it: every second of every day we lived in danger of being exposed . . . and never ever once did a single one of us falter. Talk about teamwork – we were absolutely the most efficient stars. Kev the brightest of us all, for sure.

He got very restless, waiting it out. No one can sit in a rondavel day in and out knitting babyware, even if the winter sun coming in the door is bracing. I was going up to the top field, and just draped a blanket over Kev as if he were chilly and took him along in the car to support Timothy's home side. They were playing the convict team from Sonderwater Jail. If Bairnsford Nurseries didn't beat them there was no telling what would happen. We were number three in the league, so they didn't have much chance, and I don't imagine hard labour boys are allowed decent time-off to practise their soccer, do you?

Timothy and their chief warder ran up to the car as we approached and cleared the spectators away a bit for us to get a good view from right under the thorntree at mid-field. They were all warmed up and ready for the great contest. All was so orderly and . . . bloody marvellous. When you think what old toothy Timothy has done for the morale of this Valley, and how our boys used to look. You would not believe those springing, bouncing, champing bloody stars were the drudges who plod through our greenhouses with squeaking wheelbarrows all week. Jannie bought them their jerseys from Mrs Leibnitz, actually in the nursery colours, just to demoralise the opposition. As for the Sonderwaters, they were used to wearing stripes, I suppose, and must have been saving up their pocket money for boots cause most of them were barefooted. That makes an irony, cause when our supporters let rip you know what they sound like: '*Bare-foot! Bare-foot!*' I assure you, our team has the most fabulous boots.

Hell, but even the hard cases looked so ready to go. Onto the patch runs the dapperest, most prancing ref you've ever seen, and does he blow his whistle!

We were the only whites there, too, let me tell you, except for Richie who came. He seems to know most people already. Jannie was serving at the nursery with not one soul to help carry. I shouldn't have risked taking Kev, but what the hell? Obviously the whole nursery knew from Ou Sara and Belinda . . . Ou Sara took him early morning tea, after all, and had overheard us a thousand times . . . I don't know, white people, she just shook her head. She never used to question the kinds of things we do. Belinda missed Fiona, that's all, but she and Kev just behaved *normally*. We all behaved perfectly normally. What else were we supposed to do?

'But you shouldn't have taken him up there when hundreds of people who *don't* know us were around,' said Jannie.

'Why not? Nothing happened,' I said. It all went in perfectly good spirits, as a matter of fact, through to Richie clasping their hands in that lovely double African shake, and me distributing free beer to queues of sweating, happy people. Rank paternalism, I know . . .

'What did Kev do?' said Jannie.

'He just leant out of the window and whipped the caps off for them,' I said. He did.

The only reproach you could make over all this is Timothy thought of it first. I don't mind betting he made some tidy winnings. Because we won: 16-3.

Taking courage from his first public appearance in that condition, Kev had Jannie do his hair properly and he wore a doek to cover his shaving shadow and lots of powder. I didn't witness this, but Jannie told me they went to the Co-op just to make a few purchases. Mrs Leibnitz didn't spot a thing. Jannie introduced her as his sister, Fiona, and they even had coffee at the bar.

'Bet Kev remembered to cross his legs on those high stools they have,' I said.

'Let me tell you Fiona had the finest pair of legs to show in the whole of the Transvaal,' said Jannie.

'And what did people do if they got too close to her?' I said.

'Actually people are quite polite to pregnant women. They

just moved out of range when they saw her coming,' he said.

This may be a joke to you, but of course it *had* to work. If Fiona had been exposed, we'd not have been able to show our faces there again.

All you do is play it for real. I'd go to the Trescott on Friday nights after Jannie had brought her in for her check-ups. The receptionist would say, 'Ah, your wife's in the waiting room, Mr Vermaak. Your brother-in-law said you'd be coming.' I didn't bat an eyelid. Of course Fiona was my wife – and of course Jannie, her brother, was perfectly naturally friendly with me. (She was registered as a patient of Alfie's as Fiona Vermaak, which later made endless muddles since they'd had a previous Fiona who hadn't yet paid her bills, and a certain Kevin got lost in there and incinerated by accident?)

There was old Kev looking absolutely smashing by the fountain – Italian silk scarf, eyelashes down over his book, a modest ruff on the smock, skirt to just below the knee, seams of her pantihose running straight, sensible heels.

'Sorry I'm so late, my love,' I trotted in, 'taxman kept me.'

'Oh, there you are,' said Fiona, putting her fiftieth child-care paperback in her handbag.

'Come, let's go, Fiona, my dear,' I said, and she lightly put her arm in mine.

She made one stumble, and people looked up from their *Fair Ladys*. 'Oh, my feet are so tired,' she said, and off we went.

Outside I said, 'Well done, but you need a shave.'

'Don't tell me,' said Kev, and we drove off.

'How's Alfie?'

'He's fine. Sends love.' With great relief Kev sprung the heels off his feet. 'He wants to take one of those scanner photos they do from inside – you know, to tell what sex it is.'

'Oh, and?'

'The only drawback is – I ain't got the hole to insert it up.'

We had a good laugh about that.

'And your vitamin intake?'

'Says I just mustn't overdo it.' He sank in the seat with his hands holding the mound. 'Otherwise, everything's fine . . . And you? Did you have a good week?'

'Busy, but everything went well. Sanctions giving us a bit of trouble. You know . . . nothing to worry about . . .'

'Well, I'll cook you a lovely supper myself when we get home.'

Another Friday I fetched him on time and we were leaving past reception when in comes one of the Pink Flamingo crowd. (You don't know him, but quite a good friend of

Kev's and I've seen him around. Gays didn't seem to use that hospital, thank goodness, but maybe his mother was having a hysterectomy.)

'Well, my my!' he goes – the whole number, contemplating us, hands on hips.

Kev thinks *this is it*, my dear – now the entire world will know, and so do I. I stood rooted to the spot, but Kev – he merely sails past him all unconcerned.

He passed. The guy was puffed up at *me*.

'Honestly, why didn't you *tell* me?' he hisses. '*I* didn't know you were *married*.'

'Come on, you flirt, help me down the steps,' said Kev.

I gave the guy a wink and called: 'Coming, darling.'

'Pigs can fly,' said the guy.

But if I have one image of Kev it's in the winter sun, under a floral hat in a deckchair, him with his smock raised to catch a bit of tan, his fingertips feeling little Betty Boop or Simon the Slugger in there, kicking away. And talking to it incessantly, in the walled garden where no one could see. Those nails were so well kept, that smile so all-consuming. Perhaps I learned what husbands out in the real world do feel for their wives and forthcoming attractions; I'd have killed to keep them from harm.

Belinda brought us coffee on a tray.

'Die kind wil nie stil bly nie,' I said.

'Ja baas,' she said.

Of course she knew how it felt. 'Jy weet hoe dit gaan.'

'Ja baas,' she said, depositing the tray. Belinda never talked much – a bit like Kev! – but she added: 'Baas, daar is net een ding wat ek nie verstaan nie. Waar gaan Baas Kevin melk vir Baas Kevin se baba kry?'

She had a point.

'Aah,' I said. 'Belinda, jy weet – Barefoot Nurseries is 'n baie baie spesiale plek!'[1]

She nodded and scuttled off. I suppose she hadn't heard of cows!

I went back to the Sunday papers.

'You know, there's just one thing I really miss,' Kev said.

I hoped he wasn't going to say Henno. 'The girls at the factory, you mean,' I said. 'There must be things women share that a man can never give.'

'Yes,' said Kev. 'But it's my mother and my sisters. I'd really like to pay them a visit at Parys.'

---

1. Ask Paul for a translation!

'God, you must be mad,' I said.

'They'd understand. They'd understand,' he said.

'And what about your father,' I said.

'You could meanwhile take him out for a beer,' he said, 'and explain how you made an honest woman of me.'

'Kevin,' I said, 'that will not do. Anyway, you only had a foetus-implant, not a sex-change operation.'

I flipped over another page.

You know why we didn't want the story to get out? Not just because of the way the Sunday papers would hash it up. But because the press would alert Henno to where Kev was. We lived in mortal terror of him. Yes, we did. With every reason, as it turns out.

Playing games so well is fun, but you're in trouble when they become too real. You have to have a point somewhere where you say, now *that* is the solid truth, otherwise you really lose your bearings. Our only solid truth left was – Henno, if he finds out we have his baby, will kill it. If he couldn't have it, he'd make damn sure *we* couldn't. A bunch of screaming queens hijacking his sperm; that's what it amounted to.

But we made a vast mistake in *not* letting the story out. A baby makes its presence felt long before it's born, let me tell you, with precautions and planning. If everyone had known Henno's baby was due, he wouldn't have dared touch it.

By bad luck it was the night Kev was staying over in my flat to have more tests in the morning. It was a Thursday actually, then on the Friday we were coming back to Barefoot Nurseries. It was the time of evening when you're between things: not yet got the merger plan (in my case) out of your head before deciding what to do with yourself. Kev was in the bath, relaxing.

When there is a grinding of the bell. There are many others in that block going through the same thing, so I think it's somebody got the wrong door. Some quite interesting types roam the corridors there, and I'm usually only too willing to help.

It's Henno. He'd changed a lot. You don't come back from fighting the MPLA and look the same. Short hair. Deeply tanned, making his eyes *blue*. At least he was in his old clothes, not a uniform.

'Oh – hello,' I said, 'it's you.' Any other night I could have handled it fine.

'I thought it was the wrong flat,' he said.

'No, this is the one,' I said. 'Er, look, nice to see you, but I can't have you now.'

Henno looked in over my shoulder, and by a stroke of fortune there were Kev's highheels on the floor and his handbag open on the couch. 'Ah, you got someone,' he said.

'Ye-es,' I said, 'so it's not convenient . . .' Conspiratorially I added, and I haven't a clue why: 'Just – just don't let on to Jannie.'

'How's Jannie?' he said.

'Oh – he's fine . . . though there's nothing whatsoever happening out there now.'

'Listen, sorry to disturb you,' he said. 'But I jus' come back . . . and haven' you gotta job for me?'

This would take a little time and I didn't want the voices to go higher or Kev'd hear in the bath. Even though I was in my socks and vest (and trousers, of course), I stepped out, thinking to walk him to the lift. There were enough ficas, rubber plants and dracaenas on the way to hide behind; that block was an indoor jungle.

'Well, it's hard times, you know. Things have gone down since you were last here – because of the war.' I could see that was not the first time he'd been told that.

'All right, please man,' he said, 'so jus' tell me where's Kev?'

'Kev?' I said.

'Yes, Kev – you were at his place for dinner, man. He always has a welcome for a ou.'

I pressed the lift button. 'I think he's at Margate Sands. Third Beach you'll find him on.'

He'd heard that one before, too. 'All right, where's Jannie's sister, then? She always has a welcome for a ou, and you can say that again. Isn' she living in the Brow?'

'Oh, you mean Fiona.'

'Yes, Fiona.'

The lift came and the doors opened.

'Um, we don't talk to Fiona anymore. She's . . . into so many men. We . . . don't even want to know where she is.' I thought he was going to step in, but he didn't and the doors closed. 'Listen, I can't stand here all night like this.'

I pressed the button again, but it would take a long while to return.

He was thinking hard, a desperate man. He said: 'I thought you were into . . . squeezing me . . .' He looked me hard in the eye.

'Go and find someone else to squeeze your . . . there's a good boy,' I said, patting him on the shoulder.

'Otherwise I don' come, I carn' come,' he said, 'that's the trouble.'

'You should be so lucky,' I said. 'Most of us come if you so much as click your fingers.'

A couple in full party kit let themselves into the corridor and headed for the lift, concerned not to be late. Those socialites you see on every page – the Connerys, in this case.

'Just, just,' I said. I scuttled for the fire stairs to wait it out there.

I could hear their conversation dip as they approached Henno at the lift. 'Good evening,' 'good evening,' 'evening,' they all said.

The lift eventually came – ping. 'After you,' 'after you'.

I waited until the doors closed and emerged with relief. The coast was clear. I made for my flat.

'Pst, pst!'

I stopped. 'Didn't you go down?' I said.

'That would be spoiling the evening for those fat cats – me in the lift with them,' he said.

He had a point, but I said: 'You're spoiling my evening, too, Henno.'

'Please, man,' he persisted. 'Haven' you jus' got fifty cents so I can get some *bread*. I got no place to *stay*, I got no money for *petrol* –'

'No money for a drink-up.'

'I got nothing, man. Please, please.'

The body doesn't lie: he was fit but emaciated, stringy. I thought he had malaria. Everything he said was true. If he'd been a bit brighter he would have tried blackmail next. It's your Christian duty . . . (not that I'm one of those). But none of us wanted him to get at Kev and *that* whole thing starting up again.

'*Please*, man. I don' wan' to sell my *bike*.'

'Like Kevin had to sell his flat, hey?'

'Jus' a few rands.'

'What will you do with them?'

'Go back to Cape Town and see my mom.'

With that I reached for my wallet. 'If I *pay* you, will you do that? I'm sorry, Henno, but that's all I can do.'

'What?'

'Go back to Cape Town.'

'Yes, man. I haven' seen her for a long time. I don' think Joburg's so good for me.'

'Things are calmer at that lower altitude. People more friendly. Shit.' Of course my wallet was in my jacket in the flat.

Henno stood there, expectant.

I know what he saw. As I rumbled around in my pockets,

the beginning bulk of desire. Does it ever, ever end? There's a very complicated thing here, because *he knows* how men get their kicks from keeping other men down. What do you think those boys on Gino's list were making their living out of? I had to be cruel, but not *that* cruel. At least he hadn't realised that if he had to submit, he could make a lot of money out of his humiliation.

But the lift decided the moment. Ping – and the doors opened.

I shoved Henno into the depths of the indoor plants and bustled towards my door.

Just as well I did. It was Connery.

'Oh –' I said breezily, as I approached my door. 'You must have forgotten some little thing!'

'Ah,' said Connery, approaching. 'Thought I'd check up. Never can be too careful.'

'Check up on what?' I said, pushing on my door.

'That – lounger wasn't still about. Don't want to come home and find our Bulgaris gone, do we?'

Of course my door was locked from the inside. To make conversation I said: 'I suppose you carry a gun, to defend your – Bulgaris' (whatever *that* means). This was getting ridiculous: Henno cowering in the rainforest; Connery late for the Oppenheimers, prowling after a trespasser; me in my socks, shut out; Kev shaving his legs in the bath.

'I do,' he replied. 'Least until they put proper security in this block.'

'It's all right, he's gone,' I lied. 'I was just – pretending to water the plants and I saw him go. Have a lovely evening.'

Connery looked relieved. I thought he was going to say, Next time you water the plants do you awfully mind being fully dressed?

'I'm sure we will,' he said.

'What?' I said.

'Have a splendid evening.' Ping. He was gone.

I hauled Henno out of the pots.

Justifiably he was getting angry. 'Shit, man, shit,' he wiped his hands. 'That's what you get when you been defending this bloody country – no job, no money, no *welcome home*, Henno hey – you done a *good job*.' Through his teeth, restraining himself. 'I killed more fucking Communists with my own bare hands than he's even thought of to protect his – what? *Bulgarians*? Shit, shit, no shit, and next thing he's going to shoot *me*! No I've had enough, I'm up to here, I've *had* it. Shit, shit, it's all *blerrie kak maan!*'

'Don't look at *me* like that. I just saved your bloody life!' He was going to carry on. 'Keep your voice down.'

Then we heard Kev pull the bathplug out and the water gurgle.

'Just *give* me the *money* you promised and I'll *go*. *I* don't want to stay in a place like this, honestly, *honestly*.'

'Can't,' I said.

'Why not?' he said.

'Locked out,' I said.

'Well,' he said, almost on the brink of tears, 'jus' do me a favour. Jus' ring the bloody bell!'

I moved some of the Thuja plicatas straight.

'Please, man . . . leave the plants alone now. What does a ou have to do, hey? Go down on his knees – and beg.'

'Shush, you're making a scene.'

He was trembling all over. He bit his lip and it was going to be any second now. 'What do I have to *do*? Jus' tell me what a ou mus' *do*? *Please*, man.'

If I'd had a whip in my hand, his face would've been slashed in two. Down on your knees, take that and that and that. And while you're about it, take this in your mouth, you disgusting wretch.

I suppose that's what combat's all about – keeping your power and counting the bodies.

His eyes were glistening.

I said, 'Can't you even get a job with a *security* company?'

'They don' want me, man.' He held his face tight. He was going to say, Just give me the money and I'll go forever. And the lift was going to ping and Kev come looking for me. Besides, I could not do what I should have done, even to Henno.

I tapped him on the shoulder with my forefinger.

'No, I'm not going to hide again.'

'Sh, just stay there.' I passed him and went to my door, rang the bell.

I waited, Henno waited where he was.

Kev tripped to the door, opened it suspiciously, was going to shriek.

'*Shut up*,' I said. 'Let me in.'

He did, and I closed the door.

'Heavens, I –'

'Just shut up,' I said.

'– looked everywhere. Thought you must have fallen out the window. I'm so . . . relieved,' went Kev like a record running down.

'Did you hear me? Keep your trap shut and don't you ever open the door with nothing on again,' I said.

109

'Your paisley dressing gown is not nothing. I think it's rather fetching.'

'Get in the bedroom, lock the door on yourself, put on a proper dress.'

Kev gasped.

'If I hear one more squeak out of you, I will *kill* you.'

Kev flounced out of there, closed the door, turned the key.

I counted five to calm down. One . . . two . . . three . . .

Went to my jacket and wallet. Pulled out fifty rand. Four . . . Added twenty. Petrol's gone up since he last did the trip.

I went to the door, opened it, making quite sure I clicked back the lock this time. I didn't think to dress properly myself. I checked the corridor for clearance.

Approached Henno with the money in my fist. It was twilight and the lights flickered on.

'Here,' I said, 'and I'm really sorry I can't do more.'

Henno couldn't help himself. Tears literally shot out of his eyes. He turned away to conceal this, and folded the two notes.

That's when he should have left. It would have been the perfect solution.

'She's giving you uphill, hey?' he said as a sort of friendly joke. 'Jus, they all the same.' He tried to convey he was chuckling. He didn't want me to see he was crying, and turned further. He sneaked a finger across his nose. 'Thanks for the cash, no really, hey,' he said. 'I'll go now.' His head rose for a convulsive sniff.

I patted him on the back; well, if I'd comforted him more he'd have broken completely. I was not cast to be the torturer.

Then I heard it coming – the wheeze of the lift levelling off. Ping.

Whichever of the wealthy burghers, my neighbours, stepped out of the lift saw only a rather panicky leather-boy rushed like a pass-offender into the back of a van and the door close and lock.

Was this ever going to end? Now Kev was in the bedroom and Henno in the lounge and me in the kitchen knocking over glasses for a bottle that was full. I got one, broke the cap, 'Pst, *in here*,' I said, and Henno came into the kitchen. I shut that door behind us.

I shoved a glass in his hand, tried to pour without clattering the glass. 'Drink up, it'll make you feel better.'

'I don' wan' disturb if you got problems –' he said, looking at the glass, tears plopping into it.

'Drink, drink,' I said, downing mine. When I put aside the glass, my eyes were now full of tears. 'Fiona – died,' I said.

'What?' he said.

'Yes, she did die, shortly after you, you know –'

'Ag no,' he said, simply.

'In a terrible way, and she was very brave, right to the end. Braver than you or I would be.'

'*Ag no*,' he said. 'And she was such a *lovely* thing.'

'Yes,' I said, giving a big swallow of phlegm. 'If you're into girls, I suppose.' I poured two more.

Henno took his. 'I don' know. When a ou gets back from *that* place all he wants is the people at home to be *happy*. Know what I mean? And now Fiona – she isn't happy, she isn't even alive.' He took a gulp and wiped his nose. 'That's – terrible.'

'Yes it is,' I said, taking one of those breathy heaves. I looked up and felt drowning at sea. 'Terrible, especially cause she was carrying your baby.'

'My baby. Fiona.' He looked as if he'd been hit in the chest by a Cuban cannon-ball at close range. He crumpled. 'Ag shit man, my baby also.'

He certainly didn't look relieved, which would have been the first reaction of some philanderers I know. None of her other lovers cared if she was pregnant or not. Come to think of it, he himself was somebody's anonymous handiwork – no father had ever stepped up to claim him. So I suppose he really *did* know about the responsibilities of paternity.

He ripped open his shirtfront as if he couldn't breath. 'Oh no,' he went.

I crouched on my knees, swallowed hard. 'Are you sure that's what you feel?' I said.

'Why didn't you tell me she was having my baby?' he said.

'Would you have looked after her?' I said.

'Of course man . . .' he said. 'If you'd let me back at the nursery.'

'You didn't even know her name properly,' I said.

'Yes I did. That was only a game. Anyway, it's Fiona.'

'Fiona who?'

'There you got me,' he said. 'But she'd be Fiona Wassenaar, wouldn't she, and I'd be looking after her like a man should.'

'You couldn't, you were in the war.'

'Ag give me a break, man. I don' know how I'd be looking after her then, but I'd be looking after her when I came back. Wouldn't I?'

I thought, Don't say you can't now, she's dead.

A crying jag came over me. Now I sat on the floor.

He got up and went for the bottle. He held it up to see if I wanted more. I nodded, and said, 'Help yourself.'

He put down the bottle and sat cross-legged opposite me. 'Hey, hey,' he touched my knee. 'Isn't she . . . going to . . . weren't you going to the movies?'

'Never mind about her right now,' I said. 'Henno, are you sure?'

'Sure what?' He waited, then tapped me with his glass. '*You* don' have to feel so bad for my sake. Drink up, hey.' He set the example.

I still wanted to know: 'Would you really have looked after her and the baby?'

'I said I would've if I could've. I don' know how. Maybe you'd let me work at the nursery or something. What else do you want me to say? I could do security for you.'

'It's too big a risk,' I said.

He draws a line on the floor. 'Anyone sets foot there, they're dead, man – as a Muscovy duck.' I suppose that's how the boys on the border talk.

'The baby didn't die,' I said. I took my slug.

'What?' said Henno. 'How's that –'

'Kev's carrying it for you.'

'– I beg your pardon,' he said.

'Just don't ask how but it's true,' I said.

He gripped his glass, put it down. 'Kev?' he said.

'Yes, Kevin Vermaak who loved you so,' I said.

'Oh Kev,' he said, relieved. 'But how – you . . .'

'Don't you trust him?'

'Of course I trust him, but . . . you know . . . how can . . . I mean, Kev dresses up and all, and you may not think it. But he is a man.'

'That why you raped him, like a real man does?'

Henno faltered. 'Shit, I don' know where this conversation's going. I didn' rape him.'

'Tied him on the bed in the dead of night and scratched on his back with a bloody *screwdriver*!'

'I beg your pardon,' said Henno.

'Well, what happened then?'

'It wasn't like that,' said Henno. 'He asked for it, that's all.'

'Careful, you're on dangerous ground. That's what all rapists say. It was actually provocation.'

'I think you better go to the movies . . . and I'll jus' go to Cape Town.'

'Like you did after fucking Kev up, just because you can't come any other way.'

'Shit man, I was *scared*.'

'Scared – of what? That you'd be associated with being in bed with a *moffie*, even if you did *rape* him?'

'Er, listen, can I jus' have another drink? Then I'm going. Thanks for the money, thanks for everything and I'm off.'

'Don't dora your way out of this,' I said. My head was full of stickiness and salt, so I blew my nose.

Henno stretched his hand out and blew his nose deeply, gave me the handkerchief back. I folded it up: 'Ag sis, man, haven't you even got one of your own?'

'I was scared such a little chap should want that done to him. I was scared I would split him apart. I was scared he was going to be disappointed. Make me a baby, make me a baby. Go on till you make me a baby. Tie me down so I can' get away . . . It was completely terrible . . . You got that streak in you, too. Well, if you ask me to tie your legs to – that kitchen table, right now, and shove the plug up your arse and switch it on, even for a thousand rand – I won't do it. And you know what, you wouldn' have a baby, either. All you'd have is an electrifying experience.'

'Henno, how can you *say* such things?'

'It's not me, it's Kevin,' he said. 'When you were gone he talked like that all the time.'

'And the letters on his back – how do you explain that?'

'He wanted that so all the world would know even a moffie can have a child.'

'What?'

'Yes, yes.'

'All right, I see now,' I said. 'Have a drink.'

'You satisfied now?' he said. 'Jesus, you're a doos. Don' you understand one thing about yourself?' He tapped my sock with his boot. 'Can I have some ice?'

Of course Kev for the last half hour had been listening to all this. I'd heard the bedroom door unlock, I'd heard him trip on one of his heels. Then, like the old crone in the Free State on a chilly eve, he'd huddled down behind the door. There wasn't a keyhole that you could see through. I'd heard the rustle of his party dress as he sank down. He had a *lot* of explaining to do.

I stood up to go and open the door, but the blood drained from me and I had to pull out a kitchen chair. Henno broke the ice and plunked the tray on the formica.

'Can I sit?' he said, and I said, 'Of course, as long as you don't ask for my hanky again.'

He went to the basin and dampened a cloth, wiped his face. Then he rinsed it out. 'You want?' he offered.

I took it, wiped my face and threw it back into the sink.
'Ah, I don't know,' I sighed. 'Sometimes it's all a little much.'

'Don' have a heart attack about it,' he said with a quiet laugh in that awful butch way that sounds so threatening, but isn't. It's quite companionable, in truth.

He poured over the blocks in both glasses. 'What, she think you're making her a surprise dinner to take to her in bed? Asparagus, artichokes . . .' he looked along the tins. 'Cheers.'

'I think there's something she wants to tell me before bed,' I said.

'What, she doesn' want to work in the kitchen anymore?'

I smiled. Hell, he was astute.

'But I'll say this, one thing you shoulda learned years ago, whatever you think – moffies carn' have children. It's a basic, scientific fact of life. They haven't got tubes and things. Sorry, have I offended you?'

'You know what, Henno. That's the only detail where you're wrong. Every single other thing you've said I accept. Just that bit – there's where you made a mistake!'

'So how can Kev be carrying my child?'

'*I* don't know. Ask Dr Alpheus and the finest surgical team in the land – *they* know how. They've been practising on lesser forms of life for years.'

'Oh ja, I seen something in *Scope* about that.' He was as drunk as I was. 'They put it in with – microwaves.'

'Hardly,' I slobbered.

'No no no sorry, micro*chips*.'

'Hardly, Henno,' I said. I had a big laugh coming on and shook my head.

'He's got my *bung in his oven*,' he roared out.

'Microwave!' I burst a bit. 'I don't know, maybe we better have something to eat with this.'

I was going to raid the fridge, but he held my wrist. 'Hey, I know you friends with Kev and hiding him, but I would like to see him. I won' do him any harm, even if you think the worst of me. Is he really at Margate Sands?' he said.

'No,' I said, and I had totally unstoppable laughs. 'He's . . . *right behind that door*!'

I could not contain myself anymore; I'm sorry, it was all far too ludicrous and far gone.

'What!' says Henno. '*What!*'

'Yes, open it and see for yourself!'

'What! What!' like bullets from the hip.

All we needed now was the joyous reunion.

Henno strode to the door and hesitated as if I was putting

him on. He turned the handle, slowly drawing the door forward.

He looked back at me, puzzled. Then he opened it wide. 'You jus' having me on,' he said. 'There's no one there.'

'Let me see.' I stopped laughing.

I inspected the passage. The lounge: shoes and handbag gone. The bedroom door open and no coat and doek on the bed.

The curtain over the window was moving. For a dreadful swaying moment I thought the stupid bitch had got fully dressed just to take a swallow dive into Fox Street.

Ping. I distantly heard the lift and it was going down.

'What, she walk out on you?' Henno said, coming through. 'Hell, this is a nice place you got.'

I checked around more. 'Evidently she walked out,' I said.

'Probably found out you're gay!' said Henno.

'Very funny,' I said.

'No, I got nothing against gay people,' he said, 'not even Kev.' He sprawled across the sofa and took off his jacket and one boot.

'Before you take off the other,' I said, 'come look here.'

We dangled out of the window, ribs together. Kev stepped out from the awning and jaywalked across, his back to us. The travelling case I would have thought was the give-away.

'Jees, that's some broad,' said Henno. He leaned farther out and gave the longest, lowest wolf-whistle ever heard in downtown Johannesburg. Kev froze in midlane – one miffed lady! Thought better of aiming a V-sign six floors up. Strode on and briskly round the corner.

I hauled Henno in by his seatpants.

'Shit, that was some lekker broad,' he said.

'Let's open some tins,' I said, but we went straight for the second bottle.

I suppose we should have climbed on Henno's bike, and gone wobbling after Kev. It was highly negligent to let him go off like that into the night. Too deep in the booze, my dear; besides, I was a little off Kev right then.

Henno hobbled in. He loosened the top of his pants. And me – well, I was already half nude as you know. I just took off one sock.

'Something you moffies'll never learn,' he said. 'You don' do it up your bloody backside. That only hurts, hey. There's other places.'

'Oh, like where?' I said.

'I learned it in the SADF.' He pursed his lips inside and waggled his tongue.

'In the army. Well, I must say!'

'Yes, but you got to keep your lips so, otherwise you can hurt him with your teeth.'

'Oh Henno, why don't you just go to Cape Town?' I said. I biffed him with a pillow.

'I carn', he yelled.

'And why not, may I ask?'

'Because you've got the hots for me!' he said.

I biffed him another shot. 'I have *not*,' I said.

'Then why're you shaking, tell me that?'

'I have high blood pressure, you fuckhead. Get me another drink.'

He went while I arranged myself and the cushions.

He came back with two glasses and only his snow-white briefs. Crumbs, talk about a specimen of manhood.

'You should get a job in a gay bar,' I said. Consumption would double at the sight of him.

'I'm always willing and able,' he said, packing up.

Actually, that's where I'll end that lengthy and appalling scene. Certainly none of it was foreseeable. I had a feeling some tables had turned.

I leave you with this last thought. That creature, that killer . . . we did him a frightful injustice. Oh yes, we did all gang up on him so that he didn't stand a chance. Vengeful bitches!

But he was the most loving and gentle man I'd ever known.

(There, you've really *learned* something now.)

Next day (Friday) I was not performing efficiently at work. Between sorting out a hangover and the events of the night before, I didn't give the corporation's books much of a chance. This would have to stop. But another thing I had to learn: a hangover is easier to get rid of than a baby. Until noon there was a board meeting, as well, and I came out of there as if I'd been in a sauna. Anyway, a long weekend was coming up, so no one concentrated.

Over lunch I figured what to do about Kev. I got through to Alfie, who said Kev was having his tests, but what the hell did I think I was doing leaving him to walk the streets? Did I realise the technology, the thousands of man-hours, etc., that were at stake? I just had to grow up now, said he.

The trouble was I'd left Henno a spare set of keys to the flat. I whipped over to get them back, but he was out looking for a job . . . and hadn't left the keys. That was reasonable; he wasn't going to find employment over a long weekend exactly, and could return them to me after that. I showered and packed my things so that I could make a quick getaway. (No, if you must know . . . we had slept in the same bed, but he couldn't get it up. There were only two conditions he stayed on: that he didn't answer the phone, and didn't bring women there.)

I spent the afternoon with Dave Bennington, getting things done after a fashion. No matter how I tried to formulate it, I couldn't arrange the words correctly. I suppose I wanted to explain how wrong I'd got the situation that terrible night of the pizza intervention . . . about Henno's tendencies, when they were devious Kev's all along . . . Ten times I was about to start: 'You know that night when I saved you . . .' I'm far more able with figures than words; figures at least *add up*.

What does add up is this: that one straight guy, with no particular skills or qualifications, affable enough . . . Henno with little more than a prodigious cock . . . could slowly drive a lusting queen crazy. He'd done it to Kev, right down to taking over his flat, and now he was doing it to me. On Tuesday it would stop. At five o'clock I couldn't get out of the city fast enough.

I pulled in at the Trescott, thinking at least to have the Kev business sorted out as soon as possible. It would be no more than a drive to the nursery full of sulks and recriminations, and we'd have to have the *big scene* sooner or later . . . But the most important thing, after all, was to get the baby back to its sanctuary. No more games, just some routine and discipline.

I popped in at reception and the lady nodded – in the waiting room. Gathering my coat about me, I strolled in. Kev was there, deep in another how-to book. Fit a nappy, I think. You lift the baby's legs and work the straight edge under first.

I nearly said, Ah Kev. 'Ah Fiona, my dear,' I said, 'at least I'm not late this time.'

Kev closed his book. I should have known something complicated was up, because he didn't have his overnight bag. But I couldn't say, Where have you been, you dilly queen? There were people around. I said, 'Looking gorgeous . . . as usual.'

Kev closed his book and slipped it in his handbag. He looked up, past me. Other *Fair Lady* readers' eyes looked past me, too.

Then you've never seen so many *Fair Ladys* go into spasm.

Kev got up, ignoring me, and swanned past. There in the door were two of the burliest men you've ever seen, with scars, loose-fitting tops and tight jeans . . . steel-rimmed boots! Efficient they looked, arms crossed beneath their chests. They had not come to collect their doubtless exceedingly athletic wives; they had come to collect Kev. 'Hello, ma'am,' 'Evening ma'am, this way . . .'

I have never been so snubbed! 'Er –' I thought I'd better explain to those in the waiting room, *in case* any of them had been watching. 'Quite all right, she's honorary president of their Karate Club.' And I trotted after them.

Kev was signing out the book at reception. 'Ninjas!' the lady exclaimed.

'Ninjas!' I said.

'Yes,' Kev cooed to the lady. 'Licensed to kill.'

I shut up and followed them out. They weren't frogmarching Kev; just escorting him, a bit behind and to either side.

'The car's over there,' I called to their backs . . . but they proceeded down the pavement in the opposite direction.

I trotted after them. 'Fiona . . .' I said, 'they're not – kidnapping you, are they?'

On they strolled. Clearly they weren't. I should have known it. They were Martie and Danny's. Obviously Kev'd taken a taxi straight to their flat and the rest had followed. The flat was close by and that is where they were headed.

I struggled to keep up with them.

At the corner I called: 'Fiona, please . . . stop this now immediately. You know you're wanted at the farm. Dinner is waiting for you.'

Kev paused. The two ninjas turned and scowled. This display gave me the idea: if Kev lifted his little finger, I'd be dead before I knew what to do next.

'Don't you sell us out to Martie and Danny . . . no good'll come of it,' I said.

The ninjas stepped towards me.

'I'm in perfectly good company,' said Kev, 'so fok off.' The ninjas' eyes positively glinted.

'You're only going to *gossip* all weekend,' I said. 'You'll miss your *pills*.'

'Oh yes,' said Kev, 'I think I will.'

He gave a little flounce, eyed the bloody ninjas, said, 'Come on, chaps.'

And off they sailed, turning the corner.

I don't think I'll forgive Martie and Danny for that. Not even if they grovel at my feet for half an hour. I won't give my forgiveness, *even then*. Meddlesome, disloyal shits. But if you think that's the *end* of the trouble they caused . . . which they'd never breathe a mention of . . . just wait and see, wait and see.

Instead of going straight home, I went to Bennie Goldberg's Bottle Store and bought a *case* of J and B on account, and put it in the boot. Of course I meant it to stock up the flat. (Well, at least I had a *drinking* partner in Henno, who really took to decent booze . . . and heaven knows how long he was going to stay.) But it was going to be oh so difficult to explain to Jannie what had happened. It would be much easier to explain if I went into Bennie Goldberg's and bought a *second* case.

When I arrived back at the nursery Jannie was chronically busy, what with the long weekend and all. He gave me a peck and said put it in the cellar. He had a whole box full of print-out labels (oh yes . . . so you don't need to return Disc 1; it's redundant and the prices have all changed). He was going to put them on by gaslight.

'Where's Kev?' he said.

'Oh . . . just staying overnight with Danny and Martie,' I said casually. 'He wanted a change.'

'I suppose you know what you're doing . . .' he said. 'Your supper's on the table.'

'Thanks,' I said.

Later I went to help with the labelling at the nursery, but it's quite finicky getting the tab around the stem without breaking it, and then back in the hole . . . so I thought I'd better watch a video.

By *Saturday* night I'd seen seven videos and was really pissed.

Jannie came in from a good day's business.

'You need a shower,' I said.

'And what about *you*?' he said.

By the *Sunday* night I'd seen seventeen videos . . . If you drink to extinction, even your sexual perception goes. When Jannie came in after a hard day's business I couldn't for the life of me see why I'd ever seen one thing about him that was attractive. He was a huge blob to me, like a beanbag.

And you know what, if he'd run in and said, Surprise! Guess who's here?

Kev? – no.

Alfie and Richie? – no.

Dave Bennington – no.

In my mind they were all beanbags.

Who then?

All the way from Switzerland, surprise, surprise – *Klaus* is here. And you'd walked right into the living room, fit and well and beaming, all arms out for joy!

Well, *even you* would have looked like a beanbag.

(I'm sorry . . . how can I *put down* such things?)

A whole nother day to go . . . oh God. How many videos had I seen? Well, there were only two bottles left in the one case and an awful lot more in the car. It wouldn't have been so bad if Jannie had sat beside me and sunk a few himself, but he was incredibly busy.

On the *Monday* morning he woke me and screamed: 'Guess who's here?'

Let me tell you, I really fought to think who it could be.

'Alfie and Richie – they always pop in when they need something,' I said.

'No . . .'

'It must be Dave Bennington, with his wife and kids – and her granny,' I said.

'No . . .'

'Klaus all the way from Switzerland, and Paul, I bet you.'

'*No*,' he said. 'You better get yourself shaved and decent, because you'll have to handle them. I'm busy.'

'I don't want to spend the morning talking shit to Danny and Martie,' I moaned.

'It's *not* them,' he said.

'So Kev isn't back yet?'

'Yes, Kev is,' he replied. 'And he's brought with him two ninjas for a start. And the rest correspondents from the London *Sunday Times*.'

'My gosh,' I said.

'And a camera team from the BBC,' he said.

'The BBC,' I said flatly.

'Yes, one does lights, the other sound and the third the actual camera. Quite nice buns you should see when he actually crouches over the lens.'

'Oh Jannie . . .' I let out air like a flat tyre. 'I'd rather it was lovely old Klaus.'

Klaus, where are you when I need you?

'Get up! Get dressed! This is *your* side of the business. I've got customers with ten-ton trucks!'

'The staff hasn't checked in?' I said.

'We run a place called Barefoot Nurseries, don't you know? They're all playing soccer.' He shoved me under the shower without even taking off my pyjamas.

'Tell them to come back tomorrow,' I said.

'They can't, they're flying back to Lusaka.'

'I mean the journalists . . .' I said, and the word journalist . . . journalist . . . went round my head.

Half an hour later when I'd figured out why my pyjamas were so soggy, I'd also worked out what a journalist was: a nice little old lady who opened her pad and asked nice questions you could answer interestingly . . . Well, if you still think the world of the media is like that, you'd better go to a re-education camp.

I presume, when you're going on the slippery slide, and you're getting everything wrong, you just have to keep on going till you hit the very bottom.

I made sure I looked sparkling as a new pin . . . and you know what, suddenly all of Bairnsford Nurseries was on a slope. I didn't know we'd bought fifty acres in the Magaliesberg with such drainage. Better still, it sloped whichever way I went.

Down it sloped from the bedroom to the patio. Ou Sara and Belinda had the tables out and platters of scones with nets over them to keep the flies off. You know what I should have done? – fire them on the turn.

I went down the slope to the rondavel. Kev wasn't there, but certainly there were enough lamps and batteries and exposed films sealed up and technological mess. You know what I should've done? – burn the place to the ground.

I didn't. I spotted Kev's pills on the dresser. Something came terribly clear to me: he'd forgotten those for an awful long time. I picked them up and dropped them; picked them up one after the other and shoved those I could find in the box and securely put it in my pocket.

While I'd been counting pills I thought, Well, they must have Kev in a quiet corner of the nursery, which the customers can't see, where Jannie has the most beautiful display of indigenous flowers. The ground sloped that way now, so I had no trouble getting there. We do have a gorgeous arbour, and it's total bliss. Bit dazzling on the eyes, though; I suppose it would give them too much flare.

Jannie was wheeling a barrow on the other side of the hedge. 'Where they?' I said.

'Aren't they down at the river?' he said.

The river . . . that's miles away. Down the slope. Half an hour later I'd worked out they must have Kev in a bathing costume propped against the waterfalls . . . so that his pregnant belly and hairy chest would show together. How else could they prove to the world that he was what he said he was?

(Just incidentally, do you remember that birth control campaign with a man looking ruefully at his bulging womb . . . and the caption something like, If it was you, wouldn't you be more careful? Now, take off the guy's sweater. Imagine if there's wasn't a *pillow* stuffed under it.)

Where could they be? In the office by the sheds where this word processor would end up? I prayed the ground would slope *that* way (but it didn't!). Half an hour *later* I caught a breather nearby and they weren't here, obviously. I was near the pit latrine, sweet-smelling. Well, they couldn't be there. I went down the (genuine) slope to where I knew the baby's grave was, and for some reason pointed my finger at it and said, Well, I helped you. Now you help me.

There was only one other place: the kraal where the dogs were barking. That's where they were. I thought, A bit cool, without asking permission, but still there was nothing wrong with it, I suppose. I hadn't been there for ages myself . . . one didn't want to intrude.

But by the time I got to the kraal, they had their reflectors out . . . and, well, a whole bloody movie set. Toothy Timothy was running down with armfuls of potted plants to dress it up a bit. But they didn't want his nice, neat bungalow or any of that, oh no. They didn't want even the biggest syringa tree in the Valley that hangs over the settlement like a blessed canopy.

They were busy, so Timothy and I didn't interrupt. All they wanted was the *worst* shack, which isn't even occupied any more, except by some rather terminal chickens. And they wanted the garbage and broken glass in front with a few bodies propped against the corrugated iron. (I mean, that was our goalkeeper, and he had every right to be groggy; Barefoot Nurseries had just won the cup, hadn't they? I don't know who the other two wrecks were; Kierieklapper's, probably.)

Kev was supposed to walk into the frame with the interview lady. Now Kev . . . I find it very hard to forgive Kev, too. I *have* forgiven him, but not in the depths of my heart, if you know what I mean. Kev was not wearing a bathing costume or his now habitual drag. There was nothing about him that looked queenly and regal. He had on his old tracksuit with the zip-top half undone, just a hint of the chest and the bulge beneath. So that it wouldn't be offensive, I suppose. His hair was tight back in an elastic band, so that he didn't have a hairdo anymore, but was sort of a hippie with a ponytail!

The interview lady was meant to lead with: 'In South Africa where such fortunes are spent on white medicine, what about blacks?' She was a really raw American.

And then the camera was meant to show what it was really like for them.

This all took so long our goalkeeper tried to hop off to get into his togs and bring the floating trophy. But one of the ninjas told him to stay where he was.

'Hey, that isn't fair,' I said, but the other ninja had me marked, I may say. (I never got their names; I just called them Justerini and Brooks.)

They shot it again, because this time Kev stood on the wrong marker. (Yes, he was quite enjoying being the celeb, but had lots to learn.)

'In South Africa, where there is such an immense gulf between rich and poor . . .'

'Cut, cut,' said the soundman. There was an international flight coming in overhead.

They took it again. 'In South Africa, where for every rand spent by the state on white medicine, one cent is spent on blacks. How d'you feel about that?' She held the mike towards Kev.

'Yes, for AIDS-sufferers it's even more aggravated, of course . . .'

AIDS-sufferers, I thought – they're really laying it on thick.

'Sorry, cut,' said the girl. 'Make it anything but AIDS, Kevin. We *don't* want our viewers to think the baby may be infected.'

Kev pursed his lips. 'Malaria?' he said.

'Perfect,' she said.

'Malaria and malnutrition,' he said.

'Perfect,' she replied, and they retired off screen.

'All right everybody,' and the goalkeeper and his buddies passed out on the garbage again. '*Take five.*'

You know what? I should have thrown that lot right out. Not for malicious defamation and selective propaganda – nothing like that. Just for plain old trespassing. (Well, how would you feel if they took the only non-functional toilet in a block of Turkish guest-labourers in Zurich, and said *that* was Switzerland for you, home of the cheese fondue?)

At least they weren't the SABC, supposing they'd been allowed to get within a mile of Kev. *They'd* have made him up to look like Zola Budd trying out her new Adidas for the Korean Games.

They weren't the London *Sunday Times* or BBC, either, though I like to think we'd have had some fair coverage from them. They were some dreadful press agency (Beta) using freelancers who had only 24-hour visas restricting them to a *medical* story. No wonder they had to get all of apartheid in one shot.

When Kev came off set I gave him his pills.

'Thanks,' he said, 'I've got others in my purse.'

We hauled everything back to the patio. I waddled alongside Kev. Eventually I got Justerini, or Brooks, to take my arm.

'Kev, can I speak frankly to you?' I panted.

'You always do,' he said.

'Kev . . .' I said, and he slowed down. 'Look, just because I chatted your boyfriend up, doesn't mean . . .' I gestured at this total invasion of Bairnsford Nurseries – our security, our privacy gone for ever. 'Isn't this going a bit far?'

'They're not interested in you, they're interested in me,' he said. 'So let me handle it.'

'And I have to spend the rest of my life giving the press corps of the world tea? I do have a job, you know.'

'When you're a star, you're a star,' he said. 'But it only lasts a few weeks, so come on.' His ninja offered to help him over an irrigation canal, but he hopped across.

I took advantage of having my ninja around. I got him to *carry* me over.

'Please mind the fleabanes there,' I announced to the rest. 'This is my property, you know.'

Where were the dogs when you needed them? Over at Kierieklapper by now, wrecking their periwinkles.

'You don't understand,' said Kev. 'This is an *exclusive* story. No one else can come. Not until six weeks after the delivery.'

'How much do you get?'

'A million,' said Kev. 'On condition the baby's born alive, and nobody knows till then.'

Obviously the ninjas knew all this, so I kept talking. Presumably they would get their share (all worked out by Danny and Martie, who really know how to fix such deals). 'And what if – the baby's born dead?'

'Only a quarter of that,' he said.

'Oh,' said I. 'Dollars or rand?'

'Which do you think?' he replied.

'I'll go and put the kettle on,' I said.

He followed me into the kitchen, leaving the ninjas to work out a bit on the lawn. The others went round.

'Ou Sara,' I said. 'Tea, lots of it.'

'It's not what you think,' said Kev. He put pots of jam on the tray for the scones. 'Belinda, you take this . . . I don't want to look feminine in front of them.'

'Ja miesies,' said Belinda.

'Master.'

'Ja master,' she bobbed.

'So all is forgotten and forgiven, both ways,' I said. 'I do hope so, Kev.'

'When I heard Henno in there, my heart nearly broke,' he said.

'I'm so very sorry . . .' I said.

'All right . . .' he said. 'But you know the only thing that's important to me now? This baby. I have to have it, and I have to show it to the world.'

'Will they come back and film it all?' I said.

'Only the nice parts,' said Kev. He looked in such good shape, but his back was giving him hell.

'You'll have to get Henno out here,' he said. 'That's part of the deal. Then they fly out by eight tonight.'

'But what will you say to him?'

He plunked the little bowls of farm butter on another tray. 'I don't know. Anything they want me to say.' He gave the tray to old Sara.

'Doesn't look as if it's going to be a gay story then,' I said.

'You know what?' said Kev. 'They're even more afraid of mentioning gays than they are of AIDS.' He clicked his back. 'Henno's meant to be Fiona's widower, and I'm his brother-in-law who stepped in. Can you believe it?'

'Because of the unequalness of apartheid?'

'No, because their readers can't venture outside the middle-class family unit. I really think we'd all better take the money and run.' He counted out ten teaspoons.

I was watching the kettle. 'Kev,' I said, 'I'll say one thing. All this business has made you talk, at last.'

He smiled. 'Once this is over, I'll never say another word.'

'Why not?' I said.

'I won't have to, will I? The baby will say it all.'

Once the tea was out and they were photoing again, they wouldn't let Kev sit with his legs crossed and little finger in the air. He had to crouch as if he was having a crap, and hold the cup like a mug.

Kev persuaded me to get the New Year snaps Jannie had taken over dinner. They were just silly colour ones, mildly indiscreet – but isn't that part of the fun of parties? I opened the envelope, thinking maybe I should keep some of them back. There was me as a crooning beanbag and Kev on my arm. But that interview lady quickly had them out of my hands.

This is what she rejected on the teacloth: all drag pictures for a start. Old Val lurking behind a column, blowing someone a slobbery kiss. Steffie van der Merwe with his leg crossed over the Malawian in blue on the couch. Alfie toasting the camera with his eyes lit up.

'That the surgeon?' she said.

'Yes.'

She threw it out. I suppose he looked more like a ganger there.

Martie and Danny before the Rolls with their toy-boys on the bumper. Richie with his wholesome arm round Ou Sara's neck, helping himself to a glass. They were out, too.

She found the one of Kev, Fiona and Henno at the table. She cropped it down with her fingers to Fiona. That was one of the worst quality flashes Jannie had ever taken.

'Haven't you got one of the wedding?' she said. What wedding? Who was this? She hadn't even said good morning to me.

'There wasn't any wedding,' I said.

'Haven't you got one of her in high school – graduation picture?'

'No,' I said. 'She never finished school.'

She looked at me for the first time, as if the dogs had dragged me in. She placed her fingers around Fiona's head again.

'What did she die of?' she said.

'Big C. There she was already half-gone.'

The woman took the picture without asking. (It was not mine to give: it was Jannie's, and she had no business.)

She showed it around. 'Guys, I've got the only pic of the deceased. Now doesn't that look like the perfect car-crash victim?'

That was my lesson in what it's to be a *real* hard-hearted bitch.

I should have mobilised those ninjas. They'd have cleared the place of scum.

'Please get Henno,' Kev said. 'Please, now.'

I went to the phone and eventually got it ringing in my flat. Of course I had told Henno not to answer it. I let it ring for quarter of an hour until he twigged. Maybe I should phone Connery and ask him to bang on the door and give him a message! Someone further up the party line broke in and said: 'Ag no, it's my turn now.'

'Sorry,' I said and hung up.

There was nothing for it but to get back into town. I packed my things without thinking, really. I gave Jannie's filthy paw a squeeze at the nursery and shot off down our corrugated road (that was not going to become as famous as I thought ... Only you from the pictures could pick out the odd details in the background, like the grandfather clock you gave us).

Henno's bike wasn't in the basement. Wouldn't you know it? Nor was he anywhere to be seen in the flat. He'd left the keys on the kitchen table with a note saying thanks. So he'd got a job with a security firm on a public holiday? – they must be desperate. I heaved the case of J and B onto the counter. I thought, this stuff is killing me. More likely he'd finished the old booze and gone to Cape Town, for real this time.

I phoned this through to Kev, explaining they'd have to play happy families next time round, when the Beta Agency came back for the kill.

'Thanks, anyway,' said Kev. So business-like, so butch!

I sat really depressed. The flat was quite empty now. It wasn't worth going all the way back to the farm. If I'd got the terminal in and learned how to type at that stage, you know what? – I'd have written a letter to you, and gone to bed early.

Phone Bennington. No, he'd be having a lovely family time.

I put on a tape and showered. Listened to another tape.

Central Johannesburg is completely deserted at a time like that.

I went out for a pizza.

'Two margherita with ham extra?'

'No, though they're delicious. I'll try something else – Number 28.'

'Try something spicy for a change – Number 20.'

'Fine.'

Amazing how few words you can use to tell a story. Kev's right. Gino in one word: obliging.

Next morning (Tuesday) I was faced with a very full week's work and only four days. By lunch I was a quivering mess. I cried off and went to the flat.

Don't ever try to sleep in the afternoon when you're meant to beat work. Your conscience gives you bad dreams.

I managed to get Richie round for a consultation. I didn't want to cadge favours from him now that he was setting up private practice in their home, brass plaque on the gate and all. He very proudly told me of his patients: whooping cough, measles, whooping cough ... and a woman with oedema (swollen ankles) who didn't realise she was four months pregnant. We chatted about Kev's progress; Richie said it was now thought possible by the few who were monitoring Kev that, as a result of certain technicalities, men might be better childbearers than women (because they're not susceptible to swollen ankles, eclampsia, etc. and so forth). The hitch is that they don't have the natural equipment to go into labour and the whole unbelievable business of heaving the product out into the world. So babies in men have to be surgically removed at great expense, or they just go on growing. I don't know ... I believe everything they tell me.

Richie said Kev would get what they call a bikini cut, so that it didn't ruin his bathing.

His own first few weeks in white suburbia compared with his weekends on their farm was interesting: septicaemia, TB, ring worm, more TB ... Richie had little time to spend on fashionable diseases: TB still killed more South Africans than anything else, and booze. Heart next. Then car-crashes. Nothing to tell the world about, is it? – except that the big killers are all basically non-racial!

Richie's cure for me was a week at sea level and short, fresh walkies. Cool the petrol, in other words, getting back into shape. I said should I check into a hydro, where they pump out all the dreck and sharpen up your senses on lettuce leaves and fruit-juice! He said no, because the one thing I needed most was good companionship.

I like Richie: we just had a scotch and soda or two each, and talked most amiably about this and that. He is unflappable; his unruffled and so gorgeous presence actually tells us we are all right. He's not a practising Catholic, but he'd been typecast by his upbringing long before: Sister Richie of the Sanatorium, Patron of the Poor! We talked of the Pope's visit to America. He clutched up an AIDS-baby in his merciful arms, but would he touch a genuine homosexual? – God forbid! (I hadn't realised that, had you? I suppose it'll wipe out the Vatican if they *will not* use what they should ...) Richie also told me about his father, the judge, who loves the Pope, of course.

By *Wednesday* I couldn't stop trembling and applied for sick-leave for the whole of the following week. So I spent all of *Thursday* and *Friday* filling Dave Bennington in on what to do then. There was no other way of getting out of a holiday, and it fit Jannie and Kev well, too. Jannie had to come, to drive, so left Timothy in charge – and although we worried a lot he managed perfectly.

So we set off on a non-drinkers' trip. That was no problem for Kev, but he had the backache a weightlifter gets. Every two hours we stopped to let him stroll a bit. Jannie and I had not been away together for eleven years; we worked it out. Kev, of course, although he knew more inland towns than you thought were on the map – worked here, worked there – oh Harrismith, you should see *Bethlehem!* . . . had never been to the sea!

We didn't choose Margate Sands, because of the publicity. We went further down the South Coast to somewhere private and really old-fashioned. Then, for the first time, Kev did see the sea.

'What's that the Indian Ocean?' he exclaimed.

'No sir,' we chorused, 'the Indian Ocean's up by Durban. This is the ocean reserved for whites!' (Old South African joke.)

You poor dumbheads are landlocked in Switzerland! Did you realise we have such magnificent beaches all round us?

We found the perfect, hidden place – it wasn't old-style, just old and really rundown. Until the following weekend we were the only visitors, so it kept going only on the bar-trade. Even a one-star joint like that is desegregated now, and a couple of nice-looking blacks came in for drinks, nobody batting an eyelid, as far as I could see. Even a *mixed* couple came in – they were en route from Durban to Cape Town – and that was accepted. Although nobody showed it, maybe the locals thought *we* were an odd trio. (Kev just kept his doek on, with the wind always blowing, and wore slacks and sensible shoes under his mac.)

I wish the timing had been better on this, and it had been a bit more in season. Or better still, we'd already had the baby with us. Then we could have built sandcastles for the tide to come up and devour, and collected shiny objects for it to . . . yes, have taken out of its mouth. But it was hell of a relaxing all the same. We so decompressed we could hardly keep awake the first days . . . two deep-sea whales on their single beds, beached in the blankets . . . and one pregnant cow upside down in his. (We had an open suite with a balcony giving onto the whole sweep of the bay.) Hell, we were even having quick kips after *breakfast*. That's how loss of altitude gets you, and drying out. We just had white wine with our shellfish at night . . . not just six at a time, but *buckets* of oysters, and you know what? – they are not fattening. (Kev had his own special food lined up – endless fresh fruit as far as I could see – bananas.) Can you believe it? We also played cards! (Rummy.)

One of the Indian lads came off the rocks and offered me a can of wriggling garbage. I suppose he thought I was a great fisherman. After Achmed the Spice-seller who puts tang on your tongue, let me tell you, I'm not indifferent to bait pickers whose wares are not quite so wholesome. Besides, this one – his name was Lonnie, and about fifteen, with *long* legs – was about the most beautiful youth I had ever seen. His father, he said, was a panelbeater up at the main road. (You know what panelbeating now also means in South Africa? – torturing a political detainee to death without exterior evidence.)

Anyway, Lonnie sort of seduced us all onto the rocks where his equally ravishing friends had caught a shark. That thing was so tough to bring in, even for the sand variety. I thought they'd break their only rod. They took turns at it, letting it play out and hauling it right in. Then they'd take it for a walk to tire it.

We all became *engrossed* in this whole procedure. We had to see it landed. They towed it right from the hotel all the way practically to the sugar refinery . . . and we were following, *staring* at this hulk break out during a lapse of swell, then steam off again towards the horizon! They were nice kids those, with nothing better to do all day, and they didn't mind us tagging along. Kevin and Jannie were forever in rock pools up to their knees, and I actually found some sinkers and nylon that had got snagged off and Lonnie tried to unpick it. By midday they still hadn't caught the shark and we traipsed off to lunch. They didn't land it until the evening, bloody miles away . . . it *was* a sandshark.

Lonnie popped up occasionally – like us, he and his friends had nothing to do, but we all pretended the horseplay was directed at some urgent purpose. We invited them to our balcony one day when it was hotter, and got around to introducing ourselves, sitting with our salty, sandy feet in a clump, and drank *Coca-Cola*. They were really nice kids, concerned with their schooling and normal things.

Why when it was all so completely relaxing and pleasant I should have such bad dreams I don't know. I suppose it takes a long, long time for all the buried horrors to surface. When you let them, they do. I had recurring nightmares about going into the pit-latrine after that baby. I could smell it in the room. Why? Why, when I had done my best? Anyway, I'd wake up convinced the entire room was flooded with shit and it *was burning* my skin. Why *then*?

The last thing I want to do is burden you with my heebie-jeebies (anyway, they're over now). But it is curious, isn't it? I hate it when people go off into recounting their dreams and you can see *right through them* . . . generally inadequately described, and all about absolute give-aways, like fame, fear, ambition, shame, which otherwise cannot be admitted into civilised conversation. But I'd like to think . . .

I flatter myself . . . my worst one wasn't like that. It was Belinda, of all people, and she was being raped that night by those three . . . I took the image of our (friendly) goalkeeper and those two the TV team made use of, and just turned them into her assailants. How could it be *them*? She wouldn't go round serving tea as if nothing had happened if her three ravishers were lounging about, having their pictures taken.

Jeepers, what a muddle. They were absolutely smashing her to ribbons and doing it – don't know where on the farm, except it was lit by flares, don't even know how. But the *damage* they were pounding into her. *She* wasn't screaming (I think she was beyond it . . .), *I* was screaming and it wouldn't come out of me. Then I woke up, but into another layer of dream, which any moment was going to be a wet one.

If you know how long it is since I've had one of those you'll realise I was totally shattered.

That wasn't such a good night, cause Jannie, who had eaten far less oysters than I, had taken in a poisoned one. Poor guy, up to the loo with me running after him to see if he was all right, he running to pass out in bed and me trying not to wake Kev. Back and forth. Oh God, so imperative on the body. Kev just smiling on his back, serenely above it all, Jannie sweating and oysters evacuating hardly digested. Holidays are a bit more than one can take, sometimes! But Jannie was quite all right next day. Better than a hydro!

Dreams are the sort of mental equivalent, I presume. And sometimes the mindblast connects with the bodily urge, or the body prompts the mind to race. All right, I'll stop now! I'll leave you with that profound thought.

But wait . . . oh yes, don't let me forget. We picked up this wonderful story (true) in the *Natal Mercury*. (Jannie wouldn't let me read the headlines, or even the stocks and shares.) Well, it just *made* the whole trip! There was this old geyser accused of getting his girlfriend in pod but in his defence he said he simply could not have – it must have been somebody else – because he was impotent, totally!

She claimed that was *not* her experience of him, and she had certainly not slept with anyone other than him. Exhibit A was the state she was in.

(Can you imagine all this coming out before the Natal Bench!)

So she was advanced and he was impotent, and *he* certainly couldn't produce any alternative cock and balls as Counter-Exhibit B. I imagine the prosecution and defence had more refined ways of summarising the dilemma.

She testified that his own were functional enough to beget on her. He swore they were a useless lot of old leftovers.

So why don't you try the postage stamp test? says the prosecutor to the magistrate.

The postage stamp test? says his learned eminence. (Querulation round the court.)

It is a well-known fact, says the prosecutor, that all who have hair on their chest, deeper voices and a glint in their eye, on account of their balls having dropped and their cock nestling down neatly over them, can never be content with this state of preparedness for very long.

Alas, interjects the lawyer for the defence, preparedness passed into dormancy years ago in the case of his client, and dormancy into inertia – the point being, you stupid prick, his client has a *fucking useless cock*.

(Can you believe it? In the newspapers! In Natal!!!)

Yes, yes, yes, says the magistrate, but – the question that is on everyone's lips – What has this to do with *postage stamps*?

The prosecutor then explains: it is also a well-known fact that the average male of the species has three to six major erections a night during his sleep, not counting innumerable twitches and feints as he goes after the nymphs of his fluent desire . . . Everybody knows that, even the accused knows that, and just look with what inconvenient and long-lasting results!

Are you trying to suggest he rose up in his sleep, without provocation and without knowing it? from the defence.

(Hell, we had fun coming back in the car playing the parts. Kev of course was the lady who sued, Jannie the legal team and me the magistrate, lowering over the wheel, asking if they should be mail stamps or revenue stamps.)

So what they did, I swear, was put this old toothless geriatric into bed at night with a whole page of stamps stuck around and over his groin.

The first morning all went well for the accused. On waking, he'd not even split a perforation. In fact, the stamps were in mint condition.

The second night the same: he sat up in bed and wiped his eyes. The stamps were not only intact; they were a bit creased, but perfectly reusable.

You see, you see, the defence lawyer exhibits them in triumph. Not even a pinhole pierced.

But obviously she had a good prosecutor on her side, for, not discouraged, they insist upon a third application of stamps.

Next morning the defence lawyer looks really downcast.

Magistrate instructs him to open his briefcase and the entire population leans forward.

Know what? – that old geyser, he'd not only bust through the sheet – he'd *licked them as well*.

I leave you with that thought . . .

That was our family joke for days afterwards. You know how these silly vogues persist: 'Seen any good postage stamps lately?' 'Ooh, Cape of Good Hope triangular blue! – that's a real collector's item.' Till you've squeezed the last drop of wit out of it.

Then you just forget it.

Pity you can't come back from a holiday and troll about the streets for a bit, picking up anything that catches your attention. Not when you've got a wife who's about to pop, a nursery that you're in partnership with, and the corporation you happen to be financial director of has just done the merger you probably read of (Rand High and Solid Gold also became ours). Bennington was not coping, and I've never been plunged into work more express. There are twenty-eight people in our accountancy department, but do you imagine one of them thought of leaving it to anyone but me to sort out? Oh no, boy . . . it was sixteen hour days and weekends, too. This had to stop.

It did, when the doorbell went.

I opened it. 'I thought you were in Cape Town.'

'I was, but my mom gave me money to come back.'

'Look, I can't see you now . . . really, I can't. I'm not making it up.'

'What's with the box of J and B?' It was still on the kitchen table. 'Aren' you gonna even open it?'

'No, I've gone dry,' I said, trying to close the door on him.

'I'll open it,' he said, with his boot there. 'I gotta knife.'

He had – one of those shiny blades muggers hold at your heart.

'Henno, if you threaten me!' I gasped.

'What'll you do? What?' he said. He raised the knife above his shoulder as if he would strike me. '*What'll* you do??' he said.

'I'll call the –' But I didn't have time to complete the thought.

Connery shot him from down the corridor. Wouldn't you just know it.

I didn't tell you the worst dream I had on holiday. I had to do this egg-and-teaspoon race. It was all uphill. The egg bobbling in the teaspoon was getting bigger and bigger.

Damn! Now it's hailing. Will have to get up to shut the windows. Hope it doesn't get the glasshouses, like last time.

I poked my head out of the door of the flat. They'll really go for this, the media. The baby due any minute and the father sprawled out backwards in the biggest mess of maidenhairs and Beaucarnea recurvatas.

I closed the door and went back to work. Well, there were enough people screaming out there, and I had first the *knife* and then the *bang* to digest.

Now you can see it really coming down. Bouncing off the roof of the car. My nice duco! Anyone for ice-tennis?

Do you realise how much damage a hailstorm can do? If it wasn't for hailstorms we'd be making a million out of this place. People in glass houses shouldn't throw stones. But that's a bit unfair on *plants*, isn't it? Total damage: in five minutes, all but under seven thousand.

That isn't very good bookkeeping, is it?

Without that hailstorm we'd have made a clear three thousand this quarter. Rands.

A million, did I say – *dollars?* Who kidded Kev he was in for a million of anything.

A million cents was more like it, with Exhibit A – the tool of the happy father – bleeding to death in the corridor outside. Not U.S. cents, either; South African.

Connery sprang through my door, d. j. flying, handgun smoking.

'What, are you going to *shoot me, too?*' I screamed.

'Ah, awfully sorry . . .' he veered to a halt. 'Are you *all right?*'

'And who do you think *you* are, my dear – James bloody Bond? Wretched Pom!'

'Ah . . . um . . . ee . . . er . . .'

Why can they never bloody talk when there's something to say?

'Put that *away*, Connery!'

'But it's licensed!'

'Tell that to the judge!'

'But I've just – saved your life.'

'Go and play in your own flat, Connery . . . or at the bloody

Oppenheimers if you insist.'

'But he – ah he – um he –'

'Pulled a knife on me?'

'Yes. I waited until he – was ready to plunge.' There's the legal mind for you. 'Then – I let him have it.'

The knife had bounced in. I picked it up, folded it back. 'A knife? Call that a *knife*? That's what South Africans use to pick their teeth.' I put it in my pocket. 'If you don't go back to your little wife this instant,' I said, '*this instant*, I shall have you run in for the trigger-happy *menace to society* people like you, who come here and profit from apartheid, are. Now, git.'

'But –'

'Git – git – git.'

Know the one about an Englishman, an Irishman and a Jew? – in a plane that's crashing with only two parachutes. The Jew goes first and the Englishman says, I couldn't my boy, after you.

But how can you make such a sacrifice, sir?

I didn't, you stupid git. That was your bedroll I gave him.

I'll do that again, not to be racist. An Englishman, a South African and a Swiss were going down in a plane. Two parachutes. The Englishman goes first.

'You know what, darling?' says the South African. 'Just before we go down together, there's one thing I'd like you to give me.'

'What?' says the Swiss, eyes atwinkle. (That's you.)

'A lovely little Swiss roll!'

(The Englishman took both, of course! *Boom*!)

'All right, all right, all right . . .'

Back to their kennels with the rich wailing bitches. Couldn't they even give the guy a hand out of there?

Connery was not a very good shot. He'd aimed for Henno's temple, but got him in the balls. Yes, those delectable furry famous nuts, splashed to smithereens. Next time Connery aims at you . . . everybody, *jump*!

Henno wasn't dead, but he would have preferred to be. Squirming round in the roots, tearing at his pants, 'Where my eggs, where my eggs?'

Better than Angola. There they plug your breakfast in your mouth.

Should have give him R70 and a figleaf, and told him to go back to Cape Town. Try his luck there with a knife on some other little old lady.

I encouraged the last members of the block to climb in the lift and go away.

'There, they've all seen you now, so you'll never get inside *this* block again.'

'Jus' help me up, man . . . I'm in agony, jus' –' His eyes rolled back in his head.

I gave him the nearest hand. 'You see, you can stand,' I said.

'Ja, you put me on my feet.' He aahed in agony.

'Some hope.'

'Jus' let me sit down in your flat for a momen',' he said.

'Not until you've replanted every pot, you hear. Then you can come and knock nicely for your knife.'

I closed the door and went back to work.

I phoned Richie and asked if he could come and soothe a bit of scorched testicle, but he had a patient whose bag had burst.

'Tell her to get a stronger bag,' I said.

'Tasteless bitch,' he said. 'She's in *labour* now.'

'Sorry,' I said, 'I didn't know it was called *that*.' I thought he meant her shopping bag.

'Well, I've got a pretty valuable pair of balls here. They're bleeding right into his boots.'

'Put a tourniquet round them!'

'Oh, Richie! These are the vessels that produced the first baby to be born of man in the history of the world.'

'Phone Alfie, he's been wanting a blood sample from that guy for six months.'

'Do I just collect it in a saucepan?'

'Look, I must dash. Put some TCP on it and tell him to pray like hell.'

'Oh Henno,' I opened the door. 'You've watered the plants, how lovely. And rearranged them. And got yourself all in a mess in the process. My, what a surprise. Don't you want to come in and change?'

He lumbered in and I slammed the door.

'It was only a joke,' he said.

'Well, I've got a joke for you. No drinkies tonight cause I'm busy. I mean what I say.'

'Can I jus' use the bathroom?'

'As long as you don' – I mean don't – ask me to help. Then back on your bicycle and leave me your address. If all goes well in three weeks time I shall give you a call. There'll be a little money in it. Don't ask me how, don't ask me why, but that's a promise. Good overseas money.'

'I can',' said Henno.

'What?'

'Go on my bike.'

'Not like that you can't,' I said. I had that knife of his in my hand and drew out the blade. 'Shall I cut the rest of them off? Is that what you meant to do with me, you lousy scum of shit!'

'I sold my bike, I had to.'

'Why?'

'Cause my mom said I mus' pay her back.'

'Well, at least it isn't cluttering up my garage.'

'*Jesus, you people*,' says Henno. 'You got hearts like a lump of concrete.'

'What's your mother's? The Hendrik Verwoerd Damwall?'

'Listen,' he says quietly, and very impressively. The words didn't count, but the actions did. 'If you want to stab somebody, you don' stab them like that.' He took the knife from my fingers. Showed me how to hold it fast in the palm of the hand. 'And you don' wave it around like it's a lady's fan. You hold it by your side.' He took it to his hip. 'Then you take the ou from behind . . .' He circled me. 'By the chest, so his arms are out of action.'

'Henno,' I said.

His arm enclosed me, clasping my chest. 'Then you use the front of your head to push his head down. Jus' as his back's coming up, you give him a feel of this. Feel it?'

'Yes,' I gasped. 'Yes, stop, stop.'

'Then you know what you do?'

'No! no! no!'

'You –' He clutched me under him. '– push –'

'Henno, Henno!'

'– in the corkscrew . . . nice and straight . . . and pull out the cork. *Pop*.'

You thought I was dead, didn't you? Bloody Swiss army knives.

Well, it was true. That was about all he had left, and the singed clothes he stood up in.

But still I had work to do. Didn't anyone understand that? Only acts of God could stop me, and Henno was not yet one of those.

I pushed him into the bathroom and shut the door on him.

I sat on my sofa, which I was so pleased he didn't mess,

and said to the beautiful kid by my side: Lonnie, let me stroke your glossy black hair. Lonnie, Lonnie, what if the shark never comes in? Will only a bigger one take it?

Lonnie, Lonnie, who could make a lousy world more beautiful than you?

'Gino, Gino, hello. Remember me . . .'

'Ah yessa – you enjoyed Number 20.'

'Oh, yes . . . can you deliver all the way in town?' I gave the address.

'Certainly, whatta you like?'

'Two margheritas, with –'

'I know, ham extra.'

'Lots of ham, right in the middle.'

'I can promise you, you won'ta be disappointed.'

Back to work.

Doorbell rings. David Bennington.

'Ah, Bennington, come in old chap. As a matter of fact I've got just the goods for you. Come in, come in.'

'Didn't want to rush you, but you're such a fast worker,' he said. He went to the desk where I usually put the pile.

'No, dear boy,' I said. 'In the bathroom. I have a little surprise for you.'

'In the bathroom?'

'Yes, you never did pay back that twenty rand.'

'Would you like it now?' he said.

'No no no,' I said, 'don't be so scrupulous.'

He shrugged his shoulders and went to the bathroom door. He opened it slowly. 'Good God,' he recoiled. 'Oh my good God in heaven!'

'Yes. Picked up any good rapists lately? Actually he's milder than Mary's lamb.'

David reeled backwards. Exposed! Imagine if I'd had his whole family seated there. And the Board of Directors, right on the couch.

'I think I'm going to be sick.' He literally reeled.

'Pay for your sins,' I said, 'there's a good boy.'

'Look, I know you said he was dangerous, and tried to save me!'

'Keep talking.'

'But I do have my own ways of dealing with them. I told you. I even have police protection . . . Isn't this *going a bit far*?' He spluttered and was turning hysterical.

'David, I'd do anything for you. You know that.'

'I know, I know, you bloody meddling old fart!'

'David!'

'I'm sorry, I'm sorry,' he moaned. '*so* sorry. Bloody fine gymnast, too.'

'What, what?'

'Well, just because of that . . .' he totally broke down, 'you *don't have to kill him in your bath, do you?*'

Old fart. That about fits the bill, doesn't it? Well, how was I to know he'd faint at the sight of a pool of his own blood?

Some physical force had taken a corkscrew on him, and a gallon of burgundy had gushed forth.

An Englishman, an Afrikaner and an African (black) were flying in this place, heading for South Africa. You go first, says the Afrikaner, cause you got here first. And the black man jumps.

After you, says the Englishman, cause you got here second. And the Afrikaner jumps.

Look here chaps, shouts the Englishman after them, don't you know you're meant to use parachutes?

Moral: God helps those who help themselves.

I tapped him. 'Now come on, David.'

He took his head out of his hands and looked at me cross-eyed.

'Know what Saint George gets after slaying the dragon, and saving the maiden in distress?'

'I have no idea,' he shook.

'A bloody big kiss,' I said.

He stared at me aghast: '*Oh no* . . .'

He who thought he was so cool. His lips were flapping like jelly. I pursed them together between my fingers. 'Know what that looks like?' I said. 'Looks like a pig's arse, Rosebud. Old fart, indeed.'

'But my family, my – job, my life,' he stammered. 'They'll implicate me sure as hell.'

'Not if you patch him up good as new,' I said.

He swallowed hard. 'How'm I meant to do that?'

I explained as to a child. 'Take his pants off. Take his jacket off. Keep his head out of the water until he comes round. And don't use bubblebath; use TCP. It's only a crack in his crankshaft. It'll be like bathing one of your own kids. I have work to do.'

Some of which I did.

David and Henno emerged, the latter like the walking wounded, his arm grasping over David's shoulder.

'What's that round your waist?' I said.

'Towel,' said Henno, 'inside my pants.'

'What did he do? Lift your legs and slide the straight end underneath?'

'Very funny,' said David.

'Say thank you,' I said to Henno.

'Thank you, David,' he said.

'Not him, me. For the towel,' I said.

'Thanks,' said Henno.

'Shall we just –'

'Hey, what's it called when a guy's underpants hang out at the back instead of the front?'

'Not now, please,' David groaned.

'What's it called?' said Henno, who always liked a joke.

'Ploughman's lunch!'

'Shall we just –'

'Put him back where your car last broke down? No, here's ten rand for you to stop at any old roadhouse.'

'What's a ploughman's lunch?'

'Buy a pair of hotdogs to teeth on.'

'It's a totally ersatz light pub snack.'

'There's only *one* person who can handle this, my babes.'

'I'd rather have a hoddog.'

'No don't either of you sit down because you're off off off to the Magaliesberg. Kevin's the only registered nurse I know. It'll give her something to do – plastic surgery on your peeling chestnuts, my bra.'

'You mean out at your nursery?'

'Just the place for kiddies and you know what, Dave my little junior – if I may say – not quite a fart, just a bum-creeper. The petrol costs exactly twenty rand there and back. That is if you don't break down. Then it costs your reputation, your family and your life.'

'What do I tell Jannie?'

'To lock him in the cool-cupboard till we need him for photos. And by tomorrow morning, Bennington old boy, I'll have found out exactly where you went wrong in these books.'

Henno thought of one more thing. 'What if that maniac's running loose with his gun again? Hey what then?'

I drew myself up. 'Then kick him to death with your stupid boots!' I said.

'Oh, all right,' said Henno.

'Come on, let's go,' said David.

Lonnie, Lonnie, why do you trust people in the world? Why aren't you with me now?

Look at this merger stuff. Virtually everything's totally wrong. Can't any of them follow the simplest procedure? Need daddies to pamper them through every bit of the way. Here, take my hand...

Doorbell.

Now this one I *really* had forgotten.

Two fine-looking boys (well, one spotty and the other with three exquisite bits of moustache) with pizza-baking caps on. You could see: they said GINO'S in big red letters.

'Yes, can I help you?' I said.

They nudged one another and gave goofy smiles. The lovely one held out an invoice with this precise address.

'Yes,' I said. 'But you haven't brought any pizzas.'

Nudge, nudge. Conversation behind hands.

'Yes?' I said.

The spotty one blurted out. 'He didn't say p-pizzas are i-i-included.' Heavens, a stutter, too.

'Well, better come in,' I beamed, 'it's much warmer inside.'

They entered.

'What's your name?' I said. 'Haven't I seen you somewhere before?'

'JoJo. Phew it's h-hot in here.'

'Ah yes. And what's *your* name?'

But JoJo is the talker. 'Nice place you've – you've got here.'

I look at the other one. I am so traumatised I don't hear what he says.

'I'm new,' said JoJo. 'He's teaching me...'

'I know how it is,' I replied. 'I'm old, incredibly old.'

Let's see, where am I? It's quite lekker the way you can run this thing backwards and forwards. When Jannie calls for dinner, I go. This place is getting so *orderly* and I feel so *fit* Jannie says I'm being quite creative with this machine. Well, in the beginning was the Word, and the Word was Processed...

But the point is not how I feel *now*, but how I felt *then*... after the night of the short Swiss knife... (The night of the long carving knives is still to come, of course.)

I didn't have to say much more than: 'Well, kiddoes, what you been up to? Humping in Hillbrow, bonking in Berea? Always make sure you wear your cute little caps, hey?'

It was Songs of Innocence and Songs of Experience all the way. The only thing was, as I looked then, I had to pay.

Gino proved a most congenial supplier. I worked my way through the range. Richie did say my exercise should be mild and systematic. Until I found one I specially liked, who became my regular. He has a number and a tradename, of course – but do you know what *I* called him? Apart from his beginning moustache, he had wonderful mournful eyes. Lonnie.

This was a most habit-forming, wholesome procedure. Thursday nights, 8.00 p. m. It never does to ask Gino's hustlers too much about their private lives or who else they might be seeing. Apart from the obvious precautions they must take, they're so inarticulate they couldn't really tell you if they tried. Besides, who they were soon becomes a blur to them, and who they see indistinguishable one from another.

But Lonnie was a cut above them all. He combined class with eroticism. I won't go into that now – this is Kev's story, after all. Just remember this: when at last you find the perfect call-boy, the only thing you never do with him is fall in love.

There's one more detail: now that I'm out of town, the only thing I miss is Lonnie.

What is it with older men and younger? Perhaps it's our way of recapturing our youths, though there's not much of mine I'd want to win back. I wouldn't mind *looking* again like some of them do . . . With their bodies and my brains! Alfie should be working on whole body-transplants, if you ask me.

Then I moved into thinking it was the way the part of being gay that's kept in the cupboard until last finally comes out: parenthood! Those boys turn into your own sons, with you their almighty missing father. Without *that* moffies are doomed to extinction.

It's my observation that the one thing every male gay I know wants most, and can never have, is a child. That is why the Kev thing loomed so enormous in our lives (I mean, his, Jannie's and mine). But it would become the *main event* in the lives of all the rest of us all too soon.

Like everyone else, you know the outline from here from the press, etc. But what you can have no idea of is – *what it meant to us*. Circumstantially, and in such a roundabout way (sorry!), that is what I'm about to explain.

It wasn't all happy landings, quite.

Nor did anything ever go according to any plan.

It was all meant to be a hush-hush operation, remember. No news meant Kev could go unmolested, meant Alfie and his team had no pressure on them; and the baby would not have to smile or burp until *it* was ready. For what other purpose were Stefanus van der Merwe and his men (at vast expense, let me tell you) conducting their security operation? What all of us involved thought, but never uttered, was if the first baby a certain person (male) gave birth to died, there need be nothing further said. I speak under correction, but it was that way with the first successfully transferred heart; there had been many we've not heard of before. Baboon males had been carrying implanted babies for years; no flowers for *their* tombs.

I phoned our two so-called press liaison officers – Danny and Martie. I was livid, fuming. 'You sure, Danny? A news embargo until *after* successful delivery?'

'Darling, I'm *sure*. That's what Kev signed . . . and we only get ten percent.'

'But it's a *whole week* still to go to *confinement*.'

Martie grabbed the receiver. 'That, I can assure you, is what *they* signed, too. Clause 17 (c) – I have it in black and white – Beta Agency of Los Angeles – on the dotted line!'

'Then why – you two pink and blue *poofters* – *why? why?*'

'What, why? *Don't you* get worked up now.'

'Unutterable idiots!'

'You take the line, he's always been gross and he's becoming offensive.'

'Jannie was right about you two – *incompetents!*'

'What, hello . . . Danny says you shouldn't shout on the phone. It's not polite.'

'Martie, don't you think your *timing's* out?'

'If the *timing* is a little bit *out*, my darling . . . I'm quite sure that for what Beta Agency's paying that's fully how they intend it to be. Even you should know, though you hardly have much up-front experience of the world of public relations – we did run a very profitable company, remember – *is* – that a story is only a good one if it has a *beginning*, a *middle* and an *end*!'

'That's breach of contract!'

'We are now well into the exposition. For your information the public memory can't stretch more than three weeks, so *next* week we will have the *development* –'

'– when the only type of breech is to do with birth!'

'Exactly. Goodbye.' He put the phone down.

Wouldn't you have been seething if you, in my place (Johannesburg), had just learned that people in your place (Zurich) knew more of what was going on in a place that *wasn't* theirs (Johannesburg) than the people of that place knew? It had just come in on the Reuters, datelined: GENEVA. SOUTH AFRICAN MAN PREGNANT, CLAIMS LATEST TECHNIQUE. REPORTS FROM JOHANNESBURG SAY . . .

That meant it would be on the news here that night. It wasn't going to be a gold strike. The scramble for Africa would begin again.

I had to get through to Jannie. I worked out the briefest possible message. Ringing, ringing. To Jannie I was going to say: 'The bitch that's about to lay the golden egg . . . pick her up in your arms and hide her.'

And Jannie was going to reply: 'But they'll never track her here, don't be alarmist.'

'Tonight it'll be out. She's not allowed to . . . *bark* except at people from *Beta* Kennels, does she understand that? Take her for a *walk*. Go ahead, I'm coming *now*!'

'She won't come to *heel* that easily, you realise?'

'Yes she will. She's a *dog* that knows what's *good* for her.'

'You mean they want to . . . *milk* her before she's *whelped*?' Jannie clueing in.

I couldn't get through; I couldn't even get the exchange.

Sometimes Mooinooi exchange has – you know what? – gone to the hairdressers for a quick set. They call this the jet age. Well, you know what they call it in Mooinooi? – the jet-set. (Cross my heart and swear to die – only ten minutes, R9,99 plus GST.)

Wait! Obviously that bubble of panic was beginning to burst in all of us. I do not take to stressful conditions. What was I imagining, what was eating me? Kev wasn't out at the farm at all. He was having his last check-up at the hospital. Why, even now he was *probably waiting for me* at the fountain . . .

Did I leap from my desk in that tower block? Did I fling my paper in my briefcase? Did I shoot out of my office door and into the lift? Did I?

No no no, why should I do things like that?

From the desk I rose. Neatly I stacked my papers and filed them in my case, patted it. Out of the office door I strolled. 'Going home, just a tad early,' said I.

But what's this (*what's this?*) I see? One old secretary fighting a peculiar battle. Her knitted jersey was turned into an octopus. Now it was engorging her. 'Oh, oh, oh,' she writhed.

'But my dear,' I said in some alarm.

She convulsed. 'I haven't listened to any more of your calls,

I swear.'

'I know that, dear woman. In any case it doesn't matter. Our relationship's confidential, isn't it?'

'But I couldn't resist, I couldn't resist,' she squirmed.

'You know my secrets, but that doesn't mean I have to know yours. I insist you calm down. Look at me, calm as can be.'

'How can you be? That's totally unnatural,' she wailed.

'Please, if you don't mind!'

'But *haven't you seen?*' she exploded.

'Nothing more than you're going to have to get a new jersey.' The thing was laddered.

She shoved the front page of the *Star* at me. Did I blench? Did I raise my fist to my forehead and beat my brains? (The local headline was: KEV THE COURAGEOUS – SISTER-SUBSTITUTE IN CITY.)

Calmly I looked at it and said: 'Good heavens, whatever will they think of next?'

'Yes.'

'Some gay prank, I suppose.'

'No, because *I know*! I *put it together*! I said to myself with me two and two makes far more than four!' Had she gone crazy?

'That's not very hopeful for an accountant's secretary. Please sit, and do stop kicking the wall. Two and two makes exactly four.'

'But I – but I –'

'Please stop – *butting your head* against the coffee machine.'

'The *what?* the *what?*'

I pulled her back from the valuable Africana pictures, gently and patiently. Of course I should have just laid her out with my briefcase.

She turned on me. '*Why do you never tell me a thing?*' Her chignon coming up like a fist on a spring.

'Tell you anything? How can I, if you behave like this, really?'

'I mean the *personal touch* – for years I've said Yes sir, No sir, Three bags full sir!'

'You're not the only one who has a job here, my dear.'

'You could have told *me* before the bloody newspaper! Am I worth less to you than the Johannesburg *Star*? I who –'

I had to cut this short (I mean, Kev was going to be unmasked!). 'Tell you what exactly?' I said coolly.

'That your *wife* had *died*,' she burst. 'Heartless brute! To think you had to go through so much agony, without letting me carry the burden of even a *whisper*!'

145

'Look that's terribly sweet of you, but –'

'I *have* figured it out. That night you told me to put all those calls through. Let me tell you, I'm nobody's fool! Plants from the nursery, my foot! You just didn't want me to *suffer along* with you . . . poor poor *poor* man. To think of it. KEV THE COURAGEOUS and the gentle-voiced one *I* tracked down for you are *one and the same.*'

Hoarse and bleary-eyed, she stumbled to her drawer, ripped out compacts and eyeshadow and enough hairclips to rebuild the scaffolding.

'There,' she slammed down the present. 'I am *the first.* I know I won't be the last, but one day . . . when you look back on this . . . and cast your wonderful mind over the debits and credits of your wonderful life, I now know you'll be able to say, By God, she may have been the last to know, but she certainly was the first to *give!*'

With the end of my finger I pressed the present on the *Star.* Through the wrapping I could feel a ring. The ring held a stand-up column. When I let go it jumped back into position.

'For your baby,' she said with incredible relief. 'May it be the finest in the world. Looks as if it's going to be the most famous. Please, may I see it . . . hold it, just once? – then in my old age I can say –'

'You've made a mistake,' I said.

'Hey?' she said.

I sat opposite her, folded my hands and waited until I had her complete attention.

'You *have* made a mistake. I've never had a wife. In fact, I've never even wanted one. I've never been to bed with a woman and I don't intend to.'

'Listen to him, how he lies . . . the biggest ladykiller in the Vaal Triangle!' She threw her head back.

'No,' I said, 'as a matter of fact I – only screw boys.'

'Boys?' she said. 'You mean, um, you screw them up if they come near your *women*?'

'No again,' I said. 'I only screw boys period.'

'But then, but then,' she looked weepy, '*who* are all the quantities of flowers for, special delivery?'

'That is none of your business; it's my partner's and mine.'

'And the flat you keep for illicit amours?'

'That, my dear, I admit is a bit hard to explain. Do you know what rent-boys are?'

'These days . . . when everything's Arthur and Martha and AD and BC. Aren't they – boys who sit the flat when you're away, and contribute to the *rent*?'

'No, dear . . .' I said, my eyes going out of focus with relief.

(It was getting time for Kev.) Isn't it incredible? – you're right in the middle of the scene you've been dreading all your life and she cannot even hear what you're telling her. People want to know what they want to know.

'Then it's –'

'No no. Are you calm now?'

'Yes . . .'

'Good . . .'

'It's only that I'm *so* –'

'Don't start again, please.'

'– so happy for you, at last.' She seemed to expire, drawing the spiderweb of her jersey close.

I waited until she'd suppressed her chignon. When she was concentrating on my hands, I toyed with the dummy. Eventually I took it up. '*In a sense* you are right,' I said. 'Woman's intuition and all that.'

She smiled wanly.

'Strictly between us now and not to leave these four walls?'

'But of course, of course, *I* wouldn't breathe one word.'

'In your old age – but only to yourself – you'll be able to say – not to a bunch of other clucking hens – *I* worked for that child's *god*father. Understand?'

'*Perfectly* clearly.'

'It's no blood relationship.'

'I understand.'

'But for the time being I don't want it known anywhere in this building. During working hours I am no more connected to Kev the Courageous than anyone else. Understand? Godfather's all, and it's a solemn secret.'

'My lips are perfectly sealed.'

'So will the baby's be, with this.'

She gave me a winsome smile and I pocketed the gift.

'Promise?'

'Promise. I just wanted to be the *first*.'

'I know that. So, many many thanks.' I put my finger to her lips.

She assumed the posture of contented conspiracy.

That was the nearest she'd ever come to her passion in life: motherhood.

On a Friday night when you're trying to make an early break, who do you bump into in the lift? When your tie's neither up nor off? When he is the last person you wish to see? When you have to be across town in ten minutes? And you've just been through the most cruel scene of your life?

Who? Out of the one thousand three hundred employees

cooped in a skyscraper that keeps them off the streets and infinite African horizons beyond, which?

The managing director, that's who.

I press the button he has already pressed for the parking garage.

He keeps up with the very latest, our m. d. He has a copy of this afternoon's *Star* (late edition) folded under his arm.

That lift could not be hurling down fast enough.

Then it stops. He presses the same button again with the end of his umbrella.

'Making an early get-away?' he says drily. His speciality is drought.

'Ye-es, sir,' I smile. My speciality is frankness.

'Not in these lifts, you're not.' Dryness with some wit.

I grin and nod, wondering how many one-liners I can take. We wait.

'That Bennington lad. Seems to be up and coming.'

'Yes sir,' I say. 'Made a bit of a hash of the merger papers, though.' Why did I feel like a senior boy betraying a junior to the headmaster?

The lights in the lift flickered; in that instant the power cut off and the emergency generator took over.

'Ah,' I said.

'Shouldn't we be computerising all of your department?' he said.

'Switchover's not quick enough,' I replied. 'That hiccup would have lost us our assets.'

'I see,' he said.

The lift would go now, but we were stalled.

'Hear you're about to become a proud father,' he said.

My first thought: there is no end to the extent to which a woman will go to betray you.

'Did you get that from your secretary who got it from mine?' I said.

'It's in the *Star*,' he said.

'*What?!*' I said. I meant, 'Er – I beg your . . .'

'That you have offered to adopt the miracle babe.'

'Oh that,' I said. 'Seemed a pretty – charitable thing to do.'

The lift wasn't going down because the button needed to be pressed again. I gently touched it.

We sank.

'Always thought you'd wind up with a string of little blighters to care for.'

'Oh,' I said.

'Look at the way you hold your briefcase.'

It was true. My arms were crossed underneath and I was

148

cradling it.

We hit the bottom. As the doors opened he said: 'Another thing. Always adopt, then you can choose. Your own are never suitable.'

'Yes, sir,' I said.

He was gone.

Rush-hour was in full spate – or rather was at a standstill, then a crawl. I had ample opportunity to buy all editions of the *Star*, and any other papers for that matter. And to read them over the wheel. If you think the *Star* was bad, wait till you hear the headlines of the *Sowetan*: PANTY BOSS'S LATEST CONCEPTION. *Vaderland* of course had NOG 'N EERSTE VIR SUID-AFRIKA: KEV TUSSEN DIE PALE.

Wait for the *Weekly Mail*: that was going to be 'In a continent where seventeen million children are starving to death, and in the Frontline States 500,000 are homeless thanks to South Africa's destabilisation policy, one Kevin Vermaak it has been announced intends to repair the damage by having one of his own. The fact that his contribution to peace and prosperity will be a white child, whereas all the others are black . . . etc.' The trouble with press censorship during a state of emergency is that even non-political news *becomes* political.

But wait for our own *Exit* paper. That was going to be: KEV CATCHES BIKER AT LAST. SAYS HE THOUGHT IT WAS TOO GOOD TO BE TRUE!

So much for the Beta Agency. Not *one word* of it came from any of us! They had a dozen copy people on it twenty-four hours a day. So locked into it were they, and I must say so good at their job (hello there, little yellow critters in L. A.) . . . that by the time I got to Parktown East they even had a treatment done and had sold it to the movies!

All this was indeed a ploy on the part of the Beta people. Our dour thought-controllers would have to give them unlimited visas now to complete their medical documentary. If not, we might just all escape and have the first baby born to a man outside South Africa. All the credit would go to, say, Botswana. That'd put apartheid in its place, now *wouldn't* it?

But the picture round the Trescott Hospital at six o'clock that night was so typically South African. I cringe for my country. Would any other produce a scene so stupendously – and dangerously – malicious? Of course most of it went unrecorded; why go out in the streets and picture and write about what's actually happening when Beta's doing it all for you? Local journalists were there by the dozen, but who can get an elbow in when they've been scooped? All they could hope for were the odd scraps off someone else's table. All they could come up with the next morning, after besieging the precincts, was: TRESCOTT SAYS PLUCKY KEV MODEL PATIENT. And a picture of the facade with an X where his ward was supposed to be.

But what we were involved in was like the storming of the Bastille, none of which could be reported. Firstly, you couldn't get near the place for blocked traffic. Secondly, if you did, you couldn't get to the front door for people cheering and stamping and then trampling one another into the plants. Thirdly, if you did make the steps, there were policemen with riot gear three deep – and little old ladies pelting them, not with tomatoes as they should, but with presents for Kev! Fourthly, the entire hospital, patients included, was putting storm windows up for a siege. The switchboard was jammed, the lobby barricaded. How the hell were we going to get Kev *out* of there without anyone knowing, and without his picture being taken?

A helicopter came in low, and I thought – They're going to smuggle him away via the roof. But no, it was *riot control*, for God's sake, with bullhorns and the usual warnings to disperse. You couldn't disperse; you couldn't even raise your hand to pick your nose, let alone give a Freedom salute. Couldn't they see – menacing idiots – these were *well-wishers* – the curious, the goodwilled, the wanting to be famous at last? 'By proclamation so-and-so you are endangering the public safety with an illegal gathering and are hereby ordered forthwith to et cetera!'

The most terrifying thing, let me tell you. Having one of those jobs hover over you like a bloody ostrich . . . and then the tearsmoke shoot out of it like feather boas. You go down on your knees, clench your glasses and take your final breath. There are no controls on *those* guys. They do what they like.

All I thought was: *Next* time that bitch gets on heat, Jannie can just have her spayed.

What comes after tearsmoke? Gunshots. Now that's a fine time to pick somebody off, isn't it?

Have you heard of the black protest movement – Free Mandela and Amandla Azania? Render unto Caesar an unworkable country? And so on. Yes, you probably know *more* about it than we do.

Here's another movement I'll tell you about. It's been going for centuries. It's called Kill Another Kaffir for Christmas.

And for your information it was not Nelson Mandela

shooting that grapeshot.

Three old ladies blinded for life, one with a leg broken when her wheelchair was crushed, and five nannies who had gone to have a chat in the park on the critical list. Put *that* in your carved meerschaum and smoke it. I hope it chokes you to death.

Grovelling on the tar is not exactly my thing, with perfectly ordinary people turned into ninepins toppling over you. Clutching my handkerchief to my nose, and my wallet in case I got mugged, as well, I thought, Well, if I've got to go, at least I'll go with the most multiracial crowd you've ever seen. We were all in this together: anxious fathers, clumps of out-patients, visitors, delivery men, passers-by, hordes of souvenir-hunters, genuine commuters on their way home, the unemployed and lounge-abouts, riffraff and now the Red Cross, too.

You know how much damage was done to the cars caught in this alone? Not that it matters. Public disorder can erupt against anything. In South Africa today the insurance companies won't pay up, and you know what political riot is classified as? – an act of God.

I don't know anything about the behaviour of mobs in a panic. Only that everyone has a motive for going berserk – the blacks from long habituation to being killed off, and the whites from seeing their life's savings dwindle to nothing overnight – and you chivvy a few hundred of that lot along a confined street with baton charges and you've got trouble. People were screaming with anger, tearing anything they could get hold of to bits with their bare hands – trying to get out. I repeat: there was no *reason* for this.

Edging through was an ambulance, the bumper coming like a great silver bulldozer up to my forehead. The siren went *pee-paa, pee-paa* . . . I clutched onto its mudguard like a barnacle to a rock. It was leaving the hospital, not entering it. The ambulance wasn't stopping for any casualties, either. It took all of twenty minutes, hooting and with the deafening siren going, to rev forward. At last some traffic cops opened a path through the retreating crowd and signalled it through. Why it should be heading *away* from the scene where it was most needed occurred to nobody.

As it sped up, I held on. Another block . . . and then it petered out up the pavement and in a hedge, the driver overcome. I plopped off it and the rest of us staggered into the fresh evening air, breathing it in gulps. Tough Richie had driven, and the tearsmoke got the better even of him. Alfie was all right, slamming his surgeon's coat as though it were on fire, wisps of smoke coming out even of his hair. He dragged Richie free and I wrenched open the back doors. This was like an oven when you've left the roast in too long. Kev toppled out in a cascade of that heavy, rotten-smelling smoke.

'Shit, did you *see* that?' he gasped.

Alfie said: 'Got us in the driver's cabin; that stuff is bloody lethal.'

'Shit, that stuff is not funny,' said Richie.

We lay in piles, feeling ourselves release gas. The ambulance smoked like a pyre, but it was the opposite effect of burn-out; it slowly smoked itself back to normal.

'Oh shit,' said Richie, reeling, 'will I ever drive again?'

'Nice shot, Richie,' I said.

'As long as you're all right, Kev,' said Alfie.

'Yes . . .' said Kev.

We could hear the incident clearing up a block behind us. The helicopter had long headed back to where it came from, but the sirens of the cop-cars yowled like mating lions. You could hear the odd shriek of rage or of pain.

'You know what?' I said. 'I think Kev should go back and show himself. Then it will all quieten down, and they can all go away, content, even the cops. Hey, Kevvie?'

'Yes, you caused all this,' said Richie.

'Too much of a risk,' said Alfie.

'Aah,' said Kev, 'aren't I meant to be saving myself for Hollywood?'

'Just wave from a window like the Queen, and they'll all bugger off,' I said.

'That's what you think,' said Alfie. 'The foyer is already packed with presents, and telegrams are coming in in fucking containers. This is not going to be waved away.'

'No wave, no photos,' said Kev. 'Let's – go and have a quiet dinner. I'm starving . . .'

'That's the spirit,' said Alfie.

'Oh God, will I ever drive again?' said Richie.

'Well done, Richie,' said Alfie.

'Please let's just go back to the farm,' said Kev. 'Results of my tests show my blood supply needs a rest.'

'That's correct,' said Alfie.

'Think for a moment,' said Richie. 'Is there any way people can find out Kev's at Barefoot Nurseries?'

'Only Beta Agency knows,' I said.

'Have they got a lot to answer for,' said Alfie.

'Danny and Martie are behind this,' I said. 'They orchestrated it.'

Richie said, 'Did you see them watching this from their flat – with binoculars? Wicked witches.'

'Every story has to have some of those, too, I suppose,' I said.

'They won't tell because the farm is beyond their control,' said Kev. 'They want it all happening here.'

'God, will I ever drive again?' said Richie. 'You know what I feel like? – as if my lungs are a dragon's. Haa, look at that.'

'A heavy smoker's,' said Alfie. 'Well, you've got to drive. The hospital must need the ambulance.'

'What for?' I said. 'All they need is to carry them in on stretchers.'

'To take the black patients to Baragwanath, don't you know?' said Alfie.

'Nonsense,' I said. 'It's legal for anyone to check into any hospital.'

'I never saw whites check into Bara while I was there,' said Richie.

'And you think our paying patients want blacks dying all over them?' said Alfie. 'That teargas really got you, hey.'

'Let's go,' said Kev, 'please.'

They rolled the ambulance back, and I took Kev to the farm.

Of course the Beta people had to get visas after that – but only two of them for a fortnight. That girl was back and the cameraman with the luscious buns. They recruited out-of-work Americans stranded here as a supplementary team. We moved Kev into the main house next to our bedroom for safety, and they could all sit it out in the rondavel.

I got leave until the great accouchement. Kev and Henno, Jannie and I became quite an unlikely quartet, marooned in our quarters. Henno was all right – subdued; he just grabbed his balls every time he coughed – and did a lot of useful things, like fix the roof. In fact, he thrived on being of use and wanted.

I tried to be diplomatic with those Beta people and socialise a bit. It seemed odd to have them as guests and not at the dining room table. They were a law unto themselves – all they wanted was fried chicken and gallons of beer. Ou Sara in the catering department learned not even to bother to change the menu. I suppose to them waiting to report a revolution or a medical wonder was all the same.

Certainly none of them liked us being gay. They cringed at the sight of us, making no bones about it. Maybe I'm unfair to them and journalists are a race apart, anyway. But once, when I asked the woman in charge if she'd like to see a few of the sights – visit Richie's new clinic, for example – she said, 'Humph, is that a *gay* doctor? No thank you very much.' I don't know why that so cut me to the quick.

We set Henno onto her, to chat her up a bit, soften her. It was spring, after all – you remember the kind of spring we have that arrives with a whoosh, then's suddenly summer. The apricots were out, then the cherries and peaches. You know how intoxicating it can be on the farm. Did poor Henno get an earful? He said if that's what American women were like, he'd stick to walking just the dogs.

Obviously something was up. Toothy Timothy was conducting all sorts of business at the rondavel he wasn't letting on about. Imagine our total amazement one evening ... when we see them build a bonfire down there under the palms. We were just having a few drinks and snacks. Ou Sara and Belinda were off early. The journalists had placed no orders. This was the Wednesday night. I don't know – we were having the usual circular conversation.

When we see a sheep come trotting through the cannas – a bleating sheep. We don't keep any sheep on the farm. Jannie called the dogs off the poor beast and said we must go and look.

There was Timothy – dressed up as a witchdoctor or something, with his hair all fuzzed out and a greasy jockstrap, trying to lead the sheep where it didn't want to go. And Ou Sara, can you credit it, with her teats hanging down to here and a whole lot of ox-tails at her waist, pushing it from behind.

'What, are you now a sangoma, Sara?' I say.

'Ja baas,' she says with a twinkle.

Belinda's got some beads on and is beating a drum. Half the soccer team's now got bodypaint and I don't know what, chanting a war cry at the top of their voices.

'The cannas, be careful!' says Jannie. But that sheep was going nowhere without being carried.

'All right, have a nice time,' I said.

Waving to us and doing the most fantastic leaps and gyrations, which I'm quite sure they invented for the occasion, off went this peculiar procession. I mean, our dear goalkeeper – you know what *he* was wearing? – a piece of artificial fur tucked over his jockeys, a couple of old tins round his ankles – and a pair of handlebars on his head!

I suppose they had to have their authentic African experience – return to their roots and all – even if it involved the live sacrifice of one of Kierieklapper's poor stolen sheep. Afterwards everyone looked very spiritually fulfilled. You can't beat a spot of voodoo on a mild spring night for deeply fulfilling spirituality. I suppose the crude outbreak of sexual fertility that had got hold of Henno in that rondavel had taken them all in a different way. It deserved to be burnt down!

On the Thursday I had my appointment with Lonnie in town. I didn't see how I could get away . . . Kev was reading to Henno on the patio (the journalists had our TV and all), Jannie was passing me piles of accounts and the drinks were going. Everything in moderation.

'I know what,' I said. 'I think I'd better go into town and bring back all those telegrams at the hospital.'

'Fine, I'll come too,' said Jannie.

'There won't be room,' I said. 'Alfie said there were about four cubic *metres* of them. You stay and look after Kev.'

'I'm fine,' said Kev. 'Henno looks after me perfectly well.'

'Ja,' said Henno. 'Nothing's going to happen tonight.'

'But I *never* get out of here,' said Jannie. 'Not since we went to the sea.'

'On Saturday you'll have a trip to hospital when Alfie comes to fetch him,' I said.

All three glanced at me as if to say since when do you run a floosie on the side.

Henno said: 'I'll come, just to keep you company, hey.'

'All right, I won't go then,' I said, and we returned to our activities.

Then I took my glasses off. 'No, but wouldn't Kev rather read telegrams than Barbara Cartland?'

'You'll only lead a lot of scooper-sleuthers back,' said Jannie.

'They're a lot brighter than you,' said Kev. 'We don't want our serenity disturbed.'

By this time Lonnie's dark hair was running through my hands like black diamonds.

'I'm going,' I said. 'I'll be quick and discreet.'

At the top of the pass I thought twice. Gazing at that wonderful, paling landscape down the sides of the mountains (wasn't *that* the Africa they wanted to capture . . .) I thought of what this would do to Jannie. Why should I be hurting him? I decided to turn back.

At the beginning of Johannesburg, when you see the city spread out like a galaxy to rival the stars, I thought for the third time. Really all that counted for the moment was Kev and the baby. Only two more days. We'd got through so much, why endanger that now? What if Kev . . . tripped over one of the sleeping dogs, broke his neck? I drew in, figuring out if *that* thought wasn't stronger than putting my arm over Lonnie's shoulders. I decided to go directly to the hospital, pick up the fanmail, and straight home.

It was twenty-to-eight. I went straight to my flat.

I had a little gift for Lonnie – something he would prize. Besides, if I missed an appointment I might never get another on his heavy schedule.

I'd taken to leaving a key in a pot outside the flat. Lonnie knew which pot, in case I was ever delayed. It was nearly half past, so he had used the key. The light was on in the kitchen. I cannot describe the warm, lapping excitement I felt at the thought that, within minutes, seconds, I would see him again. I didn't even know who he was: but behind the door was Lonnie, and he was mine. Courtesy of Gino's, for sure . . . but who thinks of such a detail at a time like that?

(I told you: *never* fall for a call-boy. They can't love you back. Their job is not to.)

Quietly I let myself in my own door. (Fatal – you should *always* announce yourself.)

He'd taken two glasses and swirled them out, put them on the kitchen table (you could see from the rings) and poured tots. One for him, one for me. The bottle was open, as if he intended to pour more.

I'll rework that. One for him, and one for JoJo or someone like that, who'd come to sit through this round before they had a joint appointment later on. (You shouldn't think at a time like this – get Connery with his gun.)

On the sofa were two pairs of pants. And shirts and socks and shoes all jumbled up. That is not the moment to sort out Lonnie's from someone else's. Leave them as evidence. The other set was not JoJo's.

The lights were not on there or in the bedroom. That is when you turn them on. Otherwise, when you hold up the other pair of pants to the romantic moonlight for identification – they were twice the size for JoJo's neat seat – the cash is liable to drop out of the pockets. That is when Dave Bennington should climb out of your bedroom window and descend the building's cladding for shame, except he couldn't do that, could he, without his pants?

The coins patter on the carpet. Their sound is covered by your favourite tape on your deck.

That is when you go and get yourself a drink. You don't do what I do: creep into your bedroom. That could altogether put them off their stroke.

On the other hand, it's always interesting to watch others so absorbed in making love they don't know you're there. Interesting to see how others use the sheets, align themselves. You can get an idea of how you'd look in the same position.

Is that how you smother your face in someone else's hair? Is that how your shoulders fold round to enclose the beloved, and the hollow of your back actually quivers? Is that really all that can be seen of the other – an elbow that won't fit in anywhere else, and a knee? Does he really, your beloved, let himself be screwed, with his startlingly white underpants still round his thighs?

I know the tape is coming to a finish, even if they aren't, and the machine will, even if they don't. I have to leave now in case they hear me breathe in the silence to follow.

That is when you go and swill out a glass, help yourself.

And when the tape runs over a corrugated patch – and goes *click* – that's the time to go into the lounge, turn it round and start it playing the other way. Then you can't hear if you've disturbed them. Even if the one is the guy who takes your beloved and next is after your job.

Even while he raises himself on his elbow to talk and won't let your beloved disengage.

That is when you don't turn down the tape or you'll hear what he has to say. 'Your secretary said you're away . . . Didn't think a Thursday appointment should go to waste. It was in your book: Lonnie, 8.00 p. m . . . Gino'll charge you for it all the same . . . I shall pay on your behalf . . .'

'Lonnie, Lonnie,' I said. 'Don't hide yourself away, my dear.'

He drew the sheet off his elegant head, sorted out his hair.

'I brought you a little something. I know I shouldn't have.'

Lonnie merely called my name.

'I shouldn't, but I love you very much, you see.'

'Sorry, old man,' said David Bennington.

He called my name. Lonnie called my name.

'He's not called Lonnie at all. Don't you know that?'

'Course I do, but he's Lonnie to me.'

What would your Lonnie do at a moment like that? When if he said go jump you would climb into the window frame and do so? If he said get us another drink, you would? If he said wait for your turn . . . *you would*.

This Lonnie, *my* Lonnie, calmly, gently called my name.

So what would you do if you heard your best beloved summoning you? Crawl between his thighs and hope there

157

was room for you to hold him, too, while he hugged you.

That's what you'd do. You, too.

Then, all too soon . . . far too soon to be human . . . he'd have to go. And your colleague would not have anything more to say. And you know what? – you'd have to pass by that hospital and collect the mail.

And you know how much there'd be. Half a ton of it, and it would come from every post office in the country and from all over the world (even Switzerland: three telegrams, one in French and two in – looked like – Schweizer Deutsch . . .).

You know what they would say? They'd all be the same. And they'd say: GOOD LUCK, KEV.

We had to clear the place of parcels later, too. People sent the most extraordinary things. One old carpenter went to the extent of making a *high chair* for the baby. There were bibs and rattles and embroidered nappies and jump-suits and exercisers and even an inflatable cot. Endless presents for Kev, as well, like aprons with hearts on and funny slippers – you would never know if they were meant genuinely or sarcastically. Steffie van der Merwe was invaluable, going over everything with those metal-detectors; you never knew if some fanatic might not try to get famous by blowing the baby up. We piled it all in a pantechnicon and donated it to creches in Soweto.

Now, no matter what you may have read, the baby wasn't born in the Trescott Hospital. That was out of the question. There was a round-the-clock sit-in outside the Trescott, like outside the South African embassy in London. This one wasn't anti-apartheid, though; they were purely waiting for Kev to arrive and deliver. They weren't going to be fooled again, the photographers, by any ambulance manoeuvres, either. They had the whole quarter staked out. It was most organised, for once, and the cops did a superb job keeping everything orderly and brisk. But for the sake of the poor hospital staff and for the patients, not to mention the neighbours, we all agreed that the operation could not happen anywhere near Danny and Martie.

Where, logically, could Alfie go that had adequate facilities . . . and was the last place on earth that people could think to look? Well, I can tell *you*, I suppose, now that it makes no difference. But I must say I had some doubts as Alfie and his team rendezvoused with Kev, Jannie, Henno and me and the Beta crew with Richie at Baragwanath Hospital, off the Soweto highway. Richie of course did his training there, and those people work so hard they deliver a child every three minutes (and one in ten by caesarian section). But how shall I say? – it looked as if this was going to be a bit of an eye-opener. A layman like me might have been forgiven for mistaking it for a meat-packing plant, those grim slabs against the polluted skyline of the largest, most ghastly and (I suppose) famous black system of ghettos.

Belinda was with us of course, and reception tried to admit her rather than the hunched-up white boy in an overcoat whom they were all too busy to have heard of. We had no police or anything . . . just unbelievably rushed, underpaid nurses and the odd stray from casualty. (One guy had a knife stuck in his skull up to the haft and was still walking around.)

Beta had the small operating theatre set up like a TV recording studio. We sat outside it and when the swingdoor opened, we'd catch a glimpse of the stricken Saturday night show. The labour ward – not so funny, I assure you. I watched Belinda . . . how lonely she must have felt in our pit-latrine. At least in there were others to grasp to, starched white caps to focus on and when all else failed a knock-out needle. Jeepers, Klaus, as I said before . . . who would be a black mammy going through that kind of rumba? No inhibitions about yelling out the blues, either, and the occasional doctor standing round saying: 'Push, sisi, push . . .' while lecturing them on post-natal care. Belinda . . . who looked as if she'd finally twigged what it was all about. What depths of sadness she must have known. She sat in her Sunday best . . . her feet in her buckled shoes, hardly touching the linoleum floor.

Somehow I felt awfully sorry there hadn't been the traditional procedures . . . the gasp for help and the last-minute dash. Though I would do anything to spare anyone such suffering, at least a bit of blind panic would make the delivery seem true. It was so clinical to cut the infant out and plonk him/her in the world at the right time.

At least Henno was getting his chance to do the traditional things. He was pacing up and down even before Kev went in. He'd get to the poster about prevention of venereal disease and give it a soft punch, and then about turn and pace to the one about poisonous snake-bites, and give that a tap.

When Kev's turn came, he stood up. 'Heck, wish me good luck,' he said.

Henno clasped him by both shoulders and gave him a peck on the forehead. 'Good luck, hey, Kev, man.'

Kev turned to us and said: 'Heck, maybe this wasn't such a good idea.'

'Too late now,' said Jannie.

'No, I meant I'm getting used to the thing,' he said.

'Little bliksem,' said Henno, giving the most edgy smile.

'Just remember, the whole world's behind you,' I said.

'Even if none of them know the truth,' said Kev. I gave him a peck on the cheek, and pumped his hand. All this with people milling around, not that they had a clue what was going on.

Kev and Belinda walked through the doors. They were sort of arm in arm. And that is the last we saw of our friend with the peculiar figure for the next three gruelling hours. The medical staff and the cameras were ready. There weren't going to be any retakes on this one.

Henno asked if we could get a drink. Well, there aren't any cosy pubs with beer on tap and tot-measures near Baragwanath Hospital. In fact, Baragwanath Hospital is there largely to patch up the results of several thousand other not very salubrious and even illegal drinking holes in the vicinity. I had thought to shove a bottle in the glove compartment of my car, so that would have to do. The next hours were punctuated by Henno or me or even Jannie tiptoeing through the weeds to make rapid inspections of the roadmap.

Henno developed the most amazing stomach cramps. Jannie said that was an old wives' tale, about expectant fathers going into sympathetic labour in the waiting room. But Henno was looking evilly pained. He'd come a very long way since his loutish days . . . He would not then have been a quivering wreck, clutching himself against the wall, one hand round his belly and the other the family jewels. 'Fetch it for me,' he gasped, 'I can' . . . go out there.'

'This is ridiculous,' said Jannie. '*Kev's* not having labour pains so how can you *possibly* have?'

'Nee God, ek gaan sterwe . . .' he slumped down to the floor. Whereas Kev received all our indulgence and more, I noticed, Henno never got any.

I tiptoed out through the mass of admissions to fetch the bottle. There wasn't a plastic bag in which to disguise it, so I wandered around looking for one. There was any amount of wastepaper, lifted and redistributed by the wind. Nothing substantial enough. I just hugged the bottle under my jacket.

One of the staff at admissions spotted me for an alkie intent on polluting the entire hospital. She tore the bottle from me. This shook me considerably.

Henno squatted in a painful lump on the floor.

'That's right, pay for your sins. Sweat it out, man,' Jannie was saying to him.

When he saw me his wonderful eyes lit up. 'Where's it, where's it?' he said.

'If you want your J and B you'll have to sniff it out of the garbage bin with your nostrils,' I said.

His face collapsed. 'Ah man, why you always so shit to me?'

'That's what you deserve,' said Jannie.

'If I was Kev you'd wheel a whole cocktail cabinet in and jus' plug me in.'

'It's not my fault,' I said. 'Truth is, I could do with a few more slugs myself.'

'Ah, ah, ah . . .' said Henno.

'It's just gripes,' I said.

'Shut up, man' said Jannie, 'you'll wake the babies.'

For a long time Jannie and I sat on the bench, our knees touching. Henno huddled himself up against the wall. 'Nearly October the First,' said Jannie.

We counted the Marley tiles cross-wise and running away from us. There was a difference between us. Jannie counted each one individually.

'One ninety-four,' he said, 'not including the end bits and at the doors.'

'One ninety-two,' I said.

'Can't be,' he said. 'I just counted.'

'Multiply by sixteen,' I said.

Then out came the U.S. journalist, pretty haggard-looking. She said: 'Can we have Mr Wasserman for a picture?'

'Wassenaar, Wassenaar,' said Henno, standing and brushing the suit we'd bought him specially for the occasion.

Jannie jumped up. 'Well, well . . .' he threw his hands out. 'Is it all right?'

'Obviously it's all right,' she said.

'But that's wonderful, wonderful!' he exclaimed.

'Ah, that's *terrific*,' I said, overcome.

'And so, and so? . . .' Jannie struck his palm.

I brushed Henno's back and straightened his collar.

'And so, can we know what it is?' he harassed the woman.

'This is a very exclusive story, I'm afraid,' she replied.

'But is it a – you know, Robert Ernest or an Elizabeth Fiona? Surely you can tell us that.'

'It could be one . . . or it could be the other,' she said

smugly. 'You ready, Mr Wasserman?'

'He's ready,' I said, patting him on the back.

'But he's the godfather, surely after all we've done we have a right to know,' Jannie persisted.

'What does that make you, the *godmother*,' she said, sweeping Henno inside. 'Like everyone else, you'll read about it in the morning.'

That really was so mean.

'Well . . .' said Jannie in a fury, 'that's the last time *she* gets a chicken salad sandwich free from *my* kitchen!'

'Hundred and ninety-two,' I said. 'Calm down . . .'

He calmed down.

'Which do you want it to be,' he said, 'in your heart?'

'You mean an Elizabeth Fiona or a Robert Ernest?'

'Yes.'

'Pity it has to be either/or. Pity it can't be a bit of both,' I said, nudging him.

'Well, whatever it is, half of it is me – genetically speaking.' That he had said a hundred times before.

'I suppose for Fiona's sake it should be a girl,' I said.

Then he would say: 'Ag, what difference does it make? Either way it'll have a good home.'

'But in my heart . . .' I said. 'I go for Robert Ernest.'

'Me too,' said Jannie. 'Not that I'm prejudiced or anything, but I'd just like there to be a little boy around the house. You know, when Kev comes out for weekends or on his birthday.'

'Ja,' I said. 'Keep things the way they are.'

'Shoo,' Jannie struck his knee, 'the first baby in the world born of a man! Tomorrow everyone, but everyone, will know. Well, early edition, Monday morning.'

'And Kev did it.'

'Good for Kev.'

A really trampled-down matron came out, rather like everyone's favourite nanny. We were onto her.

'Is it a – is it a –?' Jannie dithered.

'He means a boy or a girl,' I explained.

'Well,' clasping hands to starched bosom, alive again with naughtiness, 'it could be a boy . . . or it could be a gel.'

'But – but – but,' said Jannie.

'You mean it's hard to tell the difference?'

'No no, gentlemen, I should know that by now!' she exclaimed.

'So, so – which one is it, sisi?' Jannie burst.

'You'll have to guess. Quickly, because we have many more patients tonight.'

'It's – a boy,' I shot out.

She eyed me, she eyed Jannie. 'No . . .' she said, 'one more try.'

'If it's not a boy, is it a girl?'

'It must be,' I said.

'Congratulations, congratulations!' she danced round with us. 'It's a beautiful beautiful *gel*, ach everybody is so happy *happy*.'

And we didn't have champagne.

'It's a bloody special girl, too,' Jannie held her hand. 'You know that's the first girl ever to be carried and born that way. I mean, in the entire history of the human race, of the planet, *of the universe*!'

'No no,' she said, 'it is quite an ordinary gel. Healthy, seven pounds. No complications.'

'No,' I said, 'he means the first one that a man has given birth to.'

She looked at me quizzically. 'Oh is it the first one?'

'Yes, of course.'

'And it happens here – in South Africa, in your hospital!'

'But I thought there were lots of them,' she said. 'Overseas.'

That's the colonised mind for you!

'All right, all right, now I've got work to do,' she waved and backed into the commoners' labour ward.

We heard her clap her hands: 'No no, Mamabella, push, *push* – look like this.'

But if I have one abiding memory of that historical evening, it was still to come.

The journalists trooped out with all their paraphernalia, looking quite humanly exhausted. The cameraman said: 'Anywhere you can get a beer round here?'

'Sorry,' I said, 'you'll have to go back into town.'

The American girl sighed, as if she'd had the baby herself. 'Just so long as we get to a telex and picture-printer first.' She sat briefly.

To be friendly, I said: 'So it's all come out right for you?'

'Yes, oh sure, thank God for that,' she said. 'Come on you guys. This stuff is worth a lot of money, *lots* of it.' And they started hauling off.

'See you afterwards,' I said.

'Sure thing,' she said, 'we'll be back to do the follow-ups. You make sure he and the baby see no one else, you hear?'

'And it's a girl,' Jannie chipped in. 'We found out from word of mouth.'

'You know what?' she said. 'You should be a journalist.'

Then she softened. She softened so completely – from relief, I suppose – that she actually looked quite nice. 'Oh, and thanks for those delicious chicken salad sandwiches.'

We watched the whole span depart.

'You know what, you know what?' said Jannie. 'I don't think that cameraman's buns are so great.'

'You put the words in my mouth,' I said. 'I seen a whole lot better myself.'

'You know, Jannie,' I was going to say. 'I really love you. Just because *you are you*.'

He'd say, 'Why thank you. I haven't heard that said before.'

And I'd reply: 'We should get together some time.'

But Richie came to fetch us. He'd arranged to have his old overnight room converted into a private ward for Kev.

You know how big it was, after all those corridors and ventilators and disposal works and wards: nine by six. But that was a lot more room than any other patient had. And you know what was in it? One upright single bed with a pillow and freshly-laundered sheets, an upright chair and a lightbulb overhead. But that was also a lot more than other patients had. In the bed was Kev, as pale as someone drowned.

Alfie stopped us at the door. He was so exhausted he plunked himself across us and gasped. We patted his back and congratulated him.

'And he's the one who said it's all so mechanical,' Richie remarked.

'You've got what you wanted – you're *famous* now.'

'More like a famous wreck,' said Alfie. 'All right, so I admit. But you know what, Richie?' he said, clutching his fist. 'From here on it's – fortitude all the way.'

We shuffled in past Henno, shaking his hands. 'Thanks, man, thanks, man,' he said, in that light like a hoodlum in his pinstripes who'd never said an emotional word before.

'Kev, ah Kev, are you all right, my baby?' Jannie threw the bunch of best glads across his feet. 'Have you made it, my darling, my boo-boo?'

'Sorry, they got a bit squashed in the car,' I said.

'Barefoot Nurseries,' said Kev with a grin.

'And a one and a two and a go gal go,' I said.

'Not now,' said Kev, 'but *very soon*. I'll have to get my waist back first!'

'You don't want cellulite removal as well, do you?' said Alfie.

'Take it easy now, Kev,' said Jannie.

Richie sighed: 'Ah, what a girl has to go through, all on account of those lousy men with their – big things – and horrible hairy whiskers just everywhere.'

'He looks clean-shaven enough,' I said.

Kev pulled down the sheet, showing us how flabby his stomach was. Clean as a whistle right down to the scar. Scars always look much worse than they are.

'Nice work, Alfie,' said Jannie.

'Great piece of needlework,' said Richie.

'Gee, you're a fine surgeon,' said Jannie.

'Thanks,' said Alfie.

'Wish you hadn't shaved my balls. They're all itchy,' said Kev.

'Least you got some feeling there,' said Henno.

'Put it away now,' said Richie.

But the abiding impression was over on the upright chair. There was the famous babe, Elizabeth Fiona . . . Liz to you, since you're a friend, if you promise to respect and cherish her. Getting a firm start in this world, determined to make it as fast as she could. Really concentrating on going places. Not wasting time casting her watery blue, out-of-focus eyes around, trying to get a bead on us over-excited degenerates.

Plugged to the nipple. Latched on it.

'Can't get enough of it,' said Henno.

Sucking, sucking, sucking for life. *Draining* it into her minute little body.

'You know what, that baby's going to go places,' said Jannie.

'You can see it in the – *determination*,' said Richie.

'It's *my* baby,' said Henno.

'But everybody feels about babies like that. Just thank God it's perfectly normal,' said Alfie.

It was Ou Sara's idea, of course, so don't give me any of that about the old wives of the Valley not playing their part. Every baby's got to have a breast or two to feed on, don't you know? And it was Ou Sara said – put a baby in her arms, and milk would flow like wild honey in the desert. Belinda was flowing with all that stopped-up milk she'd been hoarding for months. Inside her it welled up, spurting forth.

'Is jy all right, Belinda?' I said, patting her on the shoulder.

'Ja baas,' she said, and she glanced up at me, face streaming with tears.

That is the moment I shall remember always.

I wish Fiona'd been there. She would have smiled.

Klaus, my dear – you do see it now? Everyone's got it wrong. Those banal bulletins from the Trescott Hospital misled the world. They caught the public's imagination, all right – stress on *imagination* – but what did that have to do with what occurred? About the only detail correct in the reports was the headline: IT'S A GIRL!! (Shouldn't that read *She's* a girl?)

No matter which (s)he was ... I must now take you to the Grand Finale. Gays are so clever reading between the lines, and egged on by their claiming acquaintance, nay, more than acquaintance – *intimacy* – with Kevin (was that the *prissy* queen, my dear, who always sat in the window-box drinking *Coke*??) ... and a few strategic phonecalls from Martie and Danny – well, before we knew it, we had a party on our hands. We'd done no catering or anything. We'd not even dusted, not had time to run up a new dress! Before we knew it, right here at Barefoot Nurseries ... cor, our *style* has gone right down since you left! – we didn't have half the shrubs in bloom – Jannie was running round with a hairdrier trying to get the fuchsias to open ... So we had on our hands the biggest party of the boys ever held in the *whole of the southern hemisphere*!

They kept coming and kept coming to welcome Kevin back. In charabancs and lorries they came, in buses and on bikes. It was like Rio Carnival! Open the door and a dozen more screaming, but *screaming* queens'd flood in and pour out gifts and bloody swamp us in perfume and high fashion. The Pink Flamingo was but empty that night – we were overrun.

Gino – even Gino – had *all* his boys out for a night off. Well, I must tell you ... (after shaking hands, pretending I didn't know them), 'What's that,' I said. It looked like a rolled up carpet.

'What's that?' Jannie exclaimed.

It was the largest pizza ever made on Broadway, Johannesburg. As big as a disco floor.

I danced with JoJo and Achmed in my arms, a kind of six-legged tarantella. I was so bloody happy I kept running with them into the mustard field until, like the dogs, I had to be restrained with a few more drinks.

We had the gay-libbers, the Market Theatre lot (including some famous names I will *not* mention), and movie queens, the railway staff and the airways numbers, horticulturalists and furriers, and Gay Athletes and all the male nurses ... and down to the lowest amateur rent ('Give us a rand, I give you a hand, Give us ten bob, I do the job') ... ask Val for the details. All the Class of 84 (blue version). Val kept a record down to the last crooked wrist. (Seriously, ask him: everyone who wasn't dead was there!) Martie and Danny (we're quits now, so all is finally forgiven . . .); they had two marathon-runners in tow, this time. All it needed was half of Dave Bennington to complete the census!

Kev made a few streaks through the place with the baby in his arms – they were in danger of being pampered to death! Well, how would you like it if you had a bevy of bathing beauties high on benzedrine after you shrieking: *'Let me see, let me see!'*?

Dave Bennington did come – with one cop in uniform (Stefanus van der Merwe) and two bisexual pseudo-Malawians. I stood firmly at the door, said: 'Sorry, no cops this time.'

'But they didn't have time to change,' said Dave.

'Sorry,' I said, 'you heard me, *no cops*, in or out of uniform. They'll only provoke a Stonewall and get torn to bits.'

'That's very rough,' said Dave. 'Think of the incredible hours they've put in just to protect Kev.'

'Better than protecting some lousy politician.'

'But – they're human beings, too,' said Dave.

'No, they're not; they're cops.'

'But – but –' said Steffie van der Merwe, his police spies nodding like dolls.

'We only want to see the baby,' said one.

'Yes, the baby,' said the other.

Where's a bloody ninja when you need one?

'Get your wives to show you yours someday,' I said. 'Sorry, private party – so git.'

They turned to go, very crestfallen.

'Not you, Dave,' I said, pulling him inside, whispering: 'Did you bring Lonnie?'

'No,' he said. 'I thought Gino was.'

'Oh shit,' I said.

'Holy caroly!' he ouched, 'will you look at that!'

Alfie had been hoisted shoulder high by a hundred left over brides and they were bursting through the creepers with him, like a rugby hero cheering himself, dogs leaping up and barking.

'Someone's going to get hurt,' I said.

They ran him across the property, hurling him in the jacuzzi. Fortunately we'd just refilled it.

Some of the really wonderful Doornfontein moffies were there (no front teeth!), stripping him off and towelling him down. I think Alfie thought he was in some unknown part of heaven (District Six!).

Henno was doing a stint on the phone which, the moment he put down, rang with our code again. The Trescott switchboard had finally become demoralised and gave out our number freely. From having quite a civilised patter to respond, ending with: 'Your good wishes are much appreciated and so thank you and goodbye,' he was down to: 'Who's it? . . . thanks, hey, bye.'

He kept a list of the callers, in rather handicapped spelling.

'Who was it that time?' I passed him.

'State President's office . . .' he said, 'No, that was External Affairs – it was the P.r.e.s.e.d.e.n. before . . .'

'State President,' I said to Kev.

'All right, I'll do a shift now. You go and eat,' he said to Henno.

By then we were not impressed by anything.

'What's this?' said Kev, pointing to a tangle on the pad.

'Checko –' said Henno, 'you know . . .'

'Slovakia?'

'Yes.'

'That'll set the Valley on fire.'

'I didn't know we had phonelinks behind the Iron Curtain. And this? This? Aus –'

'Australia, I think,' said Henno.

'Isn't it Austria?' I said.

'No, definitely not,' said Henno.

Belinda took the baby.

Richie spent the entire time opening bottles all the people had brought.

Jannie and I had everyone lined up in some kind of order at the back, with Gino really taking over like a flamboyant scout-master.

The sun was almost gone . . . and then we heard the singing. It was a bit eerie . . .

Those who had paper plates with something on them shifted round the house. Jannie broke away and put on the floodlights.

Spread out on the lawn were all the staff, from pieceworkers through to permanent, with Timothy in front, his cap in his hands. The dogs ran in and out of them, rather indifferent. Timothy and his people kept singing their sort of hymn, and by the end there were dozens of us, not eating . . . lining the edge of the stoep and staring at those statues – smiling statues. It was very impressive.

Immediately I thought, They should not be down there (blacks) and us staring at them (collected moffies) . . . It just happened that way, but seemed so confrontational.

I said to Timothy with a big gesture: 'If you're hungry, come up and get it. I'm sure there's enough.'

It was that kind of peaceful, sharing evening.

Ou Sara shambled through and tipped me a nod; no, that was not what they wanted. She joined them, next to Timothy and, gathering her skirts, knelt. These dark shapes knelt, one by one.

'They want to see the baby,' Jannie stage-whispered.

Kev gave his plate to someone and went inside.

'Didn't realise your people were so *devout*,' Dave Bennington whispered to me. 'Are they Muslims?'

'No, that's natural courtesy.' To Timothy I said: 'Master Kevin is coming now. Please, please . . . sit, rather, hey.'

But they weren't prostrating themselves for us; it was for the baby.

Kev came out with her – two tiny fists showing from the blanket. Belinda stood beside him. I can't quite analyse that scene – was it tense? *Holy*?

Anyway, as soon as Kev held the baby up and she got an eyeful and let out a crying jag, everything was back to normal. Kev wisely took her through the ranks, howling and squirming as she was, and let each one see her close up. I don't suppose any of us will forget this little procession and the adoring looks. Belinda held her skirt out and received all sorts of gifts, one by one placed there as offerings.

'If they're Muslims, that would figure,' said Dave. 'Isn't he to be born of a man, second time round?'

'Don't be silly, Dave,' I said. 'This whole thing's in danger of going to our heads.'

The phone was ringing inside. I looked across at Henno.

'Your turn,' he said.

It was a neighbour. She had a sick cow, she said. Would I please tell people to stop ringing me because she wanted to get hold of the vet.

I said I was *profoundly* sorry.

When I came out Kev and Belinda were with the staff, all singing *Rock of Ages*, which quietened the babe. Those of us who knew the words joined in.

Then Kev said it was time for the baby's feed, so it all broke up naturally.

I couldn't quite regain my buoyancy – the woman on the phone spoke so bitterly, *jealously* . . . as if we'd all personally invited everyone to phone and insult her. Maybe she thought we'd all tiptoed round and poisoned her cow.

Wandering round the edge of the garden, I half wished it would be all quickly over, and we could get back to a more normal life. Our affairs could never return to the way they had been, but that was just as well. We had all learned so much . . . As you've guessed, I found myself at the eucalyptus and sat with my feet near where you know. I didn't do anything conscious, like address the baby corpse in its overgrown, unmarked grave. I beamed to it that I knew I had a lot of sorting out to do (but of course would do nothing about it till I started putting all this down for you). I suppose you can't sort things, when you're in the thick of them. I felt bad about turning those cops away, but one has to draw the line somewhere. I hadn't realised how strongly I felt about being a sort of wishywashy collaborator. I tell you, in my dreams every time I was getting somewhere, down that helicopter would come like a chicken-hawk . . . Above all, I missed Lonnie.

Then I had a cheering thought. Any lonesome tourist in Joburg that night would be good business for Lonnie – everyone else was out at Barefoot Nurseries, sporting themselves!

I wandered up to the road, puffing terrifically. If I'd turned back to the house I'd have only gone for the booze. I had some half crazy notion that if I stood on the gravel in the moonlight, I'd see Lonnie come down it, like Kev did that night he got a lift to the crossroads where you could see our sign even in the dark. I spent a while up there, waiting . . .

Because the rest is so painful to recollect, that's where I'll end this letter, my dear Klaus. Bless your cotton socks – or lederhosen rather. The disc is nearly full and – hey, you haven't replied to my *first* one yet. Get a bleeding move-on! Or is it all too much for you? Can't you find a printer, or what?

Here I've got the whole of Transvaal moffiedom cavorting round the place in rank rejoicing. And your only reply is – *silence*!

Come on, that's not like you. You know how much I value your opinion.

To you and Paul, love from both of us.

P. S. Just to finish this:

Talk about the rural life. Jannie puts this machine to bed and lo! a frog jumps out of it. That's why he's got warts on his lips – from kissing it to see if it'll turn into a prince!

NOT TRUE – J.

Know what the new euphemism for having a shit is? — making room for someone else!

THAT I CAN BELIEVE.

III

ACTUALLY KLAUS, YOU KNOW WHAT I THINK YOU ARE? AN A1 SHIT OF THE FIRST WATER. I MEAN, HE'S BEEN STRUGGLING WITH THIS THING FOR HOURS WHICH AMOUNT TO MONTHS NOW. IF YOU WERE HAVING TROUBLE WITH A PRINTER WHY NOT SAY SO AFTER THE FIRST ONE? DON'T YOU THINK A POSTCARD AFTER THE SECOND ONE IS A LITTLE BIT LITTLE TO SEND IN REPLY? I KNOW HE USED TO COUNT TOO MUCH ON YOU, AND YOU HAVE NO DUTIES TOWARDS HIM. BUT TO GET HIM RIGHT, EVERY BIT HELPS, DON'T YOU SEE? AND PLEASE IF YOU DON'T MIND RETURN THOSE ACCOUNTS FORTHWITH. IF YOU DON'T I'LL PERSONALLY SCREAM.

My dear Paul,

Jannie's in a fury, as you can see, but I can take it more philosophically. Since our dear mutual friend seems to consider a reply such an imposition... *you* are the one to whom I'll address myself from now on, in the hope he hasn't managed to politicise out of you *all* your 'naive South Africanness' (quote-unquote), and behind the evidently newly fashionable slogans of the Swiss there still lurks some of your former easy-going *laissez faire*. Then you can interpret to him... because I'm not going to be put down – thrown out quite that easily. I know you left because you too probably felt irrelevant to the cause, but thereby you declared your irrelevance even more. Those of us who stay, *by the very act of staying*, declare our involvement. If we're suddenly all redundant to the political situation, if we're structurally guilty (quote-unquote), as Klaus says, and with no appeal – that I cannot accept; then so is snow redundant in Switzerland.

Of course it's all politics, and always has been. But Klaus is becoming very forgetful: he speaks of a happy cantonal system (about which I know nothing, so I will have the grace to make no comment) but in which even an outsider like you is now *included*. Easy for you all to be democrats. Here, since just about everyone is *excluded*, what then? I realise more than you think, thank you very much. The people of this country declared independence from their government ages ago! What has that to do with Klaus's politics? – we don't *want* that kind of politics. We live the massive fact of another life. If he's sick of apartheid, that's just because he's sick that his parents supported the Nazis during the last war. That's where 'last bastion of racism' and all that comes from – his own guilty conscience. Tell him that.

Meanwhile we, who are just as persecuted as any black, have all to climb out of it. We live in the future, not the murky European past. Keep your wretched Switzerland, home of world banking! As you walk the streets, swinging your little handbags like Heidi, my dear . . . oh so politically up-to-date, to give your ten per cent to the Anti-Apartheid Movement, like the devout used to give their tithe to the bloody church, you walk on the *vaults that hold the loot of Africa*. Square that with your selective consciences, my dear.

Unburden those unnumbered accounts! It is time to stop ripping off the people who made you that dough!

All right, so I can hardly claim to be some sort of socialist. Obviously, as former financial director of a corporation which *owned* over twelve per cent of South Africa, venture capitalism has always been more my line!! But you can never say where politics and the people meet has not been without interest to me. You couldn't show me that point when either of you were doing so well out here. Only when he went broke, and you were threatened with the army, and he took you out of here to milk the dole, did you begin to look for it, and scream Oh my darlings, all those people were so poor, *poor poor things*! Keep your tears to yourselves, chaps. Crocodiles cry, too.

I'd like you to see Barefoot Nurseries now, I really would. If coming to South Africa wouldn't be contaminating yourselves too much. You'd have to pass through some vicious, evil government controlled territory between the airport and here, I admit. You might never get a job at home if they knew you'd soiled yourselves there.

But here at Barefoot Republic we declared our independence long ago. We're not hoity-toity about it, or given to all the high principles Klaus can fill only a measly postcard with.

We're just waiting for the rest of the country to catch up!

(Tell him all this, Paul, for God's sake. Friendships are more precious than propaganda, now and for all time.)

In the Beginning was the Word, and the Word was processed into Meat. Everyone gathered around and lit a fire. The meat was roasted and all had a share, and a share was burnt for the sky and buried in the earth, for they gave us ourselves in the first place. Everything is reducible to that. Thank you, O Earth.

When Jannie and Kev were picking in rockpools (that lovely time when we were on holiday), their bloomers held up and faces flat towards the water, do you not think I saw ... two old crones, thrown out like garbage, picking through the ruins of their shacks after the bulldozer? (Four million people slated to be 'removed': that's apartheid for you.)
 When we were following those Indians with the shark, do you not think I saw the signs go by: reserved for Coloured bathers, reserved for Indian bathers, reserved for Bantu bathers, whites only? That shark towed us through the lot of them! *Who cares.* (I told you the people ignore them; the municipality had just forgotten to take them down, that's all.)

Kev's fine. (Not that Klaus asked. You see, when he gets into politics he loses interest in people.)
 So's the baby.

I'm fine, too. (Well, I can tell *you*, Paul ... you must get homesick for your ghastly heritage. Not like some passers-through I know, who make their money and run. And then give *what* per cent to the Anti-Apartheid Movement – was that *ten* I heard? When ninety per cent goes to supporting it.
 Aren't the odds a little unfair?)

I wasn't fine before. But now the baby's here. *She* makes all the difference. Come on my little Topsy-Flopsy, climb up on your godfather's knee. Now, type out your name with your little big finger.
 There: FIFI.

Now that moffies can have babies, I tell you none of the old rules on which human history has been predicated apply.
 Not so, my Boo-boo-boo? The world is a different place.

You know one thing? – she doesn't need to be changed nearly so often as other babies do. Ask Mrs Leibnitz (she taught us how to do it). She said: 'Zis child, zis is not a child, zis is a A-A-Angel.'
 I suppose angels are *very* undemanding in that respect.

We had the Beta gang in for a last session before their

contract ran out. I think they've overplayed their interest, because no one wants to interview her anymore.

They got one lovely pic of her with her fist in the air, going Amandla amandla, as all babies do in this country, and rose-hip syrup all down her bib.

But they wouldn't use it. Those people have *no* sense of humour.

Still, I'll miss them in a way.

So what's left to tell you about your past?

There's my heart attack – but I put that in my first disc to Klaus. Even *that* seems so distant now, I forget. A heart attack is a great watershed, but you know that only when you're on the other side of it. It was cumulative stress – from the baby's coming mostly, and the pressure Dave Bennington put on me, and from Lonnie's end. Plus a sustained endeavour to overeat and pickle the product in drink . . .

Lonnie's story, I suppose, just put the kibosh on a whole life's effort to kill myself quick.

I'm over *all* that now; I am a new man.

But that doesn't mean I don't have my regrets.

It all had to go up in smoke, didn't it? You could feel the right-wing backlash tightening around us. Just speaking English on the party line was enough provocation, let alone – Czechoslovakian! Even if the State President himself did get in on the act, that didn't mean he would protect us. Did it?

When your neighbours are all potential vigilantes, with years of indoctrination about terrorists under their very beds, they're going to find out what's cooking for themselves. Aren't they?

I wish they hadn't tried to shoot up so many of our guests, that's all. Don't you? Or do you feel it doesn't matter if any of us die?

It didn't help running round screaming 'This is private property so fok off' either. Trespassing is nothing compared to what you'll do when you take the law into your own hands.

Literally the Valley was up in arms. And we were surrounded. If they'd been listening to our phone, should we have been listening to their short-wave radios! They'd rallied a whole Magaliesberg Toyota-borne commando up at Kierieklapper before we'd even served the pudding. Where's a ninja when you need one? – we needed all the warriors of the Late Tang Dynasty to take on that lot.

I always think I should never have kicked out our Steffie and his boys. Maybe they should have been given the chance to choose whose side they were on – the baby's, or the rest of the Valley's. We'll never know, because once their cop car slid out of the Valley that was actually the signal for the forces of darkness to move in.

Despite their having no lights, I saw them coming up the gravel road. These hefty trucks like porcupines – bristling with rifles in the moonlight. They blocked the driveway, so that if anyone had wanted to flee, they couldn't.

This is not Johannesburg, where you can take a helicopter, my dear. This is an extremely conservative rural backwater, where tradition rules, okay? Tradition rules from the barrel of a gun. They'd always been secretly set to avenge the battle of . . . well, we're not talking of El Alamein; we're talking about Silkaat's Nek! And they'd had enough now of talk in all our parliaments about power-sharing and liberalisation. You don't share power with the cancer in your midst, nor fraternise with the visible cause when it wants to give the land you've fought and died for to . . . just a bunch of coolies!

I sent Jannie out to halt the advance. At least he speaks their language (we're a mixed marriage, don't you know). At least he was wearing a khaki shirt and shorts. Against my advice Alfie went to reason with them, too; the only weapon he could wield is a can of Peaceful Sleep to scare a mosquito. While they were parleying, the only other tactic I could think of was retreat.

'*You see*, Richie,' I said. 'Now get those dreadful queens off the trellis and take them down to the bottom of the farm.'

There was a deathly, sickly hush and the evacuation began.

'Henno! Henno!' I thought he could be in the front line. But he'd gone to Whole Earth next door; he wasn't going to be caught dead with the likes of us.

Pathetic, isn't it? The last thing you need to be when the crunch comes is caught in your party dress. They were *literally climbing back into the cupboards*. So much for the military wing of the MLF (Moffie Liberation Front).

My only thought was for Kev and Belinda and the baby. I didn't think of – the spraying sheds, the treasures in our room, the safe and the accounts, the video, this machine. I thought, when you're wearing boots, it's not very difficult to tramp down a baby. Kev had long fled into exile at Whole Earth after Henno . . . so that was all right. The staff had gone that way, too, and all the dogs! They knew a white man's war when they saw one.

Alfie charged in: 'You just can't even *talk* to them. Which way?'

'The river.'

'They say we bloody foreigners must go back to where we came from. I'm sure I'll get a great welcome home in Lithuania!'

'Danny! Martie! – quiver down by the riverside. *Run!*'

Dave Bennington: 'I'll see Jannie's all right.'

'They won't do anything if he doesn't provoke them. Gino – you're our only foreigner – git! git!'

'Whicha way?'

'Does water flow uphill where you come from? JoJo, JoJo, go!'

It was like the exodus to the Red Sea, I'm telling you – and me playing Charlton Heston! You've never seen a more convincing lot of extras, either. When I said, *Move . . . they moved.*

Dave and Jannie came round the rondavel, saying it was totally useless: what could you do with an anschluss of kraut-head Fascist Nazis wanting blood? *Give it to them*?

Still, we watched with a certain dismay as this Boer Brigade made through our house, prodding the furniture and overturning things. I suppose that's what you feel like when you're invaded: totally, utterly helpless. You feel so desperate you really *do* want to bare your breast and run shrieking into the wreckage.

I mean . . . that's what the Khakis used to do to these farms – pile all the lovely Cape Dutch furniture in the voorkamer and pour paraffin over it. But that was in our grandparents' day.

They use flamethrowers, now. Dave and Jannie and I stood there, with Alfie and Richie, and all these other queens holding their noses and diving into the waters. The rondavel went up in one conical whoosh like an atom bomb. It was quite unbelievable . . . It seemed to just blast off, the roof opening out like a silo to hurl up this shaft of flame. Can you believe people would fear the Communists so much they want to hurl them into outer space?

(No insurance, either. That whole gathering was illegal. Act of God again. Scourge of God, if you ask me.)

Well, by the waters of Magaliesberg, I tell you, you've never seen so many moffies weep in helpless frustration.

I thought, They're going to advance in ranks through the orchards and line up on this ridge, and then at some command *they're going to pick us off as they please*. They're going to purge the moffie plague in one go. For ever after this river'll be known as Moffiespruit, and our blood will turn the oceans red.

'Be brave, girls, now – be helluva brave.'

Some bright spark thought it was time for a singsong:

> She'll be coming round the mountain when she comes,
> She'll be wearing pink pyjamas when she comes . . .

'Shut up,' Jannie commanded.

They were addressing us through a megaphone.

'Jesus,' Richie said. 'I see what you mean.'

'That's just a warning. They'll be back another night to finish the job,' said Dave.

'Dave,' I said. 'Get rid of that other house of yours. It's *too dangerous*.'

We sat with our heads in our hands, contemplating what we'd have to get rid of now.

'I suppose just because they leave the rest of the farm standing, we're meant to feel grateful,' said Alfie.

'They're all – like Kev's father,' I said. 'Because they don't want their sons to wear make-up and skirts . . .' Mind you, I could see why they felt the way they did. If you'd had to contemplate that mob of sagging hairy tits and running mascara in the moonlight for very long, you'd also have been appalled!

(One of Gino's boys – the pale, wraith-like number with waterwings for an arse – to an in-flight hostess: 'But I thought if we crashed over water we were meant to get rubber chutes.'

'No, you only get First Aids, and then you're good for at least another three years.')

We could hear the Valley Vigilantes reversing out. The water was a bit cold for a health spa, so we bedraggled our way up again to inspect the smouldering remains.

There were signs of another party starting up in the glow of the rondavel, but we who lived there – and who had not expected either one or the other mass movement – had had enough. 'Please, gather your valuables and go home and lie low,' I clapped my hands.

Ah, but the baby, the baby!

'Baby's tired out now,' I said. 'Please guys . . . Rocky Horror Show's over. Get in your cars and drive carefully. Please – just fok off now.'

(Politics, I tell you. Just because you guys can walk around in public holding hands doesn't mean we're ever going to be able to. Politics, as far as I'm concerned, is for *dangerous lunatics*. Got that?)

Un Peu d'Histoire... isn't that what they call it in the *Michelin Guide*? It would be lovely now to be racing one of Hitler's little Volkswagens down a skislope... Light up a Stuyvesant as you plough to a stop in the deep rich snow. Throw aside your visor and sticks. Tramp to the lodge, scuffing snow off the window boxes with your gloves. Have a light supper with Rhine wine... among all the crooked politicians spending their unaccounted sums, and sanction-busters, picking their teeth.

Meanwhile, back at the ranch, we swelter.

Not very much Histoire, I'm afraid. To the left you have the Magaliesberg Range. They've been there since before Australopithecus robustus. He started before any European man. We've developed slower, that's all. Some interesting limestone caves, where sabretooths gnawed on antelopes. Now leopards gnaw on baboons and the occasional hiker.

Over on the right. Well, there's our mighty river, which, when its running, flows into the Great Limpopo. Many refugees have drowned trying to cross that part of it. They swim across from Mozambique. They must really like apartheid when they're hungry. Crocodiles are being reintroduced. Girls have got to have their handbags, don't you know?

Henno was sitting out the wait for the money which if you think it was a million dollars, think again. It was sufficient for Kev to lay off work until the baby's older, and we've opened a trust fund for her. Kev has undertaken to rebuild the rondavel into quite a nice modern bungalow, so that's where they stay. Henno got himself the Jag, so he's off on his travels again.

I don't suppose we've treated him too well. The solid resistance of three of us to one of him would have worn down a lesser man, but he remains irreducibly straight. He knows fully how attractive he still is to men, and we hear he is living off another hard-working decent citizen in town. Same arrangement: one provides the petrol, the other the vehicle. He never brings him here, though, for fear that Kev fills him in on some of the disadvantages.

Henno brings one or another pale-faced girl here, though, who stares flatly at the baby, saying everything's lovely. She won't have tea, she won't have a drink; they go walking in the lupins with the dogs, and you know the only words she says all day are: 'Yes, but where's the ma?' Then they have an urgent appointment in town.

Kev got Henno to sign over his rights in the baby in

exchange for the car, so there's no legal reason for him to visit, and the sentimental reasons are running dry. You can legally be a one-parent family here, so it's all resolved. We used to worry that Kev hankered for Henno . . . but there's not a trace of that. The child is Kev's sole preoccupation, and Henno, who used to be the centre, became the periphery, and then irrelevant. I suppose this is many a mother's and father's experience – nature's way of ensuring a reliable support-system for the child.

You can see what a magnet little Elizabeth Fiona has been for me, too. I tell you, for months on end I could not wait to get from town back to the farm, just to watch her take the bottle and have a turn maybe at burping her. The weekends would just go, without stress or that accumulating sense of crisis. I was absorbed in the activities about her.

Having a hangover breakfast on the patio, with little Elizabeth Fiona in her pram, we would all have some part of our consciousness – often the only part – functioning on her. Kev would position her out of the sun, but where the air was freshest. Then Jannie, going to fetch the coffee, would alter the angle of the pram slightly. Then I'd find some reason to check on her, and fiddle round for an even more ideal position, and get the toast. Then Kev would check the sun and the breeze, and check her out, moving her to position four.

A whole day could pass like this. If she cried, I tell you it was like the new fire alarm going off.

But if we could keep that part of the world decent and orderly for Elizabeth Fiona, that doesn't mean I had much to say over the way things were going in town. Dave Bennington could see how much of a crock I was becoming; this suited him, as he took over whole chunks of things. The art of management is delegation, but not when it gets to the point where the underling allows you only a look-in every so often . . . and then fixes up something simple to which you need only affix your almighty signature.

The corporation got good value out of Dave Bennington, all right. The earlier body training and fitness campaigns were channelled into prodigious work results. (He did sell his pleasure-palace on my advice, by the way, cutting his links with his origins and the gay subculture at once.) He had decided the road to success was entirely straight so, when he came to my office or flat, was there anything to talk about any more? Only the next deadline, appointment, board meeting. We acquired 52 firms that year, so no wonder I lost track.

My secretary told me the story that was doing the rounds. The managing director goes home a bit early one day, says to his wife: 'Who's that child playing around the goldfish pond?'

'But, darling,' she replies, 'that's our third son.'

He pauses. 'Adopted . . . or authentic?'

'But darling, you must remember that yacht we had in Saint-Tropez.'

Apparently the boy was named after it.

We were all getting a bit that way by then.

Dave Bennington was invited round to the m. d. with *his* kids for a Sunday braai. That of course clinched the beginning of my downfall.

For a while I still had one appointment a week that kept me going: Thursdays, eight o'clock. I'd been out at Randfontein doing an audit on two rubber companies (not condoms, alas). I always made sure not to be late again. I had more than an hour for a quick drink and a shower. But on the M1, as I was reaching the big city lane, I swear to God I broke down. Valve caps or something like that.

So who pulls up as I have my nose in the parts and arse wiggling on the flyover – you guessed it. The cop I'd dismissed from the party. He's a nice guy, old Steffie van der Merwe, and extremely good at his job. (Which does *not* include rescuing maidens in distress on the freeway – that he does out of sheer *helpfulness*.)

He parked in front of me, put his blue light on the roof, and strolled over. We shake hands rather diffidently and soon have our heads under the bonnet this time.

Immediately he says: 'Just as well it was me, hey?'

'Look,' I say, 'I'm *not* trying to pick up any cops. You should know me better than that.' Then as he checks all the terminals, to be friendly I say: 'How's your wife and the kids? You look pretty fit, even if you don't see Dave any longer.'

He looked genuinely grieved. In a rush I felt terribly sorry for him. His uniform made him like anyone else. I could see through it to his body in the jacuzzi, his dog-tag shining.

'Ag Dave,' he said, '*he's* a two-timing bastard.'

I felt so shitty being indifferent to his hurt. 'Look, for old times' sake, if you want to use my place . . . I've got a pad down there in Fox Street. It's empty weekends.'

The break had obviously been abrupt. I thought they might like time to sort it out. An unsatisfactory end leaves both parties hyper and manic. If nothing else, a little resolution would calm Dave down; I couldn't stand his unhappy sexual tension.

'There's it,' said Steffie, shoving a cap back on a valve.

'Honestly, I'd be happy for you and Dave to pop in. You'd keep burglars away.' I passed him a cloth.

'No,' he said, cleaning his hands. 'There's a big clean-up coming. Must lie low.'

The way he used the cloth on his fingers made me so sad. It was like, you know . . . afterwards, with languorous care. No one can change these give-aways – they're in your body-language, deep in your dreams. He returned me the cloth, as if to say: 'Thanks. It was fine!'

'Stefanus, honestly,' I said, 'if you'd like me to invite Dave over, and leave you two together . . . I'm sorry I gave you such a brush off at the farm. In fact, I wish you had stayed in the light of what happened. Forgive me.'

'I fixed your car,' he said.

I jumped in and started it. He held up the traffic and let me go. 'Thanks, hey, thanks a span.'

'Don't mention it,' he said and waved me on.

I was in good time for Lonnie. But he didn't come until 9.30. By then I was a bit far gone. That's right, drink to dull the despair. Then when the chance comes to cheer yourself up you can't do a thing about it.

Lonnie let himself in and, as it happens, wasn't in much shape to pull me together, either.

'I thought you weren't coming,' I said blearily.

'Jesus, I nearly didn',' he exclaimed, throwing his things down.

'Get yourself a drink and tell me about it,' I said.

He poured a scotch in the kitchen and came through. 'Jesus, I nearly didn' make it.'

'Have a shower,' I said. 'You'll be more coherent.'

'Later,' he said, and gave me a peck on the forehead.

My arms went round that beautiful, slim, wriggly . . . that boy, he had a waist like a – He pulled away.

'Come here, you beautiful, slim, wriggly *hank of silk*. Let me tousle your hair.'

'No man,' he said. 'I'm not in the mood.'

'The sexiest lay in all Johannesburg not in the mood?'

He stood at the window, staring at the street.

'Cheers,' I said.

He raised his glass and took a sip.

'All right,' I said genially. 'So tell me what happened.'

'They closed down Gino's. All my stuff's there . . . Sorry I'm late, hey, but I had to walk.'

'Who closed down Gino's?' I said. I suppose I thought it was a takeover by the coloured guys in Doornfontein. They'd been gunning for Gino. Bought him out and closed him down – that's business. 'Where's Gino?'

'Swaziland. JoJo told me. They got all our stuff. Mustn' go back there if you value your life.'

'Wait a minute,' I said. 'Gino's done a flit and is squandering your ill-gotten gains in the casino. That I can believe!'

'No man,' he turned on me, 'he escaped the police. JoJo said they just came, and Gino made it by minutes!'

'You mean – it was a raid?' I said.

'Yes, yes, that's what I'm trying to *tell* you. They went to everybody's places and hauled them in while they still asleep – Sipho and Gary and Bennie and Ferg; and Achmed with Spyker – all the stupid ones. They'll be sucking a lot of cock in jail, I'm telling you.'

'I suppose that's where they learned it in the first place,' I said.

'Yes,' he said.

'Shit,' I said.

'So I can' go back for my things. Just for tonight, can I stay here?'

'Yes, of course,' I said. 'Where's JoJo?'

'Gone back to his auntie.'

'Stay as long as you like,' I said. 'Have a shower and there's a dressing gown in the cupboard. That's about all I've got that will fit you.'

He got another drink and made me one, stripped and went into the shower. He turned all the lights on and left the glass door open. So I thought this was all some massively complicated come on to make up for his lateness. The next quarter of an hour was, I think, the most ecstatic time of my life.

I was watching someone, whose body was his only asset, look after it. A boy prostitute, whose beauty would not last for ever, ensure himself a little more future. Meticulous cleanliness was his consuming concern. (I'm sure Klaus felt that way about you, Paul.)

You know how the first drops bounce off the crown and, only when you strengthen the jet, part the hair and well up round the scalp, wetting up from the roots. The shampoo then takes quite homogeneously, spilling out at the back and round your temple. Drops on your shoulder stay little globules, then become a stream down your armpits. Your skin, like blotting paper, absorbs a bit and then, with the heat and steam, becomes shiny and porous, floating out sweat and the polluted air of the day.

You turn to get the steam full on your chest. The soap and shampoo gather above the cleft of your buttocks, before sliding between and you have to lift your balls to get the warmth underneath.

Lonnie turned the jet off for a moment. 'Haven' you got any disinfectant soap?' he said.

'Only what's there,' I said.

'Gill's,' he said.

'Sorry,' I said.

He went back to the hard-edged sponge, laving himself, all pits and parts. He was so systematic and thorough. You could almost hear him say: 'Elbows,' and he'd inspect round the elbow to check it was all there, and then the other one, and wipe it down. With his thumb full of soap he nicked round his navel and rinsed it out.

By the time he got to his toes they were pulpy and soft. Each one he scrubbed backwards and underneath with the brush, in case he could scrape away dead flesh. He used the step on the edge of the cubicle – little white digits on the blue mosaic – the dark hairs around his ankles like a collar. The steam billowed from behind him.

'Lonnie, you're totally, wonderfully beautiful and I love you with all my heart, and especially my soul,' I said.

'What's that?' he said, holding his hand to his ear.

'YOU'RE BEAUTIFUL,' I said.

'Thanks,' he said, giving a huge smile. Soap ran in his eyes and he grimaced. In his now quite adequate moustache it foamed.

He gave himself a final rinse and switched off. He squeezed his hair back. He shot the water off his limbs with the side of his hand – slash, slash, slash. Everything he did was completely, naturally masculine, which I suppose was what so appealed.

'Where's the towel?' he said.

'Reach round.'

'Thanks,' he said.

He dried his neck and shoulders first, then the hollow of his back, like a belt at a slimmer's. If you don't do the transverse move, you always get drops left between the shoulder blades. He buffed his chest up into a glow . . . I have never seen anyone dry each toe individually!

'Ready for inspection,' he said, giving a great sniff.

'Between your shoulders,' I said.

He sniffed again and did the transverse move, his armpit

flashing and coming down.

'Where's the dressing gown you said?'

I pointed round the corner to the cupboard.

He came out with it on, reaching down to the floor. He tried to do the belt up but that way he would have had to charleston. He sat on the carpet, reached over for his glass and straightened his back against my shins. I took the towel from him and gently began to rub his hair.

He gave a sniff, said 'Just a minute,' and went to the loo to blow his nose on some toilet paper. He flushed it down.

'Sorry,' he came back and resumed his position.

I towelled up from his forehead and around his ears. I will always love Elizabeth Fiona, I will always love Lonnie. They both came to me in such devious ways. Others might have come to me before and may come in the future . . . (Paul, I felt that way about Klaus, too – that's why I'm so upset about his abruptness.)

I had a comb in my jacket and took it out. I sifted between the tangled hair to find the parting. His hand took it from me and he went to the basin, ran hot water over it and scrubbed the teeth with the brush and soap. 'Sorry,' he said, 'one thing I don' want to catch is dandruff . . . Shall I do it?'

'Might as well,' I said, since he had the mirror right there. He wiped a patch of the surface with his hand and concentrated on ordering his locks. The only thing common about him was flicking it back like a ducktail. But when it dried it didn't have that slick effect.

He returned the comb, said 'Thanks,' went to fetch us another two glasses.

He sat alongside me on the sofa, arranging the front of the dressing gown neatly down the stripes. He looked at his wrist for the time.

'Shit, you know what? Even my watch was at Gino's.'

'I'll get you a new one, don't worry,' I said.

'Thanks,' he said.

'Will you miss Gino?' I said. 'Is he really gone?'

'Gone like it was nobody's business. Did that guy go? Phew, Gino . . .' he shook his head.

'I suppose it's just an ordinary pizzeria now?' I said.

'It's closed. JoJo said it won't open again until they extra – extra —'

'Extradite him.'

'Ja.'

'It'll hardly run then, if he's convicted.'

'Ja, Gino . . .' said Lonnie, stretching his legs.

'Will you miss him?'

'Ja, I suppose. He kept – you know, things safe for us.'
'Procurers do,' I said.
'No, no . . . it wasn' like that. Gino was just fine. As long as you do your job, Gino does his.'

He prodded me under my thigh.

'Listen, Lonnie . . .' I said. 'You don't have to . . . Now that you're all clean and everything . . . You've got to think of your future.'

'It's all right,' he said, 'if you want to.'

'What are you going to do?'

'Go back to working the hotels, then the bars.'

'Then the streets, and the toilets and sewers next. Oh God, I really wish I could have you all to myself!'

'You can, but you'd have to pay!' he chortled.

'I don't like you being out there on your own. But seriously, I'll help you the best I can – until you get established again.'

'I'd really appreciate that,' he said. We drank to it.

For lack of anything better to do, I turned on the eleven o'clock news (they still call it *news* . . .).

After that I went for another shower and, when I came out, Lonnie was curled up fast asleep in my bed. I curled up beside him, breathing the fresh smell of his skin, the slight dampness of his hair.

Later he shook a few times, talking a great fast jumble, mostly of the 'Leave me alone' variety. But I calmed him down, sure somehow that life was going to be all right.

But it isn't all lullabies and mother care, is it? (Hey, Paul? Certainly not in this country. I suppose that's why you ran away!)

'There's a big, bad world out there,' I said.

'Don't – I – know,' said Lonnie, relishing it.

'For God's sake, look after yourself.'

At night he'd come back late. As soon as I gave him flak (shades of Gino), he'd throw a pocketful of money on the kitchen table. He counted it and shoved it across to me.

'You keep it . . . just buy me the occasional bottle of J and B.'

'No, keep it for me,' he said. 'I haven't got – a bank account.'

I took him to the post office where he opened a savings book in his real name. It was Allan Hamlyn-Smith, if you don't mind. Lonnie was good enough for me. And for him. That's the name he operated under.

'Back to the big, bad world,' he'd say as I grabbed a cup of coffee and went to work.

He brought in some quite tidy sums; occasionally nothing at all. Every so often a bottle for me.

I thought, this is not what I hope for – him out working his butt off, me drinking myself to death. Now that our relationship had changed, all easy affection had gone out of it. The reason was he was utterly knackered. As we all know so well, there is a limit to how many times you can get it up a day! – he knew I would not push him when he *couldn't*.

Sometimes we'd go to see a movie. He liked Westerns . . . and fell asleep before the big draw at the end.

I thought, What if he starts working from my flat over the weekends? It would be hard to explain to Jannie and Kev. Saturdays were his best nights, and on Monday mornings when I got in he'd be passed out. I left a note for the cleaning lady never to disturb him.

'Lonnie,' I said. 'Why don't you come out to the farm? I'll introduce you and you can sunbathe, and have a rest.'

'Can',' he said.

'Why not? They won't think twice about what you do, as long as you don't do it with me – not that you do anymore – or try it on them.'

'Can' miss Saturday. It's my best night.'

'How much you got in your savings book?' He had five thousand, which tax free with interest, etc.

'Not enough.'

'I think that's quite enough for your needs – clothes and shampoo . . .'

'JoJo and me, we're going to buy a pizza parlour cash!' he said.

'Oh,' I said. 'Is JoJo also back on the beat?'

'No,' he said. 'That's why he'll be the cook and I'll be the pro- pro-'

'Proprietor. He'll wear the hat and you'll take the orders . . . No boys on the payroll?'

'No,' said Lonnie. 'Sucking off old guys is for the birds, man.'

'I see,' I said, going to work.

It was only a matter of time. I came home early, not thinking twice about it, feeling wretched for some reason. Opened the door, saw pants on the sofa (not Lonnie's). I thought, Not Dave Bennington into his old tricks again. The rule was: *no one* in the flat.

Lonnie was in the bathroom, wiping himself down with a facecloth, still with a half-erection going flap, flap. He pulled a towel around him, came through and closed the bedroom door.

'Lonnie,' I whispered, 'we said no guests.' I picked up the pants and shoved them at him.

'Not a guest, it's a cop.'

'A cop!'

'A cop,' he whispered. 'Get in the kitchen and don't come out till he's gone!'

I went into the kitchen, where the drink was, anyway. I thought, Won't take a brush off when they can get one free. So Stefanus van der Merwe was in plainclothes now... There must have been a premium on boy-meat after all the cleaning up he'd been doing, and he was determined to keep it all to himself. I had a few brief words to say to him as he passed my kitchen door: 'You are one hypocrite shit, my Steffie, so don't you *ever* set foot in here again!' Would he be surprised!

Well, the surprise was on me. Through the crack in the door I saw the biggest black cop you've ever seen, in flower shirt and shades. Lonnie showed him graciously out of the front door.

'Here, take this,' said the cop.

'I don' want anything,' said Lonnie.

'Take it, take it, boy,' the cop said, foisting it on him.

'Thanks,' said Lonnie, and closed the door.

I opened the kitchen door fully. 'How much did he give you?' I said.

Lonnie showed me: fifty cents.

'Better than the girls get,' said Lonnie. 'He gives them twenty cents. The difference is for protection.' He snorked.

'I don't believe you,' I said.

'You saw it with your own eyes,' he said.

'I know, but I don't believe it,' I said.

'You can say that again. Trouble is after he's been I can'...'

'All right, all right,' I said.

'I can' stop shitting blood for about three days.'

'Lonnie, this has *got* to stop,' I said.

'It will one day,' he said, 'it will.'

'You mean he gives the girls twenty cents – *like a tip?*'

'If he gives you anything else it means –'

'Means what?'

'You better stop dragging your arse or you're in chooky.'

'I'm taking you straight to my lawyer. You can spill the whole story – right from the beginning, dates, places, everything. I'll even bear witness for you.'

'So?' he said, knocking back his drink. 'You won't be in the witness box, you'll be in the dock. Not even you'd declare yourself for me.' He gave me an 'old fart' look, of which I'm not fond . . .

'Well, at least let me take you to my friend Richie. He can look you over, see there's no permanent damage. He's quite a discreet fellow.'

'That'll be the day I have a torch up my backside. What do you think I am – a bloody moffie or something?'

'Lonnie!' I said.

'Ag, it's jus' like a period,' he said. 'It comes and goes away.'

'Lonnie,' I said, 'you'll get infected and you'll die.'

'So you think we've got time for a movie before?' he said, sniggering.

'Yes, I suppose so,' I said, and the next morning over coffee: 'Lonnie, I don't know how . . . but this has got to stop.'

I went to work.

When I returned to the flat there was a note under his spare key on the kitchen table. It said: THIS IS NOT WORKING OUT. THANKS FOR *EVERYTHING*. NO REGRETS, HEY? LOTS OF LOVE, LONNIE.

My first reaction was unbounded, delirious relief (sozzled).

My second reaction was missing him indescribably badly.

I came out to the farm to recuperate.

Jannie kept saying: 'But what's the *matter?*'

I floundered, saying: 'I think I'm going to have a heart attack!'

He persisted. 'That's a *symptom*, not a *cause*.'

'Either way the result's the same,' I replied. You can imagine how that came out after a crate of Finest Blended.

'*Why?* why are you heading for a heart attack?'

'Bennington! Bennington's taken over my job.' Imagine *that* coming out.

'I'm not surprised, the way you behave,' said Jannie, his patience finally exhausted.

Once it got so bad he locked me in our bathroom. I banged on the door, screaming: '*I'm thirsty, I'm thirsty!*'

'Drink from the tap,' he said.

'*I'm hungry, I'm hungry!*' I yelled.

'Eat your own shit,' he said.

'*Get me Elizabeth Fiona*,' I banged on the door. 'That'll calm me down.'

'She's gone out for a walk with Kev in the pram.'

'I'll go with them,' I panted.

'You can't even walk three steps.'

'All right, all right,' I gasped, 'Jannie, you've finally – finally worn me down. It's not about Dave or Kev – it's all about Lonnie.'

'You mean . . . that little Indian boy down on the rocks. Maybe that's not such a bad idea. We'll go and look for him, and you can drink Coca-Cola.'

'Do you realise –' I said, 'the police have got this country by the balls and they're fucking it to death?'

'Yes, well,' said Jannie. 'That's what states of emergency are for.'

'Jannie, Jannie,' I implored, 'just don't leave me, that's all, I beg of you.'

'If you have a heart attack it's you that'll be leaving us,' he replied.

'Please unlock the door,' I said.

'Not until you wash yourself and sleep it off,' he said, leaving me there in my own filth.

There's a play by the late Tennessee Williams, which I saw once, before the playwrights' boycott really bit. (Now we get undiluted Tom Stoppard, and don't you tell me *that's* good for much.) Anyway, this one put the combined alcoholism and gay dilemma to perfection – the leading man said he could not stop drinking until the lever in his head at last went *click*[1] – then he could wipe it all out, like I can erase all the drivel on this machine. Do you think I can find the switch, achieve that *click*? Poor Mr Williams – didn't he end up choking on the cap of his tranquillisers?

(Don't worry now – I'm incredibly good at weighing out my food and walking it off briskly . . .)

That was the week of the next Thursday, when Lonnie didn't show up, not even for old times' sake and R50,00 . . . and at the Friday board meeting, sweating and glazed, I suddenly said out loud during a pause: '*I think my lover has been kidnapped!*'

Dave Bennington – yes, he was at my side in board meetings these days. He patted me to shut up.

'I beg your pardon,' several members said.

The m. d. was smarter. He said: 'Oh, and who has kidnapped your lover?'

I looked round them all: 'The police, of course,' I said.

'Well then,' said the m. d. with a smirk, 'at least she'll be

---

[1]. It was Biff in *Cat on a Pile of Hot Bricks*.

safe.' He winked at Dave to take me out.

On the Monday morning Dave's secretary was installed in the space before my office, and he had mine outside his. It couldn't have been more neatly done.

The new one came in to ask if there was anything I required.

'Yes, no phone calls,' I said. 'And get yourself a long wool jersey and start crying now, or I'll really feel lost.'

I dialled Richie.

'Darling, you won't believe this – but I've been demoted.'

'You won't believe this,' he said, 'but I've just been involved in a *murder*.'

'Nothing serious I hope,' I said.

'Well, not for me, no . . . but one does so wish it wouldn't all happen at the same time.'

'Do you know how many people depend on me out on the farm? – forty-four. I can't lose my job yet. That's not a tax loss, it's a liability. Even the dogs depend on me, the butterflies, the borer-beetles . . . the earthworms.'

'They'll all have to pull their fingers out, won't they?'

' . . . the pansies, the violets, the meanest rose that blows. Oh, Richie.'

He suggested we discuss it in full the following weekend when he and Alfie were coming to dinner.

'You got your parents with you or something?'

'Yes, sort of. But I managed to persuade them to stay in the Carlton Hotel.'

'Take Alfie to have drinks with them, break it softly that way.'

'Well, I did,' said Richie.

'I mean, Alfie's not just anyone. Quite a catch, I'd say – the hottest transplant surgeon of his day.'

'Yes, well, I'd just got to the very point – They were thrilled to meet him, it wasn't that. I was just going to say, Um, Mom and Dad, you see, I know you only want what is best for me, and the one who's best for me – is Alfie.'

'When –?'

'When – I was on the point of saying it, on the tip of my tongue –'

'And?'

'This *horrible murder* occurred.'

'You mean your Ma didn't say, *Not that*, darling, anything but that, and your father crumple into old age and never walk upright again?'

'No, no, the murder interrupted. They said was there a

doctor in the house, and my father said, You're on, lad . . . and when I came back Alfie hadn't said *one word*. Not could he make an honest woman of me or *anything hinting*, I swear.'

'So what happened then?'

'We all went to the concert and enjoyed it very much.'

' . . . Put it in your Christmas letter. They'll have got over it by New Year.' Having sorted that one out I put the phone down.

I dialled Danny and/or Martie. One of them answered.

'Guess what?' I said. 'I've been demoted.'

'You mean – you're out on the streets?'

'Not unless I jump out of the window,' I said.

'It wasn't an actual crash, it was just the nearest thing to a meltdown that anyone could ever want to see.'

'Not Wall Street, you ass – *me*, I've been dropped.'

'Lucky we made our million before, wasn't it?'

'Look, just put me through to Martie.'

'This *is* Martie, you bitch.'

'Give me Danny, then . . .'

After a lot of whispering Danny came on.

'Danny,' I said, 'what are you preparing for dinner tonight?'

'You'll have to come round and see for yourself. Come whenever you like. We were planning a quiet time, and to reminisce.'

'About what?'

'The baby, of course. What else is there?'

'I'm coming.'

I left the office.

The new secretary said: 'Where shall I say you've gone, sir?'

'To dinner,' I said. It was nine-thirty in the morning.

'Very good, sir,' she replied.

A cop running round in mufti, like a reggae rasta, tipping white boys fifty cents. Life was getting very cheap.

I didn't think I was going to like Azania, either.

The golden handshake was coming for me, only I had to wait to find out how much. I was sure it would be enough to invest in Switzerland, with a first-class ticket to get there. Yes, I was going to visit you in person. Get some advice about those famous clinics of yours.

Who knows – Jannie and I might have ended up skiing, after all. Yodelling to one another.

Tuesday I was the first one in the Pink Flamingo. Last one out. No Lonnie.

Wednesday I actually went to Broadway. That window of waiters carrying pizzas like sore arses looked pretty unenthusiastic now. Barred up. The Neapolitan frieze hooked its arm around nothing. Not even a stray tom squirting on a dustbin to mark out territory. Without the life and soul (Gino) there was no party. Broadway – what a pretentious name for a South African dump.
  Visiting hours at the local jail would be jollier.

Know what they call condoms in Afrikaans – babystranglers. And in Gujarati – change the colour of your prick. Policemen in Zulu (cause they hold up their finger and say stop).
  In Portuguese, condomsh.
  What's it in Schweizer Deutsch? – glove-puppets, I suppose.

In English, of course, they're called wedding rings.

Know the one about the dog that got its snout caught in a condom? – Beware.

And the rabbit? – Mrs Tiggy-wankle.

And the horse? – Top favourite.

And the rhino? Jeepers, you're ambitious.

Do you want the money or the box?
  'I'll take the box.'
  'It'll *double up* on the money.'
  'I'll take the *box*.'
  Treble. Quadruple. Last chance.
  'All right, the money.'
  Now look what was inside the box!
  Lonnie in a pool of semen.

Do you want the *money* or the *box*?
  'Box.'
  Double up, treble!
  'Box.'
  Quadruple, quintuple!
  'Box, box.'

193

You got the box. Now open up and see what's inside. Absolutely nothing.

DO YOU WANT THE MONEY? ... OR DO YOU WANT THE BOX?
'Money.'
Starting at fifty thou ... forty ... thirty ...
'Money, I said the money.'
Twenty ... ten ...
'Money.'
You don't know what's in the box.
Five, four, three ...
Look in the box. A HUNDRED THOUSAND RAND!!
... two, one, zero.

What is this? – *The Golden Notebook*[1]. Believe me, I can do the same in a lot less words.

What's this? – *The Penguin Book of Southern African Stories*.[2] Believe me, I can tell you some they haven't heard.

The Orton Diaries, that'll do. SIXTY-EIGHT RAND!

Thursday night I waited in the flat, with a wet cloth over my eyes, the tape on and a glass in my hand. No Lonnie ... I began to wonder if this Lonnie existed. Hadn't I muddled him up with someone else?

I went to Quartz Street where the girls hang out. You can't exactly lean out of the car and say, 'Hey, do you know where Lonnie is?' I drive slowly up. After a dozen parked cars with figures in them, a clump of girls in miniskirts. I lean out, bang my fist on the door. One comes across – dark wig, shoulder bag, miniskirt.

'Hey, can you tell me where's Lonnie?'
'I don't know anyone called Lonnie.'
'He's in the life, not a customer – dark hair, starting a moustache, goes with older men. Carries a savings book with his real name in it.'
'Oh yes,' she said, 'Lonnie ...' Her eyes flickered over the interior of the car. 'I don't know him ... Want to try something else?'

---

1. A sensitive novel by Nadine Gordimer about Rhodesian women going mad.
2. Edited by Michael Chaplin.

'No, I must find him.'
'Try Bok Street.'
'Thanks.'
'All right, bye now.'

Bok Street I try. Only an urchin shivering in shorts. 'No sir,' he says, 'no, sir.'

I go round the block a few more times ... then I see JoJo coming out of a Chinese place. I cannot get my car in until further down. I watch him stroll towards me in the rearview. He's a very together kid now. Alongside ... I see that it is not JoJo. Too broad-shouldered. JoJo would have cast a glance my way ... The Chinese dive is closing up.

Past Kensington there is a trysting-place, an old mine where Gino's boys had themselves taken on first acquaintance. A nightwatchman, bound up like a mummy, guards the barbed wire fences. Some lightbulbs in the poplars illuminate bits of the corrugated work-sheds. Past them is public ground beneath the quarry face. The grass is tall enough to hide your licence plates.

Bad Night in Gold City. There are no other cars there. (This moral clean-up has really affected the grope-and-slurp brigades.) If I had a gun, this is where I'd shoot myself – up against the palate, squeeze.

Friday there is no board meeting, so I still have not heard what is to happen to me. They cannot decide without a board meeting, finding some pretext for me not to attend it. I fully expect a directive to be out of town on some important business *all* next week. Even Dave Bennington has not popped in to play with the coffee machine. My coffee has turned to pitch, and pitch defiles. After all I have done for him, he could soften this process a bit. At least pretend he is not behind it.

Secretary comes in. 'Anything I can do for you, sir?'
'Please, get me your old boss.'
'Oh, Mr Bennington is out of town, sir.'
'With the rest of the board?'
'Yes, sir. How did you guess?'
'Not that difficult.'
'They've gone to see Aluminium Ware in Germiston. It's a new acquisition.'
'Not worth it. They're buying just for the sake of it now.'
'I'm sure you know best, sir.'

I came home to the farm. This time it took three hours. I kept pulling in and having a quick kip over the steering wheel. Slothfulness had overcome me. Maybe I'd only see the world in fits and starts from now on.

At one lay-by I was being overtaken by a donkey cart. Modes of transport! You could do a book on the way South Africans cross their vast subcontinent. Kev's Free State adventure wasn't a business trip – it was an odyssey. Now he'd settled down. My routine toing and froing was getting me nowhere. I should strike out on the open road . . . like everyone else, put my life on my head and walk.

But I felt too ill to do that, and drove another bit.

I had this fantasy – that Lonnie was hitchhiking. I pulled up and he jumped in. Jeepers, were we pleased to see one another! It came at exactly the right moment!

By the time I got to the top of the pass I was in a straitjacket, couldn't flex. I had another quick sleep.

Rolled down the hill and jump started . . . Don't have a heart attack now on these corrugations or you'll skid into the bush and no one will ever find you. Two doctors were coming to dinner, after all.

So this is what having a heart attack is like. Your heart is a hand. Now it is a fist, clasped. The fist punches your ribcage to break free.

This means, when you drive over the grit of your own nursery entrance – home at last – you haven't the strength to switch off. You can only stop the engine by letting the clutch out in gear. Then all you can do is heave open the door, pour yourself out onto the good earth.

You wait for the dogs to lick you clean. If you died they'd eat you. But for the moment they're much more interested in using you as a stepping stone to the steaks you have in brown paper on the back seat.

Belinda comes out of the kitchen. 'Get the dogs off the meat,' you say.

Ou Sara comes out. She knows the difference between a drunken stupor and a collapse, or until recently she thought she did. She has never yet passed comment on any of our behaviour. Making worried clucks, she helps me prop myself against the back wheel. She is afraid to grab and lug me. She picks my glasses out of the dirt. The lenses are covered in fine dust.

'Is die baas siek?' she says.

'Ja, Ou Sara,' I say with a sigh. 'Waar's Jannie?'

'Baas Jannie is Co-op toe.'

'En Kev?'

'Co-op.'
'Get Timothy.'
'Timothy het long weekend.'
'Ou Sara . . .' I said, forcing myself to speak, 'do you know what a heart attack is?'
'Kannie wees nie. Met 'n heart attack is jy dood, baas.'
She had a point there, I give her that.
It's the women who run this show, let me tell you. With their common sense.

Paul, I look out at the very patch where I fell from the car. If I hadn't had that lovely warmth of homecoming – the dusty cypresses, dusty lawn, dusty sprinkler click click clicking in the cannas, that battering sound as the jet hits a leaf, shoots free, hits another . . . irrigation and beat . . . irrigation and beat . . . well, I would have missed that if I'd died.

Don't you miss that now? The dry dusty veld, and the pulse of the sprinklers going? How could you leave that behind? I don't want to get all heavy, but it's the politics of water I'm interested in. African water, African dust.

Over dinner (prepare for a long scene) – it came out Lonnie was dead. This was an accidental item of news.

Funnily enough, I took it very calmly. These were the defence mechanisms. First I thought, My intuition has told me he was dead all along. Second, I congratulated myself on the accuracy of my intuition; my fears had not been groundless, after all. Third, I resolved to work far more on intuition in future – having this one reliable sense – and I suppose ultimately become a kind of prophet! If he'd walked in through the double doors, *then* I would have been very upset. All my defences would have collapsed. It would have taken me ages to be pleased to see him, put my arm around his shoulder, pull up a chair . . .

Alfie and dear Richie were happily burbling on about *their* farm. That's end of the week elation, when you have the prospect of working for yourselves for a change, away from the city which suddenly you would never like to see again.

'Yoo hoo,' said Kev, 'you're very quiet tonight.'

'He's been living behind a pane of glass for the last three months,' said Jannie. 'Like one of your old dummies in the clothing store, I promise you.'

'Stare in at him and admire the latest style,' said Kev.

'I go peekaboo, but he never responds,' said Jannie.

'Yoo hoo,' I said, waving my fingers from the top of the table.

'Why do blacks have flat noses?' said Alfie. 'Because they do so much window shopping!'

Nobody laughed.

'So, it's a tasteless joke,' said Alfie. 'Ooh, but have you seen those new outfits in Cyril's window, the sporty ones?'

'I don't miss the fashion business at all. I much prefer grading plants,' said Kev.

Little Elizabeth Fiona shook her rattle in the playpen. It was a pleasing, tinkling sound.

'You better get her to bed,' said Alfie.

'She's not tired yet,' said Jannie.

'Oh and did we tell you about the evening with my *parents?*' said Richie.

'All *your* Catholic father the judge would be pleased to hear is that we don't used bloody condoms,' said Alfie. 'Honestly, it was hair-raising.'

'All we want for you is whatever makes *you* happy, my boy,' said Jannie. 'A nice big circumcised – scalpel!'

'Is your father really that judge?' said Kev.

'That's the trouble,' said Richie. 'I think I've always been terrified of him.'

'Better than being in scrap-metal like my father was,' said Alfie.

'Spare parts!' said Kev.

'Bloody sure,' said Alfie.

'Well, if you're so tough, you were no good. Were you?' said Richie.

'But you weren't *there.*'

'I was only gone for a moment. So what did you talk about? What did he talk about?'

'The new guest conductor at the City Hall,' said Alfie, lowering his glass.

Jannie cleared away the soup plates.

'I think I'll put her down,' said Kev, and he held Elizabeth Fiona up to the assembled blokes. 'Nighty night, everybody.'

'Night.' 'Nighty.' 'Nighty.' 'Nighty.' 'Night my sweetest.'

'They bringing their staff now,' Richie said to me. 'Those bastards who burnt the rondavel down. Tomorrow morning I'll be crowded out. They send their drivers with whole bakkies full. It's coming right, it's coming right.'

'What do you give them?' I said.

'Boosters for a start. They come out all tingling. Alfie helps me if there's a difficult one.'

'That's me,' said Alfie, putting his napkin over his head. 'Sister Theresa of the Magaliesberg.'

'Ag, it's not for the money. The money's all in town.'

'You can say that again,' said Alfie.

'You know what's the biggest problem in this Valley?' said Richie. 'Ringworm . . . Thanks.' Jannie put down his plate. 'Ah, that looks scrumptious. Ringworm and alcohol, of course . . .' Alfie passed him the Brussels sprouts. 'Thanks. You remember Bara? I quite miss it now. Not the hours, though.'

'You don't miss the labour ward, that's for sure.'

'I miss the chronics in the children's. They see you coming with your stethoscope and their faces light up.'

'Help yourself,' said Jannie.

'Thanks,' said Alfie, taking two roast potatoes.

Kev came back. 'She should get to sleep now,' he said, sitting with his napkin bulged up on his lap. 'No, I'll have the cauliflower, please.'

Jannie dumped a wadge of cauliflower on my plate, and passed the bowl to Kev.

Don't go yoohoo again, Kev, I thought, but he just gave me a wink.

'What's the matter with you – on a diet?' said Richie.

'He doesn't like eating if you stare at him,' said Alfie. 'Hell, this is grand. Thanks, Jannie.'

'Tuck in, boys,' he said.

'Thank Ou Sara, she made it,' said Kev. 'What would we do without Ou Sara?'

'And Belinda,' said Jannie.

Everyone was eating. I cut my knife across a corner of steak, and spread some gravy on it.

Suddenly I found the words to say: *'Who got murdered?'*

'Oh, the murder, the murder, the murder,' said Richie. 'I clean forgot about that.'

'What murder?' said Jannie.

'Murder, she cried!' said Kev.

'Murder-murder-murder,' said Alfie.

'Yes, I'm listening,' said Jannie.

'You mean there was a *real* murder?' said Kev.

'Yes, in the Carlton,' said Alfie. 'That night when we were about to break the news to Richie's parents. Didn't we tell you?'

'He'll get off with manslaughter, or self-defence. I'm telling you,' said Richie. 'Mark my words, with guys like my father in charge. Out in two years for good conduct.'

'And you know what he said – I am a *re*born Christian. I pray for you,' said Alfie.

'I am a *REE*-born Christian. I pray for you.'

'Who?' said Jannie. 'Your father?'

'So you *did* tell him,' said Kev. 'My father just said, Well, in that case, fok off.'

'And look where it led you,' Richie pointed his knife. 'Now you're the most famous moffie in the world and, thanks to Alfie's genius, breeding like a rabbit.'

'Oh, I won't have another one,' said Kev.

'Elizabeth Fiona enough of a handful for you?' said Alfie.

'It's just that – I want to keep my figure,' said Kev.

Everyone whooped it up.

'Kev's all shy!' Jannie teased him, ruffling his hair.

'No seriously, who would you carry for this time, if you had to?' said Alfie.

Kev said, 'Belinda. If she had to die. No seriously, she's done as much for Elizabeth Fiona as anyone else. You can't just count her out because she's black.'

'Now that *would* make a story,' said Richie.

'It would go down well overseas,' said Alfie, 'but I'm not so sure about in this Valley.'

The phone rang our signal and Jannie went. The phone woke Elizabeth Fiona and Kev went.

'Don't worry, we in the medical profession are used to it. The moment you serve the phone goes. Thank God I'm not on call.'

'It's Timothy to say he's got to Lydenburg.'

'Where's *Lydenburg?*' said Richie.

'You just say that about Belinda, but you'd never do it,' said Alfie.

'Timothy is Pedi,' I said.

'I wouldn't think twice about it,' said Kev.

'Oh, that's where Bara got spinal malaria flown in from,' said Richie.

'Then you'd have trouble, my boy, they'd think you killed her for her baby, like you killed off Fiona,' said Alfie.

'Near Pilgrim's Rest, but that's a long way for your old truck,' said Richie.

'Nonsense,' said Kev. 'The point was to *save* Fiona, you know that.'

'Is spinal malaria fatal?' I said.

'Nine out of ten,' said Richie.

'You get a lot of uphill from the public if you're in transplants,' said Alfie. 'They just think you're *waiting* to *pounce.*'

'I'll have that heart while it's fresh, thanks,' said Richie.

Jannie came in. 'All right, so who's the *murderer?*'

'I'm a *REE*-born and I pray for you,' said Richie.

'How do you know?' said Kev.

'He just walked into the Clock Bar and put his room key down on the counter and said I'm a REE-born and there's somebody upstairs I pray for,' said Alfie.

'And there was blood all over the key. Room 1007,' said Richie.

'Shit,' said Kev.

'Yes, so don't blaspheme so much or you'll get prayed for, too,' said Alfie.

Richie said, 'The barman thought he'd cut his finger or something. He just said I thought he cut his finger.'

'While this guy was bleeding in Room 1007,' said Alfie.

'Who?' said Kev.

'Some rent-boy he'd stabbed,' said Alfie.

'Who?' said Jannie.

'The *RE*-born, man,' said Richie.

'Obviously didn't like being propositioned in the Clock Bar,' said Kev.

'Well, you don't have to take a rent-boy up to 1007 and stab him up the arse to show your disapproval,' said Alfie.

'REEEE-borns are like that,' said Kev.

'In the arse, right in? But why would he do a thing like that?' said Jannie. 'Was he clothed or naked?'

'Well, why would you think?' said Alfie. 'Anyway, ask Richie – he saw it. You saw it.'

'Naked. We were stuck with my parents, working to *the point*, you know,' said Richie.

'And the barman runs out and says is there a doctor?' said Jannie.

'No, the hotel detective who's been up to have a look, and comes straight to me, because my father the famous judge has already so proudly told him his son, that's me, is not a moffie but a doctor!'

'So off he goes, silly cow,' said Alfie, 'leaving *me* to pretend I've never had a thing to do with a medical matter in my life.'

'And when I come down and explain everything that caused the delay, know what my father says? . . . *Bloody pervert*, that's just what he *deserves*. You have it from the lips of the judge himself.'

'Who – the reborn Christian?' said Jannie.

'No, his father said it,' said Alfie. 'That's the whole point.'

'But *which* is the *pervert*?' said Kev.

'Well, it wasn't Alfie or me, was it?' said Richie.

'You still don't understand what we saying – was it the *rent-boy* or the *reborn* who's meant to be the pervert?'

'I'm lost now,' said Richie. 'Just pass me the wine.'

'The *rent-boy*, of course,' said Alfie. 'That's the *entire point*.

That's why the reborn will get off lightly. He knew that, the moment he gave himself up and prayed for us all.'

'*Who was he?*' I got out.

'This red's nice,' said Richie. He continued off-handedly, 'I don't know – some charismatic who was cleaning up for Christ.'

'NO, THE RENT-BOY,' we all went.

'Swartland,' said Alfie.

'It's only Swartland,' said Jannie.

Richie looked all bleary. 'He had . . . a bank book in his pants. Gee, he wasn't so poor. Allan H. Smith. Quite a nice looking guy. *Very* nice looking guy,' said Richie. 'Not into violence at all, I'd say. Spotless body, except for . . .'

'Didn't you try to patch him up?' said Kev.

'Not much point . . . when they're dead,' said Richie.

'Oh how horrible, I tell you, I tell you . . .' Jannie said. 'I tell you . . . Right, pudding everyone.'

'I won't have any pudding, thanks,' I said.

'What is the matter with you?' said Jannie.

'Ah, what's for pudding?' said Kev.

'Don't be so greedy, wait and see,' said Jannie, taking the plates and stacking them.

'Actually, I wonder we could go to the concert after that,' said Richie.

'Especially you – you'd seen it all,' said Alfie.

'Why, was it a real mess?' said Kev.

'I can tell you,' said Richie, giving a gasp, 'they won't get Room 1007 clean inside a month. It was – just everywhere.'

'Oh God,' said Kev.

'You know what you should have done?' said Jannie. 'Come down with the knife –'

'And stab the reborn in the bar while he prayed for you,' said Kev.

'What would that have accomplished?' said Jannie.

'No, no, he should have come down with the knife,' said Alfie, 'and put it in his *father's hand* –'

'– and said, Stab us both here, you old justice freak, because we're both perverts, too. Now you know,' said Richie.

I watched Jannie get out the pudding bowls. I watched his every move. His wrist bend as he scooped into the trifle. His left thumb as he licked off a bit. How he changed the spoon from right to left as he picked up the loaded bowl to pass it.

I thought, Now I have no cause to be unfaithful to you ever again.

'Pudding?' he said.

'No thanks,' I said. 'If you'll excuse me, I don't feel so well.'

The heart attack was a delayed reaction. It took until Sunday 3.00 p. m. for that fist in my chest to break loose. It was at the start of the Henry Wood Prom on the radio: Roman Carnival, to be followed by Beethoven's Fifth, how do you like that?

Jannie was there, reading a copy of the *Farmer's Weekly*. There was no one on the phone, and Richie had not gone back to town, so Jannie could deliver his immortal line: 'He's gone blue on the Persian carpet.'

Alfie had me into the Trescott *before the concert had ended*. I could hear it on his car radio, and the last bars in the wards as they trundled me in.

I imagined a different scenario: that I was Lonnie in Room 1007, and Jannie phoned Richie with the immortal line: 'He's gone all red on the double bed.' And Richie opened the window, and we flew right across the city (like Superman, don't you know). Richie could rescue me any time. I'm a little bit sweet on him.

But there with his scalpel was Alfie. Hell, that guy gets his kicks out of opening people up. Slash, slash, and the whole of your heart hangs out of its cage, I promise you.

I'll obey *any* instructions from now on, not to have to go through that again.

Jannie and I have this little joke: 'Don't touch that, don't drink that.'
'Why not?'
'Or else it'll be an operation.'
'How big?'
'A *major* operation.'

The rest you know, more or less, don't you?

Sorry . . . I've told this all in the wrong bloody order, haven't I? Just go back a bale or two of print-out and you'll be at the recuperation bit. I didn't put page numbers so I can't guide your intelligent hands. The bit with the cleaner and all. Remember at least *that*?

Well, the firm was exceptionally humane and decent about it all, I must say. (Remember them sending me wreaths and so on?) They put me on as tax consultant and advisor (same pay and benefits!) so I could trundle over and more or less do a token day's work when I felt like it. Tax knows no gender, race or religion; it's either right or it's wrong. I couldn't have been on safer ground.

Jannie lived in the flat for the duration. We could hardly move for new varieties of pots. Timothy took over the day to day running of the nursery, with Kev absolutely waggling his tail over having somebody to be of assistance to. Don't tell me, it's going to be a Henno all over again. But I've always felt a bit sorry for Timothy the way the others keep him at bay; in Kev has he just found a friend!

Obviously they put Ou Sara up to phoning us one night. I thought, Hell, what can be wrong?

She said, No, she wanted to say everything's fine!

And you could just hear them giggling in the background, even the *baby* giggling. Honestly!

I'm telling you, you don't have to supervise your staff in this place. Don't get in their hair and they run the show *better than you do*. For real. The first time we started turning a profit was when we were away from it!

Dear Mrs Leibnitz just popped in to say Happy New Year and buy some pink azaleas. She's a lovely person – *everything* is all right with her. Except your brand of German, I may say . . . I showed her your card of the Bridge over the Rhine, and she studied the caption, and said, 'But that isn't Deutsch!' So grovel, *grovel*.

During that recovery period I made a resolution to write to you, and to all our old friends . . . Mind you, after this lot I doubt the others are going to get much!

When Jannie came back here I missed him, so that's when I installed the terminal in town. But this separation wasn't going to keep working – the breadwinner in town – and all the cheeping dependents out in the little nursery nest. Besides, the tide had turned and they'd thrown Mama out of the nest long ago, and declared themselves unilaterally. Mama would have to come crawling back on hands and knees, waving a little flag, saying: FUCK THE STATE OF EMERGENCY. FLOWER POWER RULES, I DO AGREE.

The point is: I missed . . . no, not Lonnie, though even my new heart almost withered from grieving for him. I used to slump there, my pyjama front open with this terrible scar, and walk into the dark: Lonnie . . . Lonnie . . . I don't want to go into it now, because it *still* hurts . . . Somewhere within me is a category full of dead rent-boys and flushed babies and poor Fiona and – I don't know – never to be assuaged.

But it was Jannie I missed, who loves me so undemonstrably, so ploddingly on and on. (We've discussed all of this, every detail, so it's no betrayal to be so personal among friends.) We talk it all out, hour after hour, and lay it to rest. There's great healing to falling in love all over again with the man you love. Actually, it's quite superb. Affirms your faith in human life, it does. To know him from the beginning again.

(Yes, even in South Africa, you trendy jetset radicals! Here, of all places. So next time you want to get all political with me . . . GO AND BLOW YOUR ALPENHORNS!)

Here comes Timothy with Elizabeth Fiona on his arm. Must be change of nappy time. He's got quite a good figure, old Timothy, if only he wouldn't drink so much. Elizabeth Fiona's mad for his three last tobacco-stained teeth. She's totally obsessed with driving her hand in and pulling out the first one she can get hold of. Maybe she's going to be a dentist. Timothy absolutely quivers with delight. He lets her hand right in and pretends, with huge bogeyman eyes, he's going to bite her arm off, and she shrieks with delight.

There you are: they do it for show – for me outside the window. Absolute *shrieks*, my dear.

He lets her down at the doorway. One step . . . two step . . . arms out! *Here she comes, boys!*

All right, I must stop there.

Absolute love to *both* of you. You know that's true.

Also from Stephen Gray:

TIME OF OUR DARKNESS

"Gray's strength is that he does not deal in dark metaphors, but accepts South African society as it is and, without special pleading, depicts the way in which its inhabitants cope with that society. In its unpretentious way, without preaching, and more in sorrow than in anger, this book brings substance to the ever-decreasing documentary images coming out of South Africa and makes one realise what day-to-day life is really like for its many and divided peoples" – Peter Parker, London Magazine.

"*Time of Our Darkness* provides many insights, not least into how the atmosphere generated by intolerance brutalises, or at the very least de-sensitises, everyone, including its opponents" – Martin Seymour-Smith, Financial Times.

"Gray's melodramatic narrative is never less than gripping" – Dennis Walder, The Listener.

"I found it informative, surprising, and by the end, painfully moving" – Elaine Feinstein, Sunday Times.

"The book's manner is sprawling and careless and rich – rather like the way Doris Lessing used to write or a less tendentious Nadime Gordimer – and examines how personal lives are touched by outside events . . . Pete's helplessness, confusion and hard-pressed moral sense are moving, and certain scenes tenderly erotic in a way I have not seen for a long time" – Jenny Turner, City Limits.

"There is much to be admired in *Time of Our Darkness*. Its language is economical; it has an ingenious plot, sophisticated, skilfully constructed and above all, taut with unity. There is no detail or dialogue which does not ultimately fall into its ordained place in a tightly controlled narrative. Racy language, slang, expletives and the rhythms of a gay register are successfully used to bring to life the world of homosexuality" – South African Review of Books.

"Stephen Gray braids real, idiosyncratic lives of South Africans rather than symbols, giving us truths of a very high order, since they are so alive, so personal" – Kurt Vonnegut.

Recent titles from GMP:

Kenneth Martin
BILLY'S BROTHER

When Billy dies in mysterious circumstances, his brother comes to San Francisco to try and uncover the truth of his death, and is immediately drawn into the network of AIDS sufferers and support groups that Billy had been a part of. Among them, he is sure the clue to Billy's death will be found – but he is unprepared for the other revelations that his investigation reveals.

Kenneth Martin is the author of *'Aubade'*, a remarkable first novel of teenage innocence published in 1957 and written when the author was just sixteen. He wrote two novels subsequently but *'Billy's Brother'* represents Martin's first new novel in almost thirty years. In the intervening years Martin moved into journalism and then on to San Francisco where he trained and worked as a clinical research psychologist, also working with AIDS patients in more recent years.

'Billy's Brother' could not be further removed from the experiences depicted in *'Aubade'*. Set largely among the San Francisco gay community, familiar to Martin, it is a sharply observed mystery thriller, dealing with the changes AIDS has brought to everyone's lives, and raising important questions about the ways in which we all respond to its existence.

ISBN 0 85449 109 0   Price: 4.95

Kenneth Martin
AUBADE

Reprinted as a Gay Modern Classic in February 1989, *'Aubade'* created a storm of controversy with its frank revelations about adolescent homosexual feelings and consciousness when first published in 1957. It tells the story of Paul, a young school leaver, whose life is transformed when he meets a young medical student who he renames 'Gary'. Their relationship develops through the long, hot summer, to reach its climax with the approach of Autumn . . .

"Not many books by anyone so young are worth publishing, but this was" – John Betjeman.

ISBN 0 85449 197 3   Price: £4.95

Gay Men's Press Books can be ordered from any bookshop in the UK, and from specialist bookshops overseas. If you prefer to order by mail, please send full retail price plus 1.50 for postage and packing to GMP Publishers Ltd (M.O), PO Box 247, London N17 9QR. (For Visa/Access=Eurocard=Mastercard/American Express give number and signature.) Comprehensive mail-order catalogue also available.

In North America order from Alyson Publications Inc., 40 Plympton St, Boston, MA 02118, USA.

NAME AND ADDRESS IN BLOCK LETTERS PLEASE:

Name ....

Address ....

....